Everything About the Ridges Was Magic.

The minute she walked into the clearing Anne knew it was the right spot for the film's proposal scene. She saw a glittering stream, and the white perfection of dogwood blossoms.

She inhaled the sharp mountain air. Everything was right, she thought. She'd discovered the location just in time. She had to drive back to town and call her boss.

Then she sighted a deer on the opposite ridge. The creature was so lovely that she had to watch it. But there was something else at the edge of her vision.

A man. A man who would turn out to be as magical as everything else Anne had found that day.

PAT WALLACE

began writing poetry at ten. Since then she has been an actress and a disc jockey, and has worked for a labor union. Now her only job—in addition to keeping her husband and four cats happy—is to write the romance novels that have made her so popular.

Dear Reader:

There is an electricity between two people in love that makes everything they do magic, larger than life. This is what we bring you in SILHOUETTE INTIMATE MOMENTS.

SILHOUETTE INTIMATE MOMENTS are longer, more sensuous romance novels filled with adventure, suspense, glamor or melodrama. These books have an element no one else has tapped: excitement.

We are proud to present the very best romance has to offer from the very best romance writers. In the coming months look for some of your favorite authors such as Elizabeth Lowell, Nora Roberts, Erin St. Claire and Brooke Hastings.

SILHOUETTE INTIMATE MOMENTS are for the woman who wants more than she has ever had before. These books are for you.

Karen Solem
Editor-in-Chief
Silhouette Books

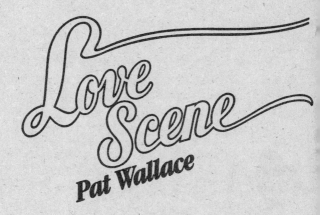

Love Scene

Pat Wallace

Silhouette Intimate Moments

Published by Silhouette Books New York

America's Publisher of Contemporary Romance

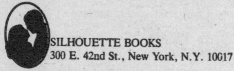

SILHOUETTE BOOKS
300 E. 42nd St., New York, N.Y. 10017

Copyright © 1985 by Pat Wallace

Distributed by Pocket Books

ISBN: 0-373-07100-0

First Silhouette Books printing June, 1985

10 9 8 7 6 5 4 3 2 1

America's Publisher of Contemporary Romance

Printed in the U.S.A.

For my cousins, the Baileys—
A.C., Vivian, Bill and Betty Anne;
for the days of Old Smoky.

Chapter 1

THE MINUTE SHE WALKED INTO THE CLEARING ANNE knew it was the spot for the film's proposal scene. She raised her binoculars, adjusted them and took a long, delighted look around.

She saw a glittering stream, and around it the white perfection of dogwood blossoms. You've got it, Anne Reynolds, she exulted. It was as right as the gloomy nineteenth-century house, the whole village of Sedgby. Lloyd Eliot, her director-boss, had sworn they'd never find the replacement location in time. But now Anne had, because she'd remembered Sedgby, high in the Smoky Mountains of Tennessee.

She inhaled the sharp, clear mountain air, pine

scented, edged with coldness; even now, in April, it was still crisp, while the city was already warming.

Everything was right, she thought, even the season. She'd discovered the location just in time. Otherwise they might have had to fake the spring scenes, and perfectionists like Lloyd—and herself, she admitted—balked at that. Anne decided to drive back to Warrenburg and phone him right away.

Then she sighted a deer on the opposite ridge. The creature was so lovely that she had to watch it. But there was something else on her vision's edge.

A man.

He was bending slightly, peering through a telescope. The telescope was trained in her direction.

Clint Ward was measuring an elevation when an unexpected object moved into the range of his powerful lens.

A woman.

The first thing he noticed when she came into the sun was a head of glorious red hair, drifting like a small bonfire around her narrow shoulders. He liked the way she moved.

"Well, well." He gave a murmuring chuckle and sharpened her image, getting a shot of a heart-shaped face. Her faintly painted lips were a bit parted, as if she were enjoying what she saw. He lowered the lens slowly, viewing a delicate neck, an open-necked gray shirt hinting at pleasant roundness, a tiny middle. The lens registered a dark skirt that neither hugged nor hid beautiful hips, then polished boots the color of mahogany caressing slender ankles and very shapely legs.

Clint raised the lens again to re-view her wonderful hair, wishing he could see her eyes, but they were covered by her binoculars.

Apparently she'd seen him; she lowered her binoculars. Now he looked into her distant eyes. They were wide and blue-gray, cautious, bright, a little sad. The telescope was so powerful that it picked up a slight dusting of freckles across her small, straight nose.

What a face, he marveled. The kind you didn't see much anymore. There was something so new about it, although she wasn't all that young. But the shape of the mouth and chin, her expression, were gutsy. Challenging.

He wanted to find out who she was, what she was doing there.

Clint straightened and raised a hand in greeting.

Anne's glasses weren't strong enough to register his face, but she got an impression of height and wiry leanness. He wore khakis with rolled-up sleeves; the raised arm was very muscular.

She hesitated before she returned his wave. This was an awfully lonely place, and he *was* a stranger. On the other hand, people waved in Tennessee all the time . . . and he could hardly be up to anything sinister with a telescope. Even the deer hadn't seemed scared of him. He was probably a surveyor, or a ranger.

A surveyor—good heavens. What if a building project was in the wind? It could be disastrous for the film. She wasn't sure yet whether this was private or public land. The specter of permits and permissions, of conflicts and problems, assailed her. She'd better get out of here and get to Lloyd.

The man was coming down the ridge, heading toward her. She turned away, starting to walk in the opposite direction.

"Wait!"

For some reason Anne stopped; his call was deep and

resonant in the clear air, ringing pleasantly against her ears. Her sense of comedy, never far away, retorted: the You-Tarzan–Me-Jane effect.

She turned and saw him approaching her. Maybe she could find out what he was up to.

He came toward her with a loose, easy stride, and suddenly it wasn't funny anymore. This was the most impressive man that she had ever seen.

There wasn't a quarter ounce of extra flesh on his tall body, yet he had an air of massive toughness. His hair was black and thick, like his heavy brows. When he came within speaking distance, he said, "Hello," and that deep, resonant voice thrilled her nerves again. He smiled.

A dazzling whiteness split his tanned face like a turned-on light, emphasizing a wide, sensuous mouth. His lower lip was full, in contrast to the firmness of his upper one below a strong curved nose.

But his most noticeable feature was his eyes. They were the golden brown of a cat's-eye stone, brilliant against his weathered skin, drawing her gaze at once.

Anne was taken off-guard; she hadn't bargained for anything like this. He'd been just a man in khakis before, a man doing something that could conflict with her own vital project. But now she saw that he was so appealing he was positively dangerous. She'd become impervious to handsome men after seven years in Hollywood, but this man was worse than handsome, she thought drily; he had power, command. She could see at a glance that intelligence rayed from those eyes.

He was admiring her openly, also something she was not used to in Glamour City, where her very lack of glamour made her noticeable but not whistled at.

"Hello," he repeated, a hint of a chuckle in his voice. "I'm Clint Ward." He extended his big, square hand,

and she found herself taking it. When the wide hand engulfed her narrow one she was astonished to feel a dart of fire move from her fingers all the way up her arm. It was incredible. For three whole years she'd been convinced that such emotions might never be reawakened.

"Anne Reynolds," she murmured. She realized that her hand still lay in his, and she pulled it out of his insistent grasp. She also noticed that he glanced swiftly at her ringless left hand.

His look flicked back to her face and hair, and she was surprised to sense the color creeping up to her face. She was absurdly tongue-tied, more like a thirteen-year-old than the woman of thirty she was.

"Do you live around here, Anne Reynolds?"

At last she found her tongue. "No. I'm . . . visiting. Are you a surveyor, Mr. Ward?" It occurred to her, listening to herself, that she sounded as if they were meeting on a reception line instead of in a mountain wilderness.

He might have been thinking something like that, too, because his eyes twinkled. "Yes."

Clint Ward wasn't very chatty.

"Is some kind of building going on here?" she pursued.

"Maybe. But not for a while."

She couldn't understand why he was being so cagey, why he didn't just say what he was working on and for whom. She'd probably have to check it elsewhere. Nevertheless she decided to keep at it while she had the chance. "A resort?"

"Far from it." His grin widened.

Well, she wasn't going to get anything out of this gorgeous clam.

"Are you an architect, Ms. Reynolds?"

Two could play his game. "No." She smiled at him, and watched his attention go to her mouth. "Not exactly." An assistant producer *was* a kind of architect in a way. She was involved in building the whole picture from scratch.

"I have a suggestion. Why don't we continue our guessing game in Warrenburg . . . over an early dinner?" The suggestion was quick and smooth, and he seemed to think she'd jump at it.

Anne felt an irrational disappointment. There had been something so exciting about their encounter, so utterly different; now it was dialogue from the singles-bar scene, which she knew only secondhand but had a great distaste for.

"I'm afraid not," she said coolly. "I've got some very important business to take care of, right away." That was true enough. She couldn't wait for Lloyd to hear the news.

"But you had time to watch the deer a minute ago." Clint Ward's teasing comment aroused her resentment. His tone questioned the urgency of her business. And why was he so secretive about what *he* was doing? That could be a ploy to impress her, to make his job seem more glamorous than it was. She'd run into that before; her all-American face had fooled other men into assuming that she was as naïve as she looked, that she'd swallow almost any tale.

"I couldn't resist," she said lightly. "Well, Mr. Ward, I've held you up long enough. I must let you get back to work. Have a nice day." She raised her hand in a casual goodbye wave and started off.

"Don't go yet." She looked back. It seemed to matter to him. All of a sudden it mattered to her, too. She was aware of the pull he exerted over her senses, the charm of his presence.

But she made herself move. "I'm sorry. I really must." And she walked away over the field and climbed the rise to the highway. At the top she couldn't resist glancing back, just once. He was still standing in the center of that green space, staring after her.

I don't need this now, she thought, not at this stage of my life. Good heavens, it's like something out of an old movie. Attraction at first sight in the wilds, two people just happening to be there at a certain point in time. And at *this* point in time, for her, there was just too much at stake for such distraction. She should have been in Warrenburg at least an hour ago.

She hurried to the compact rental car she'd parked beside the road, got in and took off her binoculars and shoulder bag, fishing in the bag for keys.

When she tried to start the car she knew she was in trouble; the engine coughed and sputtered, then died, like a big animal that had had the breath knocked out of it.

"Oh, no." Her wide general knowledge didn't cover the insides of cars. What now—ask the closemouthed, appealing Mr. Ward for help? Not that. It seemed so awkward, so tacky, right after she'd turned down his dinner invitation. She could hike back to the service station between here and Sedgby . . . but it wasn't that much farther down the mountain to Warrenburg, the resort town where there was a real garage available. Might as well go downhill all the way.

Fuming, Anne picked up her binoculars and her shoulder bag, took the key from the ignition and got out. She locked the car and started down the mountain road.

Around her were the Smokies' mighty peaks, named for the eerie, whitish cloud that swathed them, thick as drifting smoke. The mist gave their soft blue-gray forms a quality of something dreamed instead of seen. Anne's spirits began to rise. What a setting for the film.

She'd loved these mountains ever since she could remember, but now she appreciated them more than ever. When she had lived here as a child, they had almost been a prison to her, because she had already begun to love the world of make-believe.

The big day of her week had been Saturday, the main event the movie down in Knoxville. The films had been her passport to the world. She'd drunk in every scene and lived the thrilling lives of the characters on the screen, in their English castles or their city penthouses, Alpine chalets or Western ranches.

When Anne went to college her parents urged her to major in something "practical," like home economics or business or education, their ideas a generation behind hers. But from the first she gravitated toward the campus theater and television station. Too shy to pursue acting, she got involved in writing and production, helping to tie up loose ends and keep them together. She resolved that someday she'd be a director or producer in New York or Hollywood. Her whole college career centered on study and work; she made a point of getting a broad education which, she concluded sadly as a senior, fitted her for hardly anything. However, she'd saved the money she made working in the summer, and she went to New York after graduation over the protests of her parents.

There she'd lucked onto a job in a TV studio . . . and met Dan, a producer, the first man in her life. Gentle, brilliant Dan, who became her husband. They went to Hollywood together, and were working on a picture when he died. She had been able to take over.

Rounding a curve, Anne got another breathtaking view of the Smoky Mountains; an afternoon shadow was stealing over them, and they looked darker, awesome and impenetrable. She was overcome with a cold sense of loneliness and loss. After three years her grief had softened, changed; but at times like this the old loneliness assailed her with awful power.

It was at that moment that she heard a car approaching from behind, its engine a slow, heavy grumbling, more like a Jeep than a car. It was proceeding with the caution necessary on these twisting roads, where there were signs warning "Nine miles per hour" above the sheer piny canyons.

Anne got as far from the road as she could, hugging the foot of the bluff. She waited until she saw the nose of a Land Rover round the curve.

Clint Ward was at the wheel. He slowed the Rover to a crawl and called out, "Taxi, lady?" He was grinning.

She was absurdly glad to see him. "Why not?" She got in as he stopped and opened the door in one smooth motion. He leaned over her and slammed the door shut again, and she was astonished at the effect that brief moment of closeness had on her.

It had apparently moved him, too, because his voice wasn't quite steady when he said, "I thought I'd find you eventually. I saw your car and guessed what happened. What was it?"

"You're asking the wrong person." She laughed a little. "I'm much more familiar with cameras."

"You're a photographer?" His question was eager, interested. He didn't take his attention from the tortuous road, but she could feel him leaning toward her.

"I'm in the movie business," she murmured.

Negotiating an especially sharp curve, which was practically a horseshoe, he offered, "You're not an actress."

"Why do you say that?" Despite herself, she felt

slightly miffed. No one ever took her for an actress; the implication seemed to be that she wasn't jazzy enough to be in front of the camera.

She could have sworn that he read her mind; he was extraordinarily intuitive, she decided. "Not because you couldn't be," he said calmly. "You're beautiful. Because you seem . . . full of so many other things, not stuck on yourself."

It was a remarkably sharp observation, and she savored it for a moment in silence. The "beautiful" touched her.

"You belong here, too," he added softly.

"All right, I give up," she countered with a lightness she didn't feel. "You're a psychic . . . or an FBI agent."

He laughed, and she enjoyed the sound of his laughter, as resonant and strong and pleasing as his speaking voice, which was unaccented, like that of a man who'd lived in a number of places. "Nothing so exotic. I'm an engineer, that's all. I figured you belong here because when we took that last curve, you hardly noticed. And it's quite a drop."

"Neither did you," she retorted. "You drove it like a native."

"I've driven in higher mountains," he said casually. "But you *are* from here, aren't you?"

She was beginning to feel at ease in his presence. His interest was friendly and very real. She wasn't used to talking about herself; mostly she was centered on others, involved in listening—soothing the ruffled feathers of writers feeling lost in Hollywood; calming actors' nerves; stroking Lloyd's genius-tormented ego. But this was almost like talking to . . . Dan. The idea was so overwhelming that she hardly realized how long she'd been silent.

"Aren't you?" he prompted.

"Yes. I was born right up there in Jimtown," she said.

"Jimtown? I don't know that one."

"What the natives have been calling Jamestown for about a hundred years, give or take a thousand."

He chuckled. "From Jimtown to the movie business. Was it done in one great leap?"

"Hardly." She found herself telling him the whole thing, even to the grinding loneliness, the unremitting work in New York, the night courses in film at NYU, practically all of it.

Before she knew it, they were driving into Warrenburg. She stopped to get her breath; she hadn't talked about herself so much in a long, long time.

But now the sight of Warrenburg recalled her obligations; she could already feel them pressing in on her. First the car, then a call to Lloyd—and she'd probably need an entire yellow pad to contain his directions and cautions and stream of ideas. The thought was almost wearisome, and she couldn't believe her unusual reaction. She was used to being so absorbed in a new job that she could hardly think of anything else. Anne wondered if Clint Ward was the reason. But that was ridiculous; she didn't even know him. She caught the tail end of a question from him.

". . . take you?"

"I beg your pardon?"

"Hello, out there." She turned and saw him grinning down at her, and she couldn't help staring at his mouth, feeling the strong vibrations from the nearness of his big body to hers. "I was asking where I should take you first, to the car rental?"

"Yes. Yes, thank you. I'm afraid my mind was wandering." She returned his smile.

"Could you let it wander toward a drink, and dinner?"

"I may not even have time for that tonight, after I call my boss."

Clint Ward eyed her. "That sounds a bit grim." As he pulled up outside the car-rental office, he added, "Look, I didn't mean this very minute. They wouldn't let me carry a tray in this gear, anyway, much less sit at a table in the inn. I'll pick you up later . . . whenever you say." He pulled the Rover to a halt. "Where are you staying?"

"At the inn." She looked up at him again. His startling gaze was steady.

"So am I. That's great."

Not so great, she protested silently. It gave her too many outrageous ideas, ideas she had no business having . . . especially not now. She debated with herself.

"First I'd better report on the car," she evaded.

"I'll wait for you, if you like."

She started to say, "Don't bother." After all, it was only a little way to the Warrenburg Inn. But something made her answer, "I *do* like," and she saw his eyes brighten, felt her own pulsebeat quicken, sensed that treacherous warmth stealing over her again, just as it had when they met in that lonely place up on the mountain.

Anne hardly knew herself. Suddenly she hated the idea of parting from him, even for a little while, and that was a scary notion. She couldn't let herself be carried away like this. Not now, not so soon.

He got out and opened her door for her, then stretched out his hand to help her out of the Land Rover. Once more, when she put her hand in his, all her senses seemed to burn with that electric fire. Anne remembered something her grandmother had said to her when she was just a little girl. "You'll know it, child, when you meet your fate. Why, the first time your granddaddy kissed me it was like I was struck by lightning."

Anne couldn't stop staring up into Clint Ward's amber eyes. Then she got hold of herself, chagrined, and managed to say with a measure of poise, "I'll only be a minute."

She transacted her business with the rental agent in a kind of daze. Absently she received his assurance that the car would be picked up at once by a mechanic, and that a substitute car would be left at her hotel that evening. When she came out, she saw Clint Ward leaning against the side of the Rover, smoking a cigarette. He saw her, and his tanned face lit up; he threw the cigarette onto the gravel, stepped on it and went around to open her door again.

When he got into the driver's seat she found that her sensitivity to his presence was even more heightened; her heart was hammering against her ribs. It was awful . . . wonderful. She was sure he had picked up on her reactions; for the first time he was almost awkwardly silent. The warmth, the suspense, that amazing pull, were almost tangible between their bodies.

"Well," he said at last, and she could hear his voice go unsteady again, soften and deepen, "how long do you think you'll be?"

"It's very hard to say." Somehow she couldn't think at all right now; the idea of times and schedules dismayed her. Dismayed *her,* Anne Reynolds, the "human stopwatch" as Lloyd called her. But she glanced at her watch, trying to be sensible. It was already nearly five o'clock, something she found unbelievable. Time had taken on an entirely new meaning in the company of Clint Ward.

"How about seven?" he prompted. "The dining room at the inn . . . ? I can meet you in the lobby."

She turned and looked at him. He was inexpressibly eager; it seemed to be a matter of life and death. It occurred to her that he hadn't even been able to wait until he'd started the Rover. A casual man would already be driving her back, would wait until they were at the inn and then make dinner arrangements lightly. Clint was treating this whole thing with a high seriousness, and she couldn't help being touched by that.

With equal seriousness she answered, "Seven will be fine. In the lobby."

He looked enormously elated. Neither of them said anything more until he pulled up in front of the sprawling inn. "Seven, then," he murmured.

"Seven," she agreed. Anne had to force herself to walk straight in without looking back. She knew she hadn't even wanted to say goodbye; she'd had a wild desire just to drive off with Clint somewhere, to a place where there were no jobs or schedules or obligations.

And that was an idiotic way to feel at the very start of a new picture. She'd worked too hard and long to get where she was. Usually she welcomed the pressures and challenges of another film.

By the time she got to her room she was a mass of confusion. She shook her head. Enough. She had to call Lloyd this very second. Sitting on the bed, she placed the call.

As soon as she heard Lloyd's impressive, rolling tones, Anne said, "Eureka, Your Majesty. I've found it. And not a moment too soon."

After his effusive congratulations, she answered a hundred questions, then took down another hundred rapid-fire orders in speedwriting on her ever-present legal pad. Lloyd had amazing contacts everywhere, and she heard him shouting to his patient secretary, Emma Roberts, for the home phone numbers of Tennessee officials who could pull strings and intercede with the Sedgby Tourist Board for permissions and arrangements.

Anne realized that she hadn't mentioned Clint Ward's mysterious project to Lloyd and did so, abruptly. Undismayed, Lloyd said carelessly, "We'll check it out from here. Meanwhile, do your thing." Only Lloyd, she considered wryly, would go right ahead again after what had happened before. Always the cockeyed optimist.

She didn't expect to get much sleep that night. Lloyd would call a council of war at the studio, notify the waiting actors and take care of numerous other things. Anne herself would be busy alerting the production manager to get the crafts services together, and arranging transportation and accommodations for actors and crew.

"Talk to you soon," Lloyd concluded. "Don't even think of dinner." As Anne hung up, her silent answer was "Lots of luck." There was no way she'd have a sandwich in her room tonight. Nevertheless, when she recalled the glorious new location, she found herself forgetting Clint Ward, plunging into a sketchy but inspired outline of scene revisions and fresh angles.

At twenty to seven Lloyd called her back. "We've turned up an annoying little detail. Guess who's on the premises? *Associated,* darling."

Anne's heart plummeted. Associated Industries controlled Wideworld Films, Hemisphere's biggest competitor, as well as a multitude of other enterprises.

"Oh, yes. A hush-hush, big-deal survey," Lloyd went

on sourly. "So hush-hush I couldn't even find out what it is from my spies."

"Then how do we proceed?" Anne asked him anxiously. *"Or* do we?"

"Full speed ahead. Nothing, but *nothing,* is going to hold up this film. I'm calling in every favor in history. It'll be a positive joy to cross swords with Associated's wonder boy."

This was serious, Anne thought. Lloyd was the most bullheaded genius in America; once he'd made up his mind, he didn't like being confused with mere facts. She knew it was fruitless to argue at this point.

Ignoring the reluctance in her voice, which she found impossible to hide, Lloyd went blithely on to ask if she'd made the Nashville calls yet and give her fresh suggestions. It was nearly ten to seven when he hung up, and she felt like a strand of overboiled spaghetti, and slightly frantic. She was supposed to meet Clint at seven, and she hadn't begun to get ready. Furthermore, the last thing she wanted now was to see him, after what Lloyd had told her. She debated leaving a message for him at the desk.

But no, that was a mouse's way to handle it. She'd damned well keep the date, face him in person, and ask him why in the world he hadn't been up-front with her. She stripped off her clothes and showered rapidly, then applied her few items of light makeup and slipped into the only dress she'd brought along. Since this was a combination rest and reconnaissance trip, she'd brought almost nothing, only this one just-in-case dress that looked just that—dry-in-the-shower practical. But at least it was a pretty print of green and lavender; its soft lines made the most of her figure and glorified her hair.

She wondered why she was making such a production of this. As far as she was concerned, this dinner was going to be hail and farewell, anyway. It was ten after seven before she was ready.

The big grandfather clock in the lobby of the inn was chiming seven-fifteen when Anne stepped into the lobby. She saw Clint Ward pacing the little lounge opposite the desk; when he saw her his anxious scowl magically disappeared and his wide, white smile broke out, relieved and welcoming.

He was at her side in seconds. "You look . . . wonderful. I was afraid you were going to stand me up."

She was wary of how to answer. It wouldn't do, this early on, to let her resentment fly. And she was disturbed to realize that she'd been anxious too, as anxious now as she'd been before that rotten call from Lloyd. Now she had a suspicion that she would have appeared no matter what. Finally she said, as casually as she could manage, "I never stand people up. Sorry I'm late." She smiled a bit tightly, looking up at him; his expression was so serious and eager that she knew that this was really an occasion for him. She was touched by the sudden failure of his *savoir faire.* He'd probably been everywhere, could handle almost anything, but now he seemed like a boy on his first date, standing there staring at her, at a loss for words.

The same thing must have occurred to him, because he came to himself with an almost visible start. He laughed and said in a more normal tone, "Shall we?"

They walked into the dining room. His manner more nearly resembled the one she'd noticed at their first meeting—in charge, self-assured. She couldn't help noticing, as well, the covert stares of the other women in the dining room. He was, she admitted, a magnificent-looking man. A waiter showed them to a sheltered table in a lovely spot with a panoramic view of the Smokies' moonlit peaks. It was already dark, Anne marveled, yet it seemed only moments since they'd met. She had the strangest sense of rightness, familiarity, sitting there with him. An awkward, paradoxical feeling, she reflected gloomily, when they could be in conflict at any moment.

The waiter was in a flurry, according them V.I.P. treatment. Anne was intrigued by that; it certainly wasn't for *her*. Usually she included Hemisphere's name when registering and was made much of; this time she hadn't. Her scrupulous nature had prevented her from charging this trip to the company since it was mostly a sentimental journey; her discovery of the location had been mere serendipity.

She began to wonder just who Clint Ward *was*, what he did for Associated. The waiter's eyes had that celebrity-serving gleam she'd come to know so well on the Coast.

Most of all, though, she was uneasy to find herself so strongly affected by Clint Ward, exactly the way she'd been before. Maybe that was why she was postponing the inevitable discussion, feeling so indifferent about what she would eat. She murmured her selection absently to Clint and as he gave the waiter their orders she stole another glance at him.

He looked stunning, dressed with costly casualness in an ivory turtleneck, dark brown slacks and a camel-colored cashmere sport coat that fitted him with accustomed ease. He wore good clothes with the same indifference as khakis.

Sensing her look, he turned to her with a smile, and her pulses leaped when his tawny eyes lingered on her face and mouth and hair.

"You are a lovely lady." His tone was so soft it was almost inaudible; the way he said the words made them different from any compliment she'd ever had before.

All of a sudden she was thinking absurd things and wanted to say them—what his glance did to her, how her fingers wanted to creep under his. But she stifled them, striving to steady her hand to raise her cocktail glass to her lips. She was going to have to forget him as a man and think of him as trouble.

She sipped her drink with deliberation and murmured, "Thank you."

"Your work all done?" he asked companionably.

The word jarred her, but she had to laugh. *"Done?* I've just started. All I did was make some phone calls."

"What *is* your job, exactly?" The exact question she wanted to ask him. But he asked it with warm and total interest while his gaze roved to her lips and caressed the shining waves of auburn hair along her cheeks.

"I'm an executive producer for Hemisphere Pictures. I've been scouting a new location. We lost our other one," she said with slight emphasis, "and we're pressed to finish the picture before the deadline."

"And you found one?" She imagined that his eyes became opaque, that there was a certain urgency in his query. As well there might be, she added drily to herself.

"Yes," she said coolly. "And right in the middle of Associated's project, it seems."

He looked taken aback.

"What's *your* project?" she shot at him.

His face changed; she'd never seen any man look so

nonplussed. "I can't tell you. We're keeping it under wraps for a while."

Her heart sank. It sounded like a government thing; they'd already lost one location on that account. A secret project. Her imagination took off: a defense thing, a missile site, a nuclear installation? Any of those could take priority over the film.

"Don't look like that," he pleaded.

"Why didn't you tell me right away?" she demanded.

"In the first place, I didn't know what your interest was, remember?" She did, and flushed, feeling chagrined. "Besides, the last thing I wanted to talk about was my work—or yours, Anne Reynolds." His gaze held hers insistently; then he reached out and took her hand in his.

To her dismay, that light touch had an astounding result. It literally shocked her skin, and a sensation of quick, nearly painful heat traveled up her arm. The power of that amber stare blunted her determined will, melting her resolve into vapor. Even with Dan, the love of her life, she had never known anything like this excitement, this electricity that stunned her. Oh, yes, she'd joked with other Hollywood sophisticates about the "thunder-and-lightning" meetings of lovers in films, the corniness of love-at-first-glance. And now it seemed to be happening to *her*, cool, fastidious, impervious Anne Reynolds.

Her feelings were so strong that she thought he could read them in her eyes, and she looked down defensively. Her face felt as if it were burning.

"Good Lord," he said softly. "I can't remember when I last saw a woman blushing. It's wonderful." The pressure of his hand increased.

Another poignant dart of warmth coursed through

her veins, this time like a jolt of alcohol. If his slightest touch had this effect, she pondered, breathing shallowly, what would his kiss be like . . . what would it be like if he held her in his arms, against his hard and splendid body?

But all this was getting out of hand. She'd kept this date so she could confront him. She forced herself to answer lightly. "An old Southern custom."

"The lady of the mountains," he murmured dreamily, still studying her, "where the air is thin and heady."

The writer in her responded to that last, rather old-fashioned word, which wasn't, to her regret, heard much anymore. She was falling under his spell; she had to get hold of herself. To break the mood, she answered lightly, "Oh, yes, I've been heady all my life. I was raised to be drunk on air."

He smiled, but the serious look was still in his eyes. She thought, I've never seen eyes that color, eyes with such mesmeric power. An odd little chill skittered down her backbone; he wasn't easily deflected. He was someone who would keep the upper hand.

"Tell me what it was like for you, Anne . . . growing up here," he insisted softly.

It was the first time he'd used her given name without the surname. "Anne Reynolds" had been half-teasing, properly distant; now his voice caressed her first name, making her feel oddly vulnerable, as if his mouth and hands were grazing her naked skin. Almost surprised into speech, she spoke of her childhood in the mountains and the shadow they had cast upon her heart, the gloom of the sighing pines, the glory of the redbud trees in spring, the flashing bodies of the timid, graceful deer.

She stopped, embarrassed.

"Please. Go on," he urged her. His hand tightened further over hers. "It's all very lovely. Like you." He grinned. "You were born to the business of make-believe."

There was something almost condescending in the comment, as if he were speaking to a child. Strange how it hurt her, and annoyed her, too.

"And you?" she retorted. "What were you born to—facts and figures? The scientists' famous evidence of the senses?"

His eyes were still tender, but his expression was unperturbed. "Absolutely. And my senses presented me with plenty of evidence when I saw you. I'll tell you straight, I've never met a woman who hit me so hard . . . and right away."

Suddenly she wanted to believe that, wanted it badly. Her heart was battering against her ribs, and she could hardly get her breath. In all the empty years she'd never met anyone like *him,* hadn't known anything like this since she was a susceptible adolescent. Even with Dan, there hadn't been this instant fire, this ache of yearning. No, with Dan it had been a gradual, slow warmth. A cold little idea intruded: He was avoiding any talk about himself. Why?

Suddenly all her pressures and obligations were heavy on her again, breaking her excited mood. She had to find out how long he'd be working in their area. And yet, how could she? He might interpret the question as eagerness to have him stay. And maybe she was eager for just that.

Studying her, Clint demanded, "What's the matter? I've upset you."

Evasively she looked at her watch. It was nine-thirty already. She couldn't believe it. With this man hours seemed to turn into minutes. "I'd better be going," she murmured. "I have a hundred things to do before tomorrow."

"Please, not yet." Clint Ward smiled at her, and the smile went right to her heart. "I was hoping we could go honky-tonkin', as they say in these parts."

It sounded so appealing. "I wish I could," she said tentatively, and her regret was so plain that he took encouragement from it.

"Then do."

"I couldn't. I've got to . . ." There was nothing she wanted more right now than to go dancing, to forget everything for a while.

". . . have a change of scene," he finished for her. "I promise to bring you back before I change into a frog at midnight. I have an early day myself tomorrow."

She chuckled. "You talked me into it." She had an uneasy feeling he could talk her into a good deal more without much effort. The thought was disturbing, but very exciting.

"Great." He reached instantly for the check, and Anne could feel a profound excitement emanating from him, although his expression was controlled. His golden brown eyes were bright in his tanned face, and he kept his gaze on her while they waited.

Feeling that those eyes could see too much, that Clint Ward could sense her own excitement, Anne said casually, "I'll get a coat and meet you in the lobby."

He rose, nodding, and as she left the dining room she felt that warm, unchanging scrutiny upon her. When she came downstairs again with a light coat over her arm, he was standing near the hotel door; his air of expectancy touched her, moved her, and her whole body responded. Her pulses leaped and fluttered; she experienced a strange sensation of tenderness.

As they walked out into the April night, she could

almost hear her dazed reflections—in hours her whole life had turned upside down. This man had stopped her with a single word among the dogwood blossoms, melted the coldness of years with a solitary look from those matchless eyes, fired her with the first touch of his hands. Now all she wanted was to be alone with him in the bright blue darkness.

Chapter 2

CLINT WASN'T EVEN TOUCHING HER AS THEY LEFT THE INN, yet her skin sensed his fingers. Nearby the mountains loomed; the cobalt dark had not erased them, only lent them a deeper darkness, a greater majesty. They were black, gentle shapes against the midnight blue of the wide, clear sky, silvered by the moon and glittering stars.

She inhaled the thin, intoxicating air and thought of all the make-believe love scenes she'd created. Now she was playing a scene of her own. His big hand was touching the small of her back now in a seemingly courteous and protective gesture, but the slight brush of his fingers against the soft, sliding material of her dress crackled along her nerves.

She couldn't help a faint, involuntary shiver; his awareness was immediate. The pressure of his fingers increased a little. It was astonishing, she thought. Incredible. This minute contact was affecting her more strongly than an intimate embrace. She had never, in all her life, been touched so magically.

Anne glanced covertly upward. This was not a scene from a film. This was no longer play. He was staring almost grimly into the blue dark, and when she absorbed his expression, all the powerful features of his face spoke to her of seriousness, a massive resolve. From his heavy brows to his hawklike nose, his ambitious mouth to his stubborn jaw, he was the picture of a man who neither trifled nor could be trifled with. Then he turned his head and looked down to meet her rising glance, and she saw profound wonder in his eyes. This whole encounter had an aura of sweet seriousness, of sudden promise.

The fact that she hardly knew him, that they were still strangers to each other, had no relevance now at all. She struggled to make some casual, light remark, but she abandoned the effort. Her very inability to speak made her feel more helpless than ever.

He handed her into the Rover in a grave, almost ceremonial way, as if every gesture had supreme significance. Then quickly he walked around, opened his door and was sitting beside her. In the small, enclosed space, she was more sharply conscious than ever of his big body, his hands on the wheel, his arm near hers. The fine sleeve of his jacket hid but could not civilize that arm; she could still see the tanned powerful forearm, the swelling biceps naked below the rolled-up shirtsleeves, that she had seen in the dying sun of the afternoon.

Her nostrils quivered. He smelled like new-cut grass after an April rain. And when he moved his arm to start the Rover and there was an accompanying movement of his long leg, she couldn't prevent herself from staring at his muscled thigh under the tightened fabric of his trousers.

Once again she felt that he was leaning toward her, the way he had leaned toward her that afternoon when he'd driven her down to Warrenburg from the mountain. She made another effort at finding a social remark to lighten the unbearable tension, but once more the words died in her throat.

As if she'd spoken, however, he gave her a swift glance; in the dimness his gleaming eyes pressed her like a kiss. She took a quick, trembling breath, dismayed by her own loss of ease, and felt that he must know how she felt, because a pleased smile touched his sensuous, hard mouth, and his fingers moved on the steering wheel and gripped it more firmly.

Oddly his smile, the movement of his fingers, worked on her perversely. The smile looked satisfied, the gesture that of a man who knew he was in control. It came to her in a burst of intuitive light: He was a scientist; his attitudes were clinical. Touch A produces Reaction B, leading to Coalition C. What they used to call a "filing-cabinet mind" when she was in college. The idea saddened her disproportionately, made her feel foolishly hurt. But at the same time it restored some of her reason and poise, even if it smudged the previous magic.

She felt herself smile and had a wild desire to tell him exactly what she'd been thinking; then she realized that he'd looked at her again, and had noted the smile.

"Yes?" The question was so friendly, so intimate sounding, that she was dismayed anew. Already she felt quite close to him. This whole thing was getting way, way out of hand.

She answered in a voice that sounded breathless even to herself. "I'm afraid it's a little rude," she blurted.

"Try me," he said calmly, but his voice, too, was a bit shaky.

"Well," she began reluctantly, "in school the liberal arts students said the engineers had 'filing-cabinet minds.'"

Totally unoffended, he laughed. The laugh was big and genuine, and it vibrated pleasantly on her nerves, just as his call had that afternoon. "Very apt, and absolutely true," he said easily. She thought how very secure he seemed in himself. "I like it," he said. "Not rude at all."

He was really quite impervious, she reflected, and knowing that aroused her admiration even while it turned her a little cold. But at least the exchange had popped the cork of silence, she thought wryly. She could talk now, like a civilized human being.

So when he remarked, "This is your old stamping ground; I suppose you know all these places," she was able to respond more easily than before.

"Oh, yes indeed. As a matter of fact, I recognize this place very well. They've even got the same old sign." He was pulling up in front of a roadhouse she'd danced in long ago. She could hear the strains of plaintive country music, see the same blue light streaming out from inside. "So it's still here," she murmured, pleased, and saw his smile answer her own.

"Does it bring back tender memories?" he asked casually, braking. The light query seemed to mask a passionate, almost possessive curiosity, but it was impossible for her to feel offended by it. There was no way around it. His attitude excited her immeasurably, and her pulses raced.

"Not at all," she said openly. "Just pleasant ones. When I came here then, I was really just . . ." She stopped herself. She'd almost said, "Just dreaming of meeting someone like you." Instead she finished, ". . . just a girl."

"I'm glad," he answered in a sober tone, and her heart fluttered in her throat. There was nothing clinical or self-satisfied in him now, she thought.

He smiled widely. "Shall we?"

"By all means." She heard the tremor in her voice again and tried to smooth it. "Let's go, and do-si-do."

He was chuckling when he opened her door and held out his hand. But when she put her hand in his, he abruptly stopped laughing, and she herself was devastated by the simple touch.

As they walked in together, the slight touch of his hand on the small of her back sent sensations that were almost painful in their sharpness shooting through her body, and her legs felt as if they were moving through water instead of air. It was all too certain now. No one had ever made her feel like this before. She knew she had to pull herself together right now, make herself keep talking. Say anything, she ordered herself.

Finally she offered, "It's been a long time, but this place hasn't changed at all. Even the music is the same."

Smiling, she looked up at him again. He was looking at her almost blankly, as if he had to make an effort to concentrate. He didn't smile back; his eyes bored into hers. With a slight shake of his head, however, he returned her smile rather tightly and commented, "That's a blessing. About the music, I mean. The old stuff seems to be dying out."

He had to raise his voice a bit to be heard over the twang of guitars, the thumping bass fiddle, the poignant keening of the singer. Anne thought the remark sounded forced, automatic. He looks like a sleepwalker, she reflected, wondering about the source of his bemusement, hoping that maybe it had the same source as hers. But she shook off the crazy thought. Their greater problem remained, no matter how physically devastating he was; she and Lloyd would be crossing swords with him, probably the very next day.

Anne was oppressed by that recollection as he led her to a table and pulled out a chair for her. But when he sat down facing her, having casually signaled to a waiter, she began to wonder just what the greater problem would be—their professional opposition or his disturbing power over her.

Catching her mood, he reached across the table and took her hand. "What is it? I think you do have tender memories about this place, Anne Reynolds. You look so . . . sad."

His calloused palm scraped excitingly over the smooth back of her hand; her fingers felt boneless, soft as meringue, and that prickly touch echoed within her. I can't let this keep happening, she thought in desperation. He mustn't keep touching me; it makes me ready for almost anything. She gently withdrew her hand, noticing that his face changed when she did, and even that set off the wretched hollowness again inside her, making her susceptible, tender.

"I'm not a bit sad," she responded as calmly as she could. She tried to make a joke of it. "Just reacting like any good mountain gal to down-home fiddlin'."

He grinned at her, and when the waiter came, asked her if she'd have some white lightnin'. She declined, grinning back, and opted for a cola, pleased that he knew the local slang for home-brewed liquor. After Clint had given the order and the waiter had left, the sprightly fiddles and guitars came to a thumping conclusion, and a country version of a lyrical love song began to float from the jukebox across the room.

Clint gave her a questioning look and held out his hand. "We're wasting this," he said, rising.

She nodded, and got up too. They walked slowly to the small dance floor and moved into each other's arms. He drew her close to him, and her first thought was, We fit . . . we fit exactly, with an exquisite, mysterious perfection. He'd seemed so much taller before, towering over her, yet when they were close like this she found her mouth at the level of his muscular neck. She was moving nearer, moving into him.

Their steps matched, and again she had the feeling that they were moving like swimmers through thick, warm water, not like dancers through smoky air. When she moved her head slightly, her lips grazed his tanned skin, and she could feel him wince with apparent excitement, his arm tightening around her.

They were so close to each other that she could feel his trembling hardness as his thighs brushed hers until she felt as weak as water. She moved her left hand a bit higher on his shoulder so that her fingers were on the back of his neck.

She felt a stronger tremor in his body, and his hand squeezed hers more tightly. His other arm led her in smaller and smaller circles, so close now that they could no longer take full steps; their feet were barely moving. He bent his head, and she could feel his parted mouth against her temple. Anne had the incredible sensation that there was nothing beyond this moment, that she was nothing more than mist enveloping him. It was such an unreal, magical exhilaration that she felt compelled to open her eyes to see if he were really there.

Gently she moved her head away from him and looked up into his eyes. Those strange golden brown eyes, which looked astonishing in the dim bluish light, burned down into hers. He no longer looked like a man in charge; he had a beseeching expression, one of open longing. His look left her dizzy.

The music had stopped, but they still stood there, staring at each other. The next tune started, and they moved like automatons together, pacing their small, hesitant steps to the sweet and now familiar closeness.

Then, in the middle of the song, he stepped back, loosing his hold, and gave her another significant look. He began to lead her from the dance floor back to their table. Her feet, with no will of their own, matched his pace as they had in the fleeting vertigo of their dancing.

Their drinks were on the table, she noted hazily, and Clint was reaching into his pocket for a bill, then tossing it on the table. Then they were walking into the vibrant night.

Anne felt that she was crossing the border of a dream; reality, with its blue-shaded lights and faceless people, its smoky air and haunting music, had been left behind. He opened the Rover's door, handed her in and, in what seemed less than a moment, was sitting beside her.

She turned to him and raised her face to his kiss.

But to her tender delight, her deep surprise, he only took her face between his hands and with shaky fingers started tracing her features, one by one, with delicacy and lightness. As it had before, his faintest touch affected her like a hot caress on her naked body. And all that power, she marveled, emanated just from the look in his eyes, the stroking of his hands.

Just when she began to find the waiting unendurable, he lowered his mouth to hers with excruciating leisure. Finally their mouths came together, and she knew in full the taste and contours of his, so sensuous and commanding.

Gently at first, his lips took possession of hers, learning their outline with a fiery, feathery grace. She could hear a tiny roaring in her head like the sea; then the caress was no longer gentle, but strong and hot and savage, and she was answering with all her being, passionately answering with her parted mouth. She raised her shaky hands to his hard neck while his fingers traced a burning path down the sides of her quivering body.

Her thumb met the beating hollow at the base of his ear. There was a minute pounding there, and now for her it was her first kiss all over again, her earliest memory of arousal. All the years between had disappeared in this timeless, heady instant. His fingers stroked her sides, sliding upward to graze her breasts. Gasping, she raised her hands and placed them on either side of his face.

Her fingers felt a tremor along his cheek, and a fluttering thrill assailed her. Breathlessly she marveled at how moved he was. It was such a stunning fact that her whole body answered; she experienced a profound feeling of need, of tenderness, and imagined that her very veins were suffused with racing lava.

He made a hungry, pleading sound, so poignant that it weakened her with tenderness; then he moved his head back and forth in her hands and kissed her palm before lowering his face to her neck. But soon his parted mouth felt again for hers, and the demanding touch of his opened lips aroused a sharper quivering inside her.

Now he seemed beyond control. This kiss devoured her, and his hands went wild, seeking her breasts, the inward curve of her waist and the gently outward swell below. He stroked her narrow, trembling thighs, making a hoarse sound deep in his throat; she was lost then, and there was no such thing as reason, as caution.

She gave a little cry of delight, which he must have misinterpreted as pain, because at once he slackened his hold. "Darling, have I hurt you?"

"No, no, no." She was so breathless she could barely speak. Now his hands were gentle, tender on her upper arms, kneading them softly. "No, Clint. I'm . . . undone," she whispered in a parody of an old-fashioned heroine, trying to lighten the moment, struggling to regain some sanity and control.

"So am I," he said simply, with such openness that her feelings of tenderness were awakened all over again. He reached up and stroked her hair. "And this is not the place to become undone," he added. His voice wavered; he obviously was trying to bring himself back under control too. He raised a rueful brow to indicate their surroundings—other cars were parked nearby, and people were coming and going all about them.

He released her and, leaning back in the seat, fumbled for a cigarette in his jacket. He offered one to her; she shook her head. He found his lighter and lit the cigarette, and she admired his magnificent head bending over the minuscule flame. She noticed that his hands were shaking when he replaced the lighter in his pocket. He exhaled a cloud of smoke and then turned slowly to observe her.

When she met his golden brown gaze in the half-light, her heart seemed to flutter. Never, never, she thought, had she seen such powerful eyes.

"You're like a dream," he murmured. *"This* is like a dream, Anne." He extended one hand again and traced a line from her forehead to her brow, down her cheek and chin and jaw with exquisite lightness, as if she were something utterly fragile and precious. The wonder in his look was repeated in his fingers. "Please," he begged her, "come over here. Just for a moment."

He threw his cigarette onto the gravel outside and held out an inviting arm. She moved toward him and buried her head against his shoulder.

Stroking her hair with the same cautious tenderness with which he'd touched her face, Clint whispered, "I knew it, Anne. I knew, as soon as I saw you through that lens, that your hair would feel like this . . . like warm silk . . . that your mouth would taste the way it does, and your skin—"

The wildness was coming back to them, tenderness gone for the moment; he grabbed her by the shoulders and kissed her deeply. Once more her thinking grew hazy, and all her flesh softened, submitted.

Without another word he started the Rover and drew her near him; she was vaguely aware that they were moving, speeding through the darkness back to where they had begun.

Her first clear thought was that this was inevitable. It was almost frightening to realize that she couldn't bear to have him let her go. She desperately desired to be with him tonight, all night, and through all the nights to come.

But when he gently let her go and placed both his hands on the wheel, her mind cleared, and she realized that although he wanted her tonight, what of his tomorrows? A faint, reproachful memory of Dan intruded, giving her pause. How could she know that Clint would be as serious . . . as committed as Dan had been?

It was a deeply disturbing question. Suddenly her insides swooped and she had the same sensation she'd had a thousand times, as if riding in a skyscraper elevator from the penthouse to the lobby. She glanced at Clint. He wasn't looking at her now, but grimly concentrating on the road, as if their journey were something that had to be gotten over with as quickly as possible so that he would be free at last to take her in his arms again. That notion moved her, but at the same time she was disquieted by the stubborn power of his profile. This man was a stranger.

And tomorrow . . . tomorrow, waking from a night of love, they would be competitors again.

From that grim thought her mind flew back again to Dan. What, after all, was this one interval compared to all those happy years with Dan, who'd cherished her, understood her perfectly? They'd been woven from the same cloth; he had been gentle, knowing her needs as well as his own, living through his imagination just as she did.

Clint was blunt, single-minded, as unlike Dan as a piercing blade of sunlight was from dusky shadow. Clint would not, could not, understand the convolutions of her mind and emotions. That conclusion, cold and quick as a finger-snap, brought her to a kind of sense, a sad dismissal of this maddened interval. For a time it had been a sublime intoxication. She'd been high on him, drunk with his nearness.

They were pulling up in front of the inn, and the brightness of the outdoor spotlights was shocking, as sudden as the secret conclusions of a moment before that had taken the edge from the magic, like a too-bright lamp clicked on. But at least she could see herself clearly now—a lonely, vulnerable woman surprised into insensate abandon, succumbing to a stranger.

Braking, he turned to her and smiled. When he saw her expression, he asked instantly, "What is it, Anne? What's the matter?"

She was immediately thrown into new confusion. He was sensitive after all. He'd known at once that something had changed, and changed abruptly.

"This . . . can't happen, Clint," she said in a slow, hesitant tone. "There are too many problems."

He reached out and grasped her arm. "What are you saying, Anne?" The words were so stricken that she began to feel uncertain. He looked dazed, as if she'd slapped him.

"It's too soon," she responded weakly. "And then there's . . ."

"Soon is the only way," he insisted, "when things are the way they are with us. I know you felt what I did, Anne. You're feeling it again. Don't try to deny it." He reached for her hand, and she didn't withdraw it. When he felt her pulse quicken, he whispered triumphantly, "You see?"

It's true, she thought, defeated.

Sensing his advantage, he went on, "It's the evidence of the senses. You may as well argue with . . . the power of the sun." She imagined he said that with an odd and special inflection, but the brief thought was lost in whirling desire.

Clint turned her hand over, then planted a lingering kiss on her palm. In spite of herself, she gave way to an inner quivering. He was speaking against her skin now, and those hot lips against her palm started that fiery tickle in her flesh.

"I don't play games, Anne Reynolds. I don't have the time or energy for that. I don't waste time on anything that's not vital. And you're vital to me, Anne, as vital as . . . my breath."

"How can you know that . . . so soon?" she protested, weakening.

"I told you, soon is the only way. If you don't know at once, you never know. As soon as I saw your face in my lens today, I was sure."

"It's not always like that," she murmured, thinking of Dan again and the gradual warmth that had built between them.

"It is if it's true," he persisted, and lifted her hand to his face. His cheek felt hot and firm, like sun-warmed leather.

She fought against her raging senses, reacting to his certainty, his arrogance. A cold, clear voice inside her said, you cannot fall into his bed, not with all the doubts still plaguing you, not with that other thing between you.

The other thing—the picture. His closely guarded project. Now her confusion, weariness and anxiety overwhelmed her. "We must say good night," she murmured.

"We can't, Anne; we *can't*," he pleaded. "Not after everything that's happened. . . ." He stared into her eyes.

She almost melted in that piercing golden fire, but determinedly she slipped from his grasp and opened her door, saying, "I'm sorry, Clint. I have to go. Good night."

His voice followed her as he leaped from the Rover. "But, Anne, what did I do?"

She rushed up the stairs into the inn without a reply, then hurried through the lobby before he could catch up with her. At the elevator she glanced back once, and she saw him still standing by the Rover, staring after her in bewilderment.

When she reached her suite she closed the door and leaned against it, feeling drained. Perhaps she'd made a terrible mistake. Now that she was alone she was more uncertain than ever.

Maybe Clint was right about the evidence of the senses. Anne herself, for all her imagination, had never been much of a mystic; she believed in what she could touch and smell and hear, taste and see. It was that very reverence for the visible and palpable that made her films such a delight to the eyes, the ears, the senses.

As for comparing Clint with Dan—they were two different men. Dan was gone. Everyone kept telling her that she had to live again. . . .

The telephone broke into her reflections, and wearily she sank on the bed and picked up the receiver.

"Finally!" Anne recognized Lloyd's patient secretary, Emma.

"Emma. What now?"

"Plenty," Emma responded drily. "I've been dying to get you." Her relieved sigh was so loud that she might have been in the same room with Anne. "What's now is that Napoleon's on the way to Tennessee. He dashed out and chartered a plane; they'll be landing in Knoxville at some Halloween hour and he'll probably wake you up at dawn, so you'd better get your beauty rest."

"Oh, no." Anne's heart plummeted. Lloyd wasn't

easy to take in the afternoon; at the crack of dawn he was overpowering.

"Worse than that," Emma continued. "He's been after everyone he knows in Washington and called in all his industrial spies who lurk around Associated. Everybody came up with zilch about what Associated's project in the Smokies is. But it must be incredibly big, because Lloyd was able to ferret out something significant."

"What's that?" Anne asked almost fearfully.

"One of their honchos is heading the project . . . none other than the famous Clinton Ward."

Anne's heart was thumping so loudly that she was afraid Emma would hear her voice trembling if she spoke.

"Anne, are you still there?"

"Yes." She managed to steady her voice enough to answer. "Sure, I'm here. Go on, Emma."

"Well, you know who Ward *is*, of course."

"As a matter of fact, I don't," Anne admitted, thinking, Of course I know. He's the first man to interest me in years. She tried to dismiss the disruptive thought.

"You never were one for the business pages," Emma chuckled. "He's one of the Big Three brains at Associated. The engineering counterpart to Einstein, Oppenheimer and Teller, that's all. He was on *This Minute*'s cover not long ago."

"Good Lord!" Anne gave an involuntary exclamation. "And he's *here?*" Better keep up the charade, she decided. There was no point at all in telling Emma about him at this stage.

"There, and in charge of the whole shebang. I don't have to tell you what that means, lady." Emma chuckled again. "It's right out of a script. It could almost be a film. *The Battle of the Titans.*"

For once Anne was unable to enjoy Emma's wry humor; she was too stunned by this new piece of information, too apprehensive about what lay ahead. To conceal her true feelings she forced a polite little laugh and said, "The perfect title." After an instant, she added, "Well, thanks for the warning. Anything else?"

"You're a glutton for punishment. Isn't that enough?"

This time Anne's laugh was genuine. "More than enough, thank you. We'll be talking."

"And talking and talking! Good night, Anne."

After murmuring good night to the intrepid Emma, Anne hung up. She glanced at her watch and realized how long the call had been. Even Emma, she thought, must be feeling a bit shaken up; she usually kept her long-distance calls brief and businesslike. Lloyd must have really put the poor woman through her paces.

For a long moment after she'd hung up, Anne sat on her bed, feeling overwhelmed. She really ought to try to get some sleep; it was nearly eleven-thirty, and if Lloyd would be arriving at dawn, Anne knew she'd be a wreck if she had too little sleep. But there was too much to think about. Besides the many notes on her pad, there was the matter of Clint Ward.

Now, more than ever, he would be a lot to deal with, maybe more than she was capable of. It had been difficult enough to realize that he had an extraordinary effect on her. After what Emma had told her—that he was one of Associated's Big Three—Anne felt positively intimidated. Many things that puzzled her about him were explained by the very fact of his prestigious position. His air of worldiness, of elegant ease, and his in-charge ways were all-too-easy to understand in the light of that new information.

Emma had hit it right on the button. It would indeed be a battle of the titans between Clint Ward and Lloyd Eliot, the famous "bad boy" of the industry, converging on each other's battlegrounds. And Anne Reynolds —the junior titan, she dubbed herself with unfailing humor—would be right smack in the line of fire. It was a daunting prospect, when she needed all her creative energy for the picture.

Trying to shake off her stunned apathy, Anne got up and stripped, then headed for the shower. Just as she turned the water on, the phone began to ring again. Rebelliously, she decided just to let the damned thing ring. If it were Lloyd, calling from some outlandish checkpoint on the way, he'd just have to wait until morning to inspire her with his latest idea. She was going to take the phone off the hook as soon as she finished showering.

Dried and scented, she felt refreshed and new. She slipped into a nightgown and was about to raise the receiver when she heard another ring. Resigned, she picked it up and said wearily, "Hello."

"Anne?" Her heart gave a painful lurch. It was Clint Ward.

"Why didn't you tell me?" she demanded abruptly.

"Tell you what?" He sounded so taken aback that she couldn't help being a little chagrined at her own rudeness. But she couldn't let him get to her so easily.

"That you're Associated's cover boy," she pursued coldly.

'There was a short silence. "What does that mean?" he asked in a cautious tone.

"One of the Big Three," she quoted. "Ergo, up to something big right in our area."

"I've never been much for titles," he said calmly. "The bottom line is, I'm just an engineer, Anne. And I don't understand what you mean by 'our area.' Whose?"

"Hemisphere's. I told you what this location means to me . . . to us. You know we lost our last one, and we're very pressed. We've got a deadline, a schedule. How could you let me rave on and on, when all the time you knew that your very own project might trip us up?" As she went on, Anne was getting madder. It was hard to remember the sweet things that had happened between them when she thought of the larger issues.

"Because you made me forget everything, Anne." Her treacherous heart turned over. She felt that insidious warmth again, that awful giddiness. But she summoned up every ounce of her self-control.

"We've got to talk about this," she insisted. "Please don't change the subject."

Anne heard him take a deep breath; then he said gently, "All right. Talk."

"Why didn't you say something tonight, when I told you how vital this location is to us?"

"Anne, let me come to your room. We can talk in person. I've never been any good on the phone."

She almost said, "I'm not dressed," but stopped short, afraid that would sound too seductive. And it *was*, she thought, dismayed—seductive to her. But she retorted, trying to hide the quiver in her voice, "Poor Mr. Bell. After all he went through to invent the telephone. And now you say you can't talk on one."

Anne could hear the smile in his voice when he answered, "You're right." He paused, then added, "I didn't tell you because I didn't want anything to intrude on . . . tonight. Please, Anne, let me come to you."

"That's impossible," she said, trying to sound firm. "I literally have to get up at the crack of dawn."

"All right." He sighed. "But you see how it is. I knew we'd have problems soon enough, and they've already started."

"Aren't you being a little premature? We've only known each other for an afternoon and an evening."

"Premature?" he repeated. "Not a bit. You felt the chemistry between us. Don't deny it. I told you, I don't have time for games, and I'm not playing one. I intend to keep seeing you."

She was torn between amusement and excitement. If Lloyd Eliot was like Napoleon, Clint was a self-styled Alexander the Great. All she needed was two arrogant emperors in her life.

"I hope you'll let me," Clint added softly. "Even now I miss you."

Anne was swept again with that dismaying weakness, but she made herself say, "I'm sorry. I've got to hang up now." All the while she wanted to say what was really in her mind: that she wasn't a game player, either; that he affected her more deeply than she wanted to admit. That she was afraid, too. Afraid to open herself up to pain with a man who was still a stranger. Instead, regretfully, she added, "I don't see how we can keep on seeing each other under the circumstances. It's impossible."

"Nothing's impossible, Anne. You'll be seeing me, all right. Sleep well."

She sat there with the receiver in her hand, listening to the cicada-like drone of the line, and burst into tears. This was too much to deal with all at one time: finding the location at the eleventh hour; facing Lloyd at dawn;

and finally meeting, for the first time in three years, a man who really made her feel alive again. She couldn't handle it anymore . . . not tonight, anyway.

She hung up the phone and got into bed, contemplating the stack of paperback books on the bedside table. There should be some good escape there, she reflected wryly. But something kept nagging her until she remembered that she hadn't arranged with Emma to have a supply of clothes sent along. With the time difference, it was still early on the Coast, so she called Emma at home and asked her to leave a note asking the housekeeper to pack a couple of suitcases to be sent along with the transportation boss on his flight the next morning. Emma assured Anne that she'd take care of it and told her to get some sleep.

With that out of the way, Anne began to unwind. She chose an English murder mystery to read; it seemed a far cry from the movie business, the perfect way to relax. And, she hoped, it wouldn't have a thing to do with love. But in that she was disappointed. The detective-hero inevitably reminded her of Clint Ward, and he was courting a woman whose personality resembled Anne's own.

"I give up," she said aloud, tossing the book on the floor. She turned out the lamp and lay back, staring into the dark. If only sleep would come.

It wouldn't.

For a whole half hour after she had run away from Clint, Anne thought with dismal humor, it had been easy to think of him objectively. And Emma's call had helped—helped recall Anne to the reality she faced, aided in cooling her off a little to that sexy man who called himself "just an engineer."

But then, damn it, he had had to call her himself, starting it all over again. And remembering his voice on

the phone made the whole afternoon and evening
unreel before Anne's inner vision just like a film.

She could see him standing on the opposite ridge, in
the sun; raising his strong, tanned arm to her in
greeting; walking toward her over the fresh April grass
on the edge of the dogwood forest. His first hello in that
deep, unaccented voice that rang along her nerves; his
muscular height; that unique face—weathered, black
browed and hawklike.

How hokey! the objective part of her commented.
Heathcliff and Tarzan in one big attractive package.

And yet her heart replied, It was so beautiful. The
way he'd looked at dinner; the things he'd said. That
walk to the Rover, a simple act, but with something so
fated, so significant in it all.

The music at the roadhouse, and their dance . . .
Recalling that, Anne felt her treacherous body catch
fire.

"The evidence of the senses," he had called it.

Anne thrashed about in bed, seeking a more comfortable position, but there was no comfort to be had.

The whole thing was impossible.

At last a faint drowsiness began to overtake her.

Her final waking thought was an odd one: That deer,
a skittish creature, had shown no fear of him.

Clint lit another cigarette—his thirtieth of the day,
which was a real departure—and paced.

Letting go of that receiver had been like letting go of
her hand outside the inn. He tingled, thinking how near
her voice had seemed on the phone. He savored its
timbre, a kind of silvery alto that was neither high nor
low. Perfect, like everything about her. And he'd
scared her off, jumping the gun like that.

Clint swore. He stubbed out the cigarette; it had tasted stale, unsatisfying. He smiled one-sidedly. There was only one thing that would be satisfying tonight. That was to spend all of it with her.

According to a football coach from long ago, he ought to take a cold shower and drink orange juice. Well, he couldn't wake up the hotel staff for juice at this hour, but he could take a cold shower, he decided somberly. It had come to that.

He suited the action to the thought. He hadn't met a woman who'd gotten to him so much since . . . Clint thought back and concluded, Since never.

He padded back to his bedroom and suddenly wondered where her room was. He tried to locate it mentally from her extension number. Two floors away, at the other end of the hall, he calculated. He was acting like a teenager.

Hell.

If her room had been right next door it would have been too damned far away to suit him. But he didn't want to think about it anymore; he'd go nuts.

Clint put on pajama bottoms and went back to his desk in a grim attempt to go over the measurements he'd taken that afternoon. There was going to be a hell of a problem with that ridge and the neighboring bluffs. Maybe the excavation and blasting costs would be too high; maybe not. Clint had reaped plenty of results before, though, from less promising material. He spread out his area map. The heavy paper crackled harshly in his ears in ugly contrast to the remembered sound of her voice.

Damn it. There he went again. Gentle but all too firm, he concluded. She was stubborn as a mule, taking that absurd work of hers with such high seriousness.

But so lovely, so real, so charming. How someone like that could get involved with all the glitz of Hollywood he couldn't fathom.

He let the map fall.

What a waste—all that freshness, all that brightness and imagination, given to Tinseltown.

He chuckled softly. You phony jerk, he addressed himself. That's not the kind of waste that's bothering you. It's wasting this wonderful night. We should be together right now.

Clint got up and strode to the window, feeling hot. He flung open the window and took a deep breath of the heady air. She'd liked it when he used that word, saying she'd been raised to be "drunk on air."

That was exactly the way she'd made him feel— drunk just looking at her. He thought of her sweet face and her wonderful cloud of red hair; just touching it turned him on. She had him thinking, feeling, like a kid—him, Clinton Ward. And he hadn't been a kid for quite a time.

Her face, her hair, the rest of her . . . think about that, buddy, he warned himself, and you'll never sleep a wink tonight.

The worst thing was that it wasn't even that simple. There had been more to his feelings than that since the first minute his lens had picked up her face. He had the damnedest desire to take care of her. From what she'd told him, she'd worked so hard and done so much alone. A woman like her shouldn't be alone. She was so vulnerable . . . so delicate. She needed direction—his direction. She shouldn't be at the beck and call of an idiot like that Eliot.

Clint had heard that the man was always throwing fits about this and that. It amazed Clint that Eliot could produce a commercial, much less a movie. And Anne was stuck with him for a boss. Clint would almost welcome a confrontation with Lloyd Eliot; he couldn't stand the thought of Anne hopping every time the guy snapped his fingers. Clint could just picture him— short, fat, a real dirty old man.

But he realized that a confrontation with Eliot would mean a confrontation with Anne Reynolds. And that wasn't what he wanted.

Chapter 3

ANNE DREAMED OF THE BUZZ OF AN ENORMOUS BEE . . . and the sound of her phone tore the black fabric of sleep.

She reached out, found the receiver.

"Rise and shine, Annie! Big Daddy here."

Lloyd. In one of his cutesy moods. She let out a small moan and blinked at her travel clock. Seven A.M.

"Where are you?" she mumbled. "Knoxville?"

"Downstairs, sweetheart, in the Moonshine Manor. About to order breakfast. Want yours?" He sounded painfully alert.

"Yes," she exhaled in feeble petition. "*Lots* of coffee. Ten minutes."

Used to outrageous hours on location, Anne was a lightning dresser. A weather check the previous night had predicted that today would be chilly, with clouds. She confirmed that with a glance out the window. April, with its usual capriciousness, had turned forbidding and gray.

Anne pulled a gray-green sweater from another drawer, put it on with a russet tweed skirt and slipped on a matching jacket. In the bathroom she brushed her hair and dabbed on lipstick. She found her briefcase and slung it over her shoulder. It was already packed with her notes and other necessities.

She tossed a capacious sea green raincoat over her arm and checked her watch. The whole operation had taken six minutes. One detail, though—she was in her stocking feet. She laughed and zipped on well-polished mahogany boots, then hurried out to the elevator.

Feeling a bit giddy, she entered the lobby and found herself looking around for a sign of Clint Ward. She wasn't sure whether she was disappointed or relieved not to find any.

Lloyd Eliot was the only guest in the dining room. He was seated in solitary ease at a table for four by the picture window, looking almost indecently bright-eyed and handsome. He was pure Hollywood in a jacket of creamy cashmere with leather elbow patches, and an Aran sweater. The sweater exactly matched his big, styled mane of ivory hair; he was playing the exiled king at a country retreat.

Sighting her, he rose. "The lady Anne!" He hugged her and kissed each of her cheeks with the mumbling accompaniment that people in The Business seemed so fond of.

She grinned and gave him a real kiss, liking him in spite of himself. "It's good to see you." Her greetings always seemed anticlimatic after his, but his smile was genuine nevertheless. He had as much respect for her ability as she had for his, and they were comfortable together. She'd come to look on him as an incorrigible older brother.

Anne tossed her raincoat over his Burberry on one of the captain's chairs and sat next to him, putting her briefcase on the floor by her chair.

"Well, my dear," he boomed again, "you look positively reborn. What is it—this hideous fresh air?" To Lloyd the outdoors was simply a nowhere connecting places.

She temporized with a smile and started to say, "No, just utter confusion," but without waiting for an answer, he rushed on. "I'll be as good as gold and not talk business till you've had your coffee. Here." He poured her a cup and she sipped gratefully.

It was like a transfusion. The coffee, and the very sight of Lloyd, had reawakened all her energy and enthusiasm.

"Lloyd, you'll *love* the site." Before she knew it, she'd described Sedgby in minute detail, even giving him a capsule history. Then she fished her tentative shooting schedule from her briefcase and thrust it at him.

While Anne absently ate her breakfast, Lloyd scanned the schedule, commenting, "I like it . . . I *like* it."

When she came back to earth a little, she blinked, and Lloyd emitted his stage laugh. She thought fleetingly what a shame it was, in a way, that he'd abandoned his Shakespearean acting career. With his bright, dark-lashed blue eyes, his noble features and splendid voice, he was perfect for the stage. But he'd been too much of a director himself, he claimed, to take direction from others.

"I like this," he repeated, tapping the schedule with his finger, then running a glance over her accompanying notes. "But then, I expected nothing less from you. This is the sort of thing that made *The Winter Kind* such a smash. And you were 'brung up' in these parts, as the locals say. Now, when you've finished that mess"—he waved at her plate—"we'll get down to cases."

"I want my grits," she protested. She hadn't tasted them for years.

"Grits! My sainted aunt. I thought they were a *myth*, child. That sounds like *gravel*."

She laughed at his expression. To Lloyd, the South was New Orleans, Miami and an ancient premiere in Atlanta. The rest was an uncharted wilderness. "Try some," she suggested. "You've still got some on your plate."

Leaning over, she put her hand on his arm. He was examining the grits as if they were chocolate-covered ants, with such a funny face that it made her giggle.

At that instant she saw a man coming through the archway to the dining room. Clint Ward. Her heart lurched.

Clint's glance shot to her hand on Lloyd's arm. Anne's face felt burning hot. Good heavens, she thought, he looks as if he thinks we're *lovers*. Abruptly she withdrew her hand. Clint turned on his heel and stalked off.

The sudden heat drained from her face.

Lloyd was gingerly tasting the grits. "Not bad," he decided. He looked at her. "What's up with you? You look as if Dracula's bitten you, darling."

Anne *felt* pale. This was grotesque, after last night.

After Clint had kissed her, touched her, held her like that . . . and now, to see her in a scene that appeared so intimate.

Lloyd reiterated, "What's the matter, Anne?"

"Not a thing," she said tightly. "Just loss of sleep."

"Is *that* all?" Lloyd expelled a sigh of relief. She thought with wry affection, It wouldn't occur to him to apologize for getting me up so early. "Thank the Lord," he added. "There's too much to do for you to get sick on me now. Besides, I simply can't deal with all these boors and idiots without you, Anne. There's never before been an executive producer who could handle all the nuts and bolts and still come up with artistic imagination."

His praise warmed her.

"Have some more coffee," he said, "and listen to what I've already done."

She heard the astonishing list of things he'd handled since yesterday evening, amazed as ever at his ability to charm or bulldoze others into handing him his way. But she found her concentration slipping, her thoughts drifting back to Clint Ward.

". . . Suzuki, and Livie and Jack and the supports will be flying in this afternoon," Lloyd was saying. "Are you ready to cope with Jack the Gripper?"

He cocked an ironic brow at her, and the nickname got her full attention. She'd coined it for John-Mark Salem, their romantic lead, after suffering his annoying mannerism. He had a habit of grabbing women by their hands or upper arms in a bone-crushing grip almost every time he spoke to them.

"A touching fellow," Lloyd punned. Anne hooted, feeling more normal; her feet were on familiar ground again. This was the world she loved and knew—crowded and hectic, gossipy, stimulating. Last night she had been catapulted into an alien place for a little while, an odd dream-country where no one existed except one man, one woman. She tried to ignore the small pull at her heart when she remembered, thinking that, strange as it seemed, this world of make-believe was truly her reality.

"Terribly," she agreed. "You said Suzuki's coming this afternoon." He nodded. "That's marvelous," she said. The petite, unflappable Japanese designer was the only one who could come up with the designs Anne envisioned, colors in harmony with the Smokies' cloudy peaks, the dogwoods' dewy pallor and the somber gleam of the Sedgby interiors.

"We'll have the whole crew together tonight," Lloyd promised. "But our first order of business this morning is an appointment in Sedgby. That's the real reason for this ghastly early call. Not for me just to see it."

"With the tourist board," she inferred.

"None other. But it won't be an ordinary meeting. The board includes my old friend Hobie Cannon, a name that should be familiar to you since you probably studied his history texts at that school of yours. He's department head now."

"F. Hobart Cannon! Of course." She'd remembered him all this time because his books had a way of glamorizing the dullest facts, making them as vital as the very moment one lived in.

"A very prestigious historian, a *mavin* on this area. We were together at Yale; for a time Hobie wanted to tread the boards, too. Just as well he didn't—he played an appalling Cassio to my Iago in *Othello*. Ugh! Then he opted for that dreary specialty. Well, Hobie, poor dear fellow, is one of the prime movers on the board, but his *aunt*, my dear, is the chairman. Evidently a sort of Appalachian Victoria. Hobie told me on the phone last night that despite my okay from all the other powers that be, Aunty will probably cut up rough about our little project. She thinks all movie people are as decadent as ancient Romans and wear rhinestones on their eyelids. Exactly," Lloyd emphasized with a pressure of his hand on hers, "why I want such a lady as you along today. That outfit, by the way, is a masterpiece. You look like a pretty librarian."

"I should have put my hair up in a tight knot," she said, a little miffed at his evaluation of her outfit. By West Coast standards she supposed she was pretty conservative.

"But what real clout does she have?" Anne protested. "You've said you have the big okays, even a tentative pact with Associated." The latter had been on his list of the things he'd accomplished.

"Yes, but there are wheels within wheels. Aunty Hester—wouldn't you know it would be a moniker like that?—owns half the mountain, three-quarters of the private property in Sedgby, is wardress of Sedgby antiquities by virtue of being a descendant of . . . what's his name again?"

"You mean Josiah Cannon, the founder of Sedgby?"

"The very one, my dear. *And* she's a kind of tyrant-queen among the locals. Not—repeat, not—of this era," Lloyd said with gloom. "She's lethal, our Hobie says."

"Oh, no. '

"Right now it's the rental of the Sedgby properties we've got to wrap up. We'll have to sweeten the old bat, that's all. And there may still be waves from Associated."

"In spite of the agreement?" Anne asked, bewildered.

"In spite," Lloyd responded. "That high-powered

mechanic of theirs, Ward, even dictates to their brass, apparently."

"What do you mean?" The unexpected mention of Clint's name jolted her.

"He's got carte blanche in all his wretched projects; that was part of his hiring agreement with Associated. Ergo, we've got to get his cooperation too."

"I see." Anne tried to compose her expression, hoping it wouldn't be a dead giveaway.

Lloyd patted her hand. "Not to worry, kiddo. Remember, I romanced that English battle-axe into renting us her castle . . . and then there was the Italian contessa." He looked at his paper-thin gold watch and exclaimed, "We'd better be off! We have to beard Hester at ten, and I'd like to look around beforehand. Ready?"

Anne nodded. Lloyd rose and threw a bill carelessly on top of the check, too impatient to fool with a credit card. He peered out the picture window. "You'll need your pelisse," he said quaintly, swept up her raincoat and draped it around her shoulders. She retrieved her briefcase and waited for him to belt himself into his trench coat.

When they were outside, he remarked, "I trust you'll chauffeur me. Some local with the improbable name of Charon's Taxi drove me out to the Styx," he punned, grinning. "I swear I haven't been so terrorized since that demented bus ride in Sicily. I will *not* drive myself on these roads."

"Have no fear." Anne patted his arm. "I've driven here since I was fifteen, and it's just like riding a bicycle. It's all come back to me."

She automatically glanced around the parking area for Clint's Rover. It was nowhere to be seen. She fervently wished she could get him out of her mind.

Nevertheless, as she drove the winding, rising highway toward Sedgby she was conscious that her excitement over the film was coming back again. When she
recognized the shoulder by the dogwood clearing she
braked.

"Surely *this* isn't it," Lloyd protested. "There's nothing for miles."

"No, not yet. But this is the spot I've marked down
for the proposal scene. Come on . . . you can see it
from the road. We don't even have to go down there
now." She noticed his hesitant glance at his polished
ankle boots, his gabardine slacks.

They got out and walked to the edge of the shoulder.
After looking down on the clearing, at the white
loveliness of damp dogwood blossoms, Anne inevitably
glanced across at the opposite ridge. There was no tall,
lean figure there today. Her heart hammered sickening-
ly; once more she was overwhelmed with memories of
the night before. She was glad that for the moment
there was no real need for her to speak. Lloyd was
raving about the pictorial grandeur of the spot, asking
her the usual rhetorical questions.

She was newly dismayed by her inattention. Only
moments earlier she'd been full of the creative ideas
she'd had for the proposal scene, but now she seemed
to hear Lloyd as if he were far away. It almost
frightened her that the thought of Clint could be so
all-absorbing. She wondered uneasily how she was
going to bring her best to the project if he could
unsettle her like this, even at a distance.

Now Lloyd remarked again about the time and
suggested that they go on.

She was so silent on the drive that even the ebullient
Lloyd noticed it. "Are you all right?" he prodded.

"Of course. I was just thinking . . ." Anne said the

first thing that popped into her head. ". . . how strange it is that you and Hobie Cannon went to school together. Very convenient. Is there anyone you don't know?"

"Crowds of people," he conceded. "Several Watusi and most Russians. Humorless people, those."

She laughed, feeling better in spite of herself. Lloyd never ceased to resent the fact that he hadn't been allowed to remake *Anna Karenina* on location.

"Now," he said briskly, "I want Hobie to think I've been doing masses of research. Let me read back the history of Sedgby to you in twenty words or less."

He succinctly repeated what she'd told him about the history of Sedgby: The "ideal" community had been founded in 1880 by the eccentric English aristocrat Josiah Cannon, who named it for a famous English school. His fellow pioneers, other idealistic aristocrats dedicated to working for the community's common good, had given up the enterprise in only three years, not having the slightest notion of how to make a living from their farming, fruit canning and pottery making. Some die-hard descendants had remained and kept up the historic buildings; now the state and private interests were preserving it as a shrine.

"You're a very quick study," Anne assured him. "But look . . . we're here."

There was the American Gothic spire of the old Christ Church, then the old Sedgby library. Farther on they could see the sprawling Halberd Inn, reconstructed on its original foundation. Lloyd peered at its two-story veranda and the towering center gable on its third floor. "Unbelievable," he breathed.

Pleased, Anne drove around the inn to park in the rear. "The 'young bloods' kept their horses here in the old days. So you agree with me about Sedgby?"

"I'm flabbergasted," Lloyd admitted as she stopped.

"Did you know that words from Shakespeare's time still show up in the natives' speech?" Anne offered as they got out.

"Good Lord." They walked toward the rear entrance. It was all extremely casual; she pushed open one of the back doors. There was no one in attendance, but they could hear the chink of silver against china, the murmur of voices. "Late breakfast," she explained. "Sedgby's doing pretty well from the tourist trade."

"And will do even better when we're shooting," Lloyd added. "Some of the tourists will probably be offering their services as extras, and then afterward . . ."

He broke off. A slender middle-aged man with a severe pepper-and-salt crewcut, dressed in pressed chinos and an old tweed jacket, was coming toward them, smiling in the dim hall. He held a smoldering pipe in one hand. He extended the other, calling out in a Tennessee-English accent, "Lloyd Eliot, as I live and breathe!"

"Hobie!" Lloyd boomed out and strode to the man, then clapped him on the shoulder and pumped his hand.

Lloyd introduced Hobart Cannon to Anne. He stared at her hair with open admiration. "You mean this is your executive producer? I thought she was the *star.*"

It would be inhuman, Anne thought, not to react warmly to *that.*

"You've clued Ms. Reynolds in on Hester, I take it," Cannon said to Lloyd, and took a pull at his pipe.

"Oh, yes," Anne responded. "I understand her . . . opinion is very important."

Hobie Cannon chuckled. "You should work for the State Department. We'd better go in, though. All the others have arrived."

Anne's watch indicated only five to ten. Hester must run a very tight ship, she decided, following Cannon to a set of double doors farther down the hall. He pulled the doors open and gestured his guests inside.

Anne had no chance to observe the room or its occupants, except for one. One of the men rising from the table was Clint Ward.

She realized to her horror she'd stopped dead in her tracks, almost colliding with Lloyd, who was a step behind her. Her face was dyed with heat, and she felt like someone who'd been dealt a blow on the chest. Her heart pounded.

Clint looked utterly magnificent and quite at ease in a light brown corduroy suit and a dull gold sweater that made his hair look black as pitch and made his odd golden brown eyes contrast astonishingly with his weathered skin. There wasn't the slightest sign of recognition on his bland face, only a swift brightening of his dark amber gaze. Apparently he was going to take his cue from her.

From nowhere a phrase from a lovely old folk song rang across her mind: "Black is the color of my true love's hair . . ." With desperate swiftness she grasped for control, realizing with relief that all of it, the pause, the look, the fleeting observance and the memory of the song, must have taken only seconds, because no one seemed the wiser.

Cannon was inviting Anne and Lloyd to the head of the table, where a forbidding old woman in black was enthroned.

"Aunt Hester, may I present Ms. Reynolds and Mr. Eliot of Hemisphere."

Anne murmured, and Lloyd gave Hester Cannon one of his best half bows.

"Ms. Reynolds," Cannon amplified, "is executive producer, and Mr. Eliot is senior producer-director."

Ignoring Lloyd, Hester Cannon commented, "Well, it's high time the female sex came into its own. I congratulate you, young woman."

Anne smiled at Hester. The woman was unbelievable. She sounded as if she'd just discovered the feminist movement yesterday. Hester looked like something right out of a Victorian novel, except that she must have been extremely old.

"Get cracking, Hobie," she directed. "Introduce these young bucks and get the meeting started." The "young bucks" were two men of at least fifty, Anne thought with an inner laugh.

Cannon proceeded with the introductions. When he reached Clint Ward, Anne could almost see Lloyd's hackles rise; she knew, too, that hovering on the tip of his tongue was an irascible question about why Ward was present at the meeting. Clint, for his part, barely acknowledged Lloyd's presence, and he greeted Anne as would any man being introduced to a pretty woman —with a warm smile. She was suddenly conscious that she must look absolutely wild, with her humidity-curled hair billowing out over her shoulders, her flushed face and still-uncertain manner.

When they sat down she found that her chair was directly opposite his.

Clint tried to keep his expression neutral and made every effort not to stare at her across the table while he heard the old woman tartly opening the meeting.

It was damned near impossible. Her hair looked like a cloud of fire, the only bright spot of color in the somber room. Today her startled eyes looked like jade above the green sweater. Clint's thoughts astonished him—what a way for an engineer to think. He smiled to himself, then realized that the others were looking at him and vaguely heard his own name.

His disciplined mind went into instant action. "Thank you, Mrs. Cannon. I appreciate the chance to sit in. My bosses, as you know, asked me to come. The agreement they reached with Mr. Eliot is far from final. I can only give my approval after a study of Hemisphere's plans and schedules."

"Which is not the purpose of this meeting," Lloyd said crabbily, "and should be taken up privately by us. In other words, you consider yourself here to monitor Hemisphere, Mr. Ward."

" 'Monitor is a belligerent word," Clint drawled. "I'd prefer to say 'be made aware' of your plans. I'm afraid," he addressed the others, "I've not yet had the chance to approach Mr. Eliot about this. He arrived only this morning."

Anne's look seemed to say, "You had a chance at breakfast." Clint met her eyes, thinking, How right you are. And passed it up because I felt like a jealous kid, seeing you so chummy with this half-baked Barrymore.

"Gentlemen!" Hester snapped, and banged her gavel. "Let us maintain some semblance of order. Before we take up the matter of rentals and extras, I want to make my position clear, Mr. Eliot. Mr. Ward's project (whatever that may be)"—the parenthesis was dry—"has at least brought no disreputable personnel into our village. Movie people, I understand, are still prone to such excesses as those afflicting the industry not long ago." She mentioned certain scandals of the twenties as if they'd happened last week.

Clint controlled his mirth. The old girl was nuts. This

was the first time he'd ever had trouble keeping a straight face at a business meeting. But then Anne Reynolds hadn't been at those meetings, either; the combination of her nearness and Hester's outrageous remarks was enough to throw anyone off-balance.

"Aunt Hester . . ." Cannon scolded. "The rest of the board is extremely eager to conclude this agreement with Hemisphere. The revenue alone—"

"May I *continue?*" Hester froze him. Clint noticed that Anne seemed to be having trouble with her own composure, and that two of the board members were coughing into their hands. Hester quizzed Anne, who replied, Clint thought, magnificently.

When she was through, Eliot took over, and Clint had to admit he was masterful—so stately, so convincing that Hester was beginning to thaw. Smoothly Eliot went into the matter of rentals and the hiring of extras, which, he said, would create a good deal of employment in the area. The board members' eyes gleamed when Eliot named the rental offer.

"The whole operation," Lloyd concluded, "will take only a few weeks. We've done some of the filming already, and we'll be able to do the rest on the Coast and elsewhere. So we'll work here without causing the slightest problem for this lovely village . . . or Associated"—he shot a repressive glance at Clint, who found that statement ridiculous—"*and* to the enormous benefit of this treasured . . . shrine. Furthermore, we're planning a special promotion in conjunction with our own publicity as an additional fund-raiser for Sedgby. We hope to premiere in Knoxville, which will bring the area a great deal of attention."

That was overdoing it a bit, Clint judged, but the pompous idiot could be right. The discussion went on and he hardly listened; he hadn't really had to be here at all. But he'd known Anne would be, and it was the only way he could think of to see her. He couldn't have waited another hour; he had been haunted by her half the damned night.

When he heard the thawing Hester offering the three of them the "south parlor for your arrangements," he accepted with alacrity. It would be mighty pleasant business, he decided, to confer with Anne Reynolds again.

When Hobie Cannon showed them into the cozy parlor, Anne's sense of being transported back to the past was stronger than ever. The place had long ago been a "writing room"; the round antique tables still displayed quill pens and inkpots. There was an air of serenity about it all, in sharp contrast to her own turbulent feelings. The comparative smallness of the space made her more aware than ever of Clint Ward's massive presence; he seemed to fill the small prim room.

Anne hardly looked at him until they'd entered; she knew she couldn't trust herself. And while it puzzled her that Clint kept up the masquerade of their being strangers, she was also strangely glad. It was suddenly quite important that Lloyd be kept in the dark about yesterday; she could imagine Lloyd's cynical suggestions if he did know. She could almost hear him saying, "But sweetie, that's *marvelous;* now you can just romance him into staying out of our way."

What had happened last night between them had had nothing at all to do with that kind of romancing. She'd known that as soon as Clint had met her eyes an hour before. In spite of everything she'd felt the same helpless confusion in his presence, been drawn by the same inevitable magnetism he had exercised over her last night. Even now, in the gray light of the rainy morning, with so much at stake, her senses had reacted to his glance in almost the same way as her mouth had warmed last night to his hungry kisses, her vibrant body to his stroking hands.

She tried to stifle those thoughts as they pulled out their chairs, sat down and started going over their papers. To her dismay, Clint pulled his chair a little closer to hers and spread out his area maps for her inspection.

Last night was last night, she reminded herself sternly; now is now, and I've got to concentrate on the job before me. Nevertheless she uneasily acknowledged the warmth emanating from that big hand so close to hers; her flesh was dazzled by it.

Almost with relief she heard a polite tap at the door; Lloyd called out, "Come in."

A secretarial-looking woman in austere brown wool said softly, "I'm sorry to disturb you, but there's a phone call for a Mr. Eliot."

Lloyd muttered an apology to Anne and Clint, saying he'd left the inn's number with Emma. He followed the brown-clad woman out, shutting the door.

"Well," Clint said, "this is what I call a break. I'm sure it wasn't in your script."

For the first time since they'd come into the parlor, she turned and faced him. He was grinning at her, his white teeth startling in his weathered face, but there was no mockery in the grin. It was poignant and uncertain, and there was such desire and tenderness in his look that she almost succumbed to that familiar, insidious perplexity he could arouse in her without half trying.

"No, it wasn't." She couldn't help smiling back. "You didn't have to be at that meeting, did you?"

"Of course I didn't. It was just the quickest way to be

with you." His hand crept toward hers on the table. "Anne, you look so beautiful," he said softly. "More beautiful in the rain than in the sun. Your hair makes all the light that anyone could need."

She felt her resistance slide away; it was impossible to withstand a comment like that, especially with his fingers touching hers as they were at this moment. His warm glance drifted again over her bright, billowing hair as he spoke, then came to linger on her mouth.

She knew she had to speak, had to say something to help her regain her poise. "Why the masquerade?" she asked coolly. "You acted as if we hadn't met."

He stiffened. "I thought you might want it that way." Some of the warmth had gone from his look, but he didn't let go of her hand. "Under the circumstances."

"What circumstances?" she demanded, bewildered.

At last he withdrew his hand. "I thought that . . . Eliot might be the reason you ran away last night. Especially after what I saw this morning."

A hot indignation flooded her. "So that's why you didn't join us. Good heavens. Lloyd and I are like . . . like brother and sister. What kind of person do you think I *am?* Do you think I would have let . . . those things happen if I were involved with someone else?" She was getting madder and madder.

"I'm afraid I don't think very well at all when I'm around you, Anne," he murmured. His level gaze inventoried her again and, swearing under his breath, he pushed back his chair and stood beside her, grabbing both her hands in his to urge her upright.

Unwillingly she found herself rising as he made a hoarse, inchoate sound and shoved her chair backward with his foot so that he could gather her into his embrace.

"Anne, oh, damn it, Anne," he whispered, tighten-

ing his hold on her, pulling her close. Their bodies were
pressed so tightly together that she could feel the
breastplate of bone below the thick muscles of his
chest, the straining tendons of his upper thighs. She
knew a sweeter desperation, a depth of yearning far
greater than the most abandoned caresses of the last,
lost night.

Completely forgetting in that heated instant where
she was, Anne found herself submitting—more than
submitting, moving into him, letting him pull her
nearer, lifting her shaken arms until they circled his
neck. While one of her hands stroked the thickness of
his deep black hair, the other grazed his cheek with
trembling fingers.

He made a sound almost of pain and bent his head
until their mouths were touching. Gently, at first, then
not gently at all, but exploring with open lips, and
finally clinging, clinging with an awesome pressure, a
starving need that threatened to undo her.

Nothing, nothing mattered to her now but this, and
in her frenzy of forgetting she could not conceive of
ever being without him again.

Still holding her so tightly that she couldn't escape,
he raised his head at last and whispered throatily,
"Don't you see, Anne? Don't you see, darling, this is
the way it's got to be?"

Just then she heard Lloyd Eliot's voice somewhere
down the hall, raised in protest or in argument, but
even that jarring, distracting sound could not distract
her from the moment. Clint's eyes were staring down
into hers, his strong hands kneading her shoulders with
a stunning heat that penetrated the tweed of her jacket,
the soft, sliding wool of her sweater.

And under the spell of that seeking touch she
admitted in desperate silence: Maybe it's true. Maybe it

does have to be this way. Once more she was lost to every other consideration, lost in the sight and touch, the sound and smell of him as his mouth lowered to hers again.

This kiss had a more awesome power than the one before; now her delight was laced with fear. No man had ever held such sovereignty over her body and mind, her senses, her determined self. It flashed to her clearly where they really were. She began to draw back, slowly, half reluctantly. What if Lloyd had walked in just now . . . or the skeptical Hester Cannon?

Good heavens, that would give Hester the perfect ammunition to oppose the admission of "decadent movie people" into Sedgby. If Hester should see the "ladylike" producer in the arms of a man she'd apparently met less than an hour ago . . .

I've got to be out of my mind, Anne decided.

"What is it?" Clint asked urgently, still holding her by the shoulders.

"I've lost my senses," she murmured. "When I think of where we are . . . and what we're trying to settle here. This is serious business, Clint."

"Well, I'm serious, too," he countered.

She could hear Lloyd practically shouting on the phone somewhere outside. It must be something very upsetting, she decided, because he'd been on his best behavior, controlling every gesture in this sensitive situation. At least, she concluded drily, he wouldn't be bursting in on them right this minute.

"What I'm saying is serious too, Anne," Clint repeated stubbornly. She studied his piercing eyes, his determined jaw and mouth. He was still avoiding the other matter. But to her intense relief, he finally let her go.

She moved away from him and sat down in the chair

Lloyd had vacated on the other side of the table. Clint stared at her bleakly for a second, then sat down too.

He said with amazing calm, "If you've lost your senses, I'd hate to see you when you *have* them." A rueful grin split his face. "You've got sense enough to know that it's illogical for people who feel the way we do to be apart."

She couldn't think of a single thing to say, and somehow his abrupt switch from passionate lyricism and wild yearning to this cool objectivity began to turn her off a little.

"It was you, you know, not Eliot," he went on, "who turned the tide with Hester. I wish you could be as certain of us as you are about your work. . . . I wish I could turn it around and win you over the way you did that old woman."

She weakened at the sight of his rueful smile, but the fact remained that she couldn't lose her head like that again. She had too much else to lose. She must control her wild and treacherous heart.

"Please, Anne," he said more softly. "I apologize for . . . going crazy like that—and here, of all places. But you don't know what you do to me. You've got to let me see you, you've *got* to," he pleaded. "Please, let me see you tonight."

"That's impossible," she said quickly, positively relieved to have the excuse of truth. "We're meeting with the cast and crew; there are a hundred things to take care of. And we'll probably have a very early call in the morning."

"Tomorrow, then," he said quickly.

She hesitated.

"You can't work all the time," he cajoled.

Now there was a loud silence from the hall. Lloyd

had stopped talking. He'd be back before they could turn around.

"I'll . . . think about it." She heard Lloyd right outside the door talking to someone; then he was in the room again. At the first sight of his face, Anne knew that something had really upset him, also that he was plotting some new intrigue. She could always tell. He was a bit flushed, but obviously he was holding himself in, unwilling to explode in front of Clint Ward.

"Sorry to keep you waiting," he muttered. "We have a bit of a problem, Anne. We should be getting back to Warrenburg soon. Maybe you can catch me up on what you've worked out so far with Mr. Ward." He nodded curtly in Clint's direction. "Then we can find out if you're going to let us make a movie," he added sourly.

"Let's talk about it," Clint responded in such a bland tone that Anne was deeply irritated. He sounded as if he were talking to children; his calm was maddening. "You've really leaped in without looking, Eliot. It's a funny way to do business."

Lloyd seemed to be biting his tongue, but he replied in a controlled way, "We've already settled most of the details, Ward—even with your company, I might remind you."

"It's not quite that simple." Clint was unruffled. "But I think we can work it out." He shot a significant glance at Anne. Everything he said seemed to have a double meaning for her.

"Actually, we've been waiting for you," she said to Lloyd, trying to get them back on track.

"Shall we go ahead, then?" Lloyd suggested.

"Absolutely," Clint answered, smiling at Anne. Lloyd gave him a quizzical look. Anne thought that for someone who didn't like to play games, Clint Ward was doing awfully well. She could have slapped him. But now Lloyd was comparing Anne's maps to Clint's, and she gathered her wandering thoughts and joined the two men. However, she took care to stand next to Lloyd, not Clint. She wasn't sure she could trust her heightened senses.

Clint explained the color codes on his maps and pointed out areas marked in red and bright green. "This is our basic territory."

"That looks questionable," Anne said. "We're going to crisscross here and here, Lloyd. When will you be there, Mr. Ward?"

"Not till next week." Damn it, she thought, it still didn't look too good.

Lloyd interjected, "Fortunately, we'll be doing mostly interiors first, with just a little exterior work. I trust your project won't extend inside the Sedgby buildings?" he asked Clint with an ironic smile.

"Hardly." Clint raised black, contemptuous brows. The one amused word seemed to imply that real men's work was outdoors. Anne was annoyed at that bit of juvenile machismo. He sounded as if he thought she and Lloyd were playing with toys. Clint Ward was one of the most maddening men she'd ever met—one moment tender and persuasive, the next arrogant and egotistical.

"Then it would appear that we can function, at least for the moment," Lloyd said curtly. Anne was astonished at his attitude; it made her very nervous to have so little margin to operate. As a matter of fact, Lloyd seemed strangely preoccupied, and she wondered exactly what the phone call had been about.

"For the time being, certainly," Clint agreed. Anne could read a kind of ambiguity in that statement. But there was no point in borrowing anxiety now; she had enough already, both about the film and about Clint Ward, she admitted.

"Fine. Then we might as well adjourn for the moment. Where can we reach you? Are you staying in Warrenburg?"

"I'll give you my site location." Clint handed him a card. Lloyd took it with suspicious blitheness. Anne just knew he was plotting something.

They folded up their maps and stowed them away. When they entered the hall again, Hobie Cannon rejoined them. Lloyd thanked Cannon profusely, said a smooth goodbye to Clint, and then practically pulled Anne out of the inn and into the car.

"What's up, Lloyd?" He was letting his exasperation show now, but nevertheless there was a mischievous smile on his mouth.

"We have some new migraines, which I'll go into in a moment. But first, I'm up to a bit of sabotage."

"What do you mean?"

"It so happens I've got an old, old friend in a high place at Associated. Went to school with him, too. My good old alma mater . . . Anyway, my friend is very unfond of Clint Ward and all his works, thinks he's some kind of visionary who asks for, and gets, much too high a budget for his division. More wheels within wheels." Lloyd grinned. "He's based in New York. I'm going to have a talk with him tonight to see what he can do, if anything. He's got quite a bit of pull with the board. A lot can happen in a week."

"I see." So that was the reason for Lloyd's calm attitude about the shooting schedule. Still the cockeyed optimist, she reflected. "And the migraines?"

"Livie's agent's making nasty. There's a catfight

between her and Marcella"—Marcella King had the main female supporting role, playing the village hoyden who tries to seduce the film's hero—"and Jack's raising hell about his *accommodations,* if you please. He wants a special garage for his motorcycle."

Ignoring the other complaints for the moment, Anne protested, "His *motorcycle?* In this area? Good heavens, has he ever biked in the mountains?"

"He says so." Lloyd seemed to be at the end of his tether. "Do you know what'll happen with his insurance if they know he's biking on these roads? As you can see, all of these things are teapot tempests . . . but as usual, they can develop into hurricanes, and we'll be capsized before you know it."

"No, no," Anne soothed him. She could see another nervous fit coming, Lloyd's confidence and good humor vanishing in the tremors of his temperament. She realized that she needed more diplomacy with him than with any of the others. "We'll straighten it all out in no time," she added calmly. "You'll see."

"I really don't know how I'd function without you, Annie," Lloyd murmured. She could tell he was already calming.

I don't either, she retorted silently as they took the winding road down to Warrenburg. Her mind was already at work solving the new crises. When they pulled up beside the Warrenburg Inn, she realized that she hadn't thought of Clint for twenty whole minutes.

Remembering, she was shaken all over again by a flashback to that brief and thrilling encounter in the parlor of the Halberd Inn.

And in the midst of her problem-solving reflections a cold idea intruded: I have to take care of Lloyd . . . of Jack and Livie and Marcella, everyone and everything.

Who ever takes care of *me?* I just don't weigh
enough to be earth mother to the Western world. The
thought was so absurd that it restored a little of her
humor and her sense of proportion, so that by the time
they entered the inn she was feeling more able to cope
with whatever was to come.

Chapter 4

AND PLENTY HAD, ANNE TOLD HERSELF THE NEXT MORN-
ing at seven, driving Lloyd and herself up the mountain
toward the location. Almost ten straight hours' sleep
had brought her to top form again; that was a big help.

"I can't believe we're really ready to shoot," Lloyd
enthused. "You're a miracle worker."

Anne silently agreed, but she said generously, *"We're*
miracle workers, Lloyd." She giggled, thinking of
Jack's out-of-commission motorcycle. "You're the one
who thought of fouling up the bike." His booming
laughter joined hers.

"But I didn't know how until you told me," he
insisted. "Your expertise amazes me. I never could

have trusted the mechanics to keep quiet if one of them had done it.''

Strangely, for all her ignorance of cars' insides, Anne had learned about motorcycles from a cousin when she was in her teens. Last night, after they had failed to convince Jack that a motorcycle was dangerous in the mountains, Anne, at Lloyd's insistence, had furtively removed two cylinder caps from the machine and hidden them in Lloyd's room. This would effectively ground the bike for several days at least; Anne was sure no replacement caps were available closer than Knoxville. And in a few days the childlike Jack might have entirely forgotten.

She reviewed her other accomplishments of yesterday, feeling justifiably proud. Anne had a special expertise in dealing with the beautiful but insecure lead, Livie Hanson—born, to Anne's and Lloyd's perpetual delight, Gertrude Stein. Livie had gotten so involved with Anne and Suzuki in the costume conference that the matter of top billing became secondary to her. And after Anne suggested to Suzuki that additional costumes were needed to properly display Livie's beauty, Anne was convinced that the matter of billing wouldn't arise again.

Brilliant Suzuki, who reminded Anne of a hummingbird both in her grace and the speed at which she worked, zipped out new designs before their very eyes and was on the phone to her New Orleans studio before any of them could turn around, demanding the new costumes within the week. Having already had experience with Suzuki's staff, Anne knew the dresses would be flown to Knoxville well ahead of schedule.

The catfight with Marcella took a bit more doing. It was Livie's tried-and-true custom to fall in love with her leading man during shooting, to lend greater credence to her role. Jack, who took what Anne thought of as a more professional view, couldn't stand Livie personally and was now romancing Marcella. The wily Anne, with Lloyd's backing, padded both Jack's and Livie's written parts and cut a little here and there from Marcella's. Marcella had a terrible time remembering lines, anyhow . . . all she could really do, Lloyd commented, was laugh, kiss and wiggle. She did those three things so superlatively that she was a natural for the seductive hoyden, and she was patently relieved to have fewer lines.

Anne chuckled, feeling easy and elated. The rain had gone, and the early sun was scattering some of the mist from the mountains. The air smelled wonderful, just-right-cool and crystalline.

"Harri's been splendid, too," Lloyd remarked.

Harriet Payne, Anne's production assistant, was an absolute gem. She'd taken over many of the practical tasks that Anne found increasingly onerous as time went by: lining up housing for the transportation and production people, getting everyone organized down to the last grip and gaffer.

"I'm thinking she's overdue for a promotion," Lloyd added thoughtfully, "to take some of the pressure off you. The more I see of your ideas, and the more I hear you with the writers, I'm convinced you're being wasted on these banal things."

Anne felt more elated than ever. The day she'd long looked forward to, the time when she'd be on a real par with Lloyd, might be approaching faster than she'd hoped for. "You don't know how I'd love that, Lloyd. I've dreamed of it since I was just a child."

"I must confess I had my doubts when we first spoke on the phone. And at breakfast yesterday morning,

when you seemed so detached for a moment." He *had*
noticed then, she thought, dismayed. "But not now,
Anne. Not now."

She realized, when he said that, exactly how much
this film and her burgeoning career really meant to her.
She resolved that nothing, no one—not even the undis-
courageable Clint Ward—was going to get in her way.

"At the moment, though, I want to run over scene
twenty-two," Lloyd suggested. Their talk became se-
verely technical; she was so absorbed that she barely
noticed how slow their progress had become.

"Damn it, what's this?" Lloyd demanded, leaning
out of his window and staring ahead. Anne heard the
diminishing growl of the equipment Jeeps and trucks
behind them, saw Jack's scarlet Porsche slow. Livie, in
her cream-colored Jaguar just behind Jack, yelled out,
"Watch it, damn it!" The Porsche had very nearly
damaged her treasured car, which was almost the exact
shade of her naturally taffy-colored hair. Livie's temper
was certainly not improved, Anne decided, by the sight
of Marcella's dark head next to Jack's golden brown
one.

Anne peered out from her side. "Associated trucks,"
she said brusquely.

"Blast," Lloyd raged. "This is just like the time that
wretched camel parade from the Passion play got
tangled in the *Winter Kind* funeral."

"At least we're not shooting yet," Anne reminded
him. The Hemisphere procession was at a halt. Lloyd
was opening his door, getting out.

"Once more unto the breach, dear friend," he
quoted. "Come on, Annie." She got out too, and they
started walking forward.

She saw Clint Ward waving the trucks on, they were

headed on an oblique course across the film-makers'
path on the outskirts of Sedgby.

"Aha!" Lloyd cried. "I knew it . . . the high-
powered handyman again."

She couldn't prevent a slight feeling of irritation at
hearing Lloyd's name for Clint, but she had to sympa-
thize with Lloyd's feelings. Clint Ward was the last
thing in the world she needed at this moment.

As they passed Jack's Porsche, Anne heard the
incorrigible Marcella purr, *"Whooo* is *that?"* Out of the
corner of her eye Anne glimpsed the actress staring
fascinatedly at the tall man in khakis up ahead and
caught Jack's air of affronted vanity. At any other time
it would have been amusing—it was inconceivable to
John-Mark Salem that any other man could steal his
thunder—but right now Anne was too affected by the
sight of Clint herself to find the situation very funny.

She was also all too aware of the contrast between
Marcella's revealing outfit and her own oversize, casual
jumpsuit. But that was wildly irrelevant, she reminded
herself. Bigger problems awaited her.

"Well, good morning," Clint called out with maddening casualness, as if they'd all met for a picnic or
something. He hadn't given Marcella a glance, Anne
noticed; she herself tried to ignore the distracting sight
of his muscular arms revealed by his rolled-up shirt
sleeves, the brightness of his black hair in the sun.

"How long are these behemoths going to impede
us?" Lloyd demanded.

Clint studied him briefly, a one-sided smile lifting the
corner of his sensuous mouth. Anne had to admit that
Lloyd was a sight in his working gear: enormous
carpenter's overalls whose pockets were laden with all
kinds of things; over them an ancient, sagging tweed

jacket; cat-scratched cowboy boots; and an old fisher-man's cap he'd bought in Corfu. Each item was a good-luck charm the superstitious Lloyd invariably wore for shooting. "Oh, not too long," Clint responded finally. "We won't be around here for more than an hour."

"An hour! Do you realize how much an hour costs Hemisphere?" Lloyd yelled.

"Lloyd . . ." Anne touched his arm. She said evenly to Clint, "This doesn't exactly conform to the routes we discussed yesterday, does it?"

"Not in the least," Clint conceded. "But yesterday we hadn't run across the problem we found at five this morning."

"That's no excuse," Lloyd interjected huffily. "Is this an example of what we're going to face every day during the entire filming?"

"Could be." Clint's unruffled manner, his casual reply, got to Anne too. She felt herself getting hot under the collar. What was worse, she noticed that Clint's gaze was admiring her face and hair, wandering down her neckline, and she discovered that two of the buttons of the jumpsuit's bodice had come undone. She started to button herself up again, and then decided not to let herself be bothered by his staring.

"Mr. Ward," she said coolly, "we're prepared to be reasonable if you are. Maybe if we just take this a step at a time we can come to a satisfactory compromise."

"I couldn't agree more . . . Ms. Reynolds." Clint gave her a significant smile. "Nothing would please me more than to reach an agreement with you."

Blast him. He wasn't just talking about their proj-ects. She felt hot, and the fabric of her suit was scratchy on her flesh. But she managed an even reply. "Okay.

Let's start with the present. How long are you going to be blocking us here . . . and what's your itinerary for the rest of the morning?"

She was so brusque and snappish that he looked taken aback, but he answered calmly. "If we push, we can be out of here in another twenty minutes." He reached in his pocket and brought out a folded paper, handing it to her. "Here's our schedule until three P.M." His fingers brushed hers.

Anne unfolded the paper with unsteady hands and looked it over. For one horrible instant the words didn't register at all; then, to her thankfulness, the information came into focus. She nodded and passed the paper on to Lloyd.

After he'd examined it, he growled, "We can't live with this." He handed the sheet back to Clint unfolded. "Let me just remind you, Ward, that Hemisphere's got eighteen million sunk into this film. And a pact with Associated."

Clint folded the paper and stuck it in his breast pocket. "Eighteen million," he commented with an offhand inflection, ignoring the last comment.

Good heavens, Anne thought. If our eight figures cause such a nonreaction, his own job must run to nine . . . or ten. The question she'd put aside in the pressure of work surfaced again: What on earth *was* the secret project he was involved in? Then, as she had before, she forgot it; there were other things to worry about now.

But the one thing she couldn't forget was that inevitable, almost electric thrill that had jolted her at just that brief contact of Clint Ward's fingers with her own.

What happened afterward, however, obliterated even that.

They were scheduled to shoot the first scene in the dogwood clearing, because it featured Marcella and Jack alone, and by getting it out of the way they could release Marcella for a brief commercial series in New York while they shot scenes in which she did not appear.

Supervising the setting up, Anne smiled to herself. Marcella's agent had been pleasantly surprised at the ease with which he'd gotten Marcella released for the other work; he'd expected Lloyd and Anne to kick up a fuss. Little did he know, Anne reflected with amusement, that Marcella's absence was a "consummation devoutly to be wished." If it hadn't been for her outrageously seductive glamour, anyone would think twice about using her because she was such a pain in the neck.

Anne was getting a bit of that pain now, in her head as well as her neck, as she went over the scene with Marcella.

"You come on from *that* direction," Anne repeated with monumental patience.

"It doesn't feel right," Marcella complained. "Jack gets all the best sun."

Anne controlled herself with difficulty. "Marcella, dear, that's the way it's supposed to go in the first shot. We've explained it to you before—it's all symbolic."

Out of the corner of her eye she got a glimpse of Jack Salem, looking superb in his full-sleeved shirt, skintight teal blue trousers and thigh-high boots. He was glowering with impatience.

"What's holding us up over there?" Lloyd bellowed from his seat on the crane, where he'd been telling the photography director how to take pictures. The man, who was used to it by now, had an expression of suffering resignation.

"We'll be ready to roll in a second," Anne yelled back. "Now, Marcella . . ." She turned back to the sultry actress in her bodice-bursting hoyden's dress. "This will be gorgeous. George knows exactly how to get your mouth and hair"—these were the two features Marcella was most vain about—"and you'll be a knockout against those dogwood blossoms."

Valiantly Anne dismissed a sudden memory of the afternoon when she'd first seen Clint; she concentrated grimly on the matter at hand. Marcella was smiling now, preening herself.

"That's just the look!" Anne enthused. "Hold that . . . it's perfect. Ready now?"

Marcella nodded, licking her full lips, and took her place.

"Ready," Anne called to Lloyd.

"Places, everybody," Lloyd yelled.

Anne heard the call, "Take one," Lloyd's. "Roll 'em," and they were off. Marcella undulated into the clearing, out of the thicket of dogwood trees, and Anne admitted silently that the woman was tailor-made for the part, witch though she might be.

Slowly Marcella approached Jack Salem, who was seated on the grass with his handsome head in his hands as she snuck up behind him.

At that instant an exquisite doe mounted the rise beyond them in the early sun, its very motions mimicking Marcella's silent gait. Anne held her breath.

Marvelous, she reflected. More serendipity! Everything was right—the colors of the actors' costumes, the sun, the blossoms and the trees and blending grass.

Marcella had reached Jack now, but he was not yet aware of her presence. Then she put her hands on his shoulders with a sensuous touch and emitted her famous husky laugh. There was a breathless silence among the crew. Anne thought, elated, I can't wait to see this scene with the music added.

Lloyd looked jubilant.

Suddenly the deer stopped dead in its tracks, then took off like lightning.

Anne was thinking, Damn, now we'll have to cut that part, when a horrendous growling assailed her ears.

A huge bulldozer was grinding into view over the brow of the green, sunny ridge.

Everything stopped, frozen. Jack and Marcella, moving into a kiss, were caught in position like a dreadful, comic still. Anne thought wildly that they looked like fish, with their mouths open, even as she heard Lloyd bellow, "What the hell is this? Cut, cut damn it, cut!"

The bulldozer ground to a halt in the very center of the ridge. Then Anne saw Clint Ward at the head of a group of workmen.

Lloyd scrambled down from the crane and headed toward the ridge; Clint was coming to meet him. Insanely Anne pictured the moment he had come to meet her in that very spot, right after she'd first seen him. But then she came to her senses and decided wryly that this was a far cry from that first heart-lifting encounter.

"What's the meaning of this?" Lloyd roared. Clint looked almost insultingly calm. Anne moved hesitantly toward the two men.

"We're working, Eliot." At that moment Clint's resonant, exciting voice held no charms for Anne. The way he spoke made her blood boil.

And, although she usually tried to smooth Lloyd's ruffled feathers, she felt like applauding when he retorted, "And what the hell does *this* look like?" His arm swept out, encompassing the actors, the crew, the waiting equipment. "A maypole dance?"

Clint's bland expression did not alter. Blast him, Anne raged, inwardly, this doesn't matter to him at all. He acts like he's king of the mountain.

"Your wretched schedule," Lloyd shouted, "did not include *that*." He made a fist at the offending bulldozer.

"I'm not going to go into every detail," Clint responded with the same maddening calm, "but the fact is that my special man had to come in a day early from Colorado, and he has to get back this afternoon. These things happen."

Anne realized Clint hadn't looked at her. At least, she judged, he has the decency to be ashamed before *me*. Or maybe he just feels foolish, considering the way he tried to seduce me. He's probably thinking that this is not the best way to go about it. At once she was surprised at herself—mooning over personal problems at a time like this. What had gotten into her?

She looked at Jack and Marcella. Jack seemed totally off-balance. Oh, Lord, Anne thought. It'll take us hours to get him psyched into the scene again.

Marcella, on the other hand, looked mad as a wet hen. If Anne hadn't been so upset, she would have laughed out loud. There was no romantic interest in those heavy-lidded eyes now, as there had been that morning. And again an irrelevant and absurdly triumphant thought came to Anne: Clint hadn't even glanced at Marcella, whose lush breasts were practically spilling over her bodice. Maybe *that's* why she's so mad, Anne surmised.

Then she pulled herself together and walked closer to Lloyd and Clint. To her amazement Clint smiled, saying, "Good morning again, Ms. Reynolds." He was acting as if they didn't have a care in the world, putting this problem and her into tidy separate compartments.

The man was impossible. How she had ever imagined they could . . .

But now she had to handle this. Lloyd was almost foaming at the mouth. "How long will that thing be there, Mr. Ward?" she asked curtly, nodding at the bulldozer.

"We were only passing through," he explained. "Sorry it happened to be at that very minute."

"Passing through!" Lloyd bellowed. "We have an agreement with your company, Ward. A gentleman's agreement."

"I'm not a gentleman, Eliot, when it comes to my work. And my company does not dictate every step I take. To answer your question," he said gently to Anne, "we can move it right now."

Anne was afraid Lloyd was going to have a fit. She put a soothing hand on his arm. "Thank you, Mr. Ward," she said coldly. "Would you please?"

Clint looked at her searchingly, as if he were about to say something else, but then he apparently thought better of it. He turned and lifted his hand to the operator of the bulldozer, and the offending behemoth lumbered off and down the other side of the ridge. After one last glance at Anne, Clint Ward rejoined his crew.

It took another hour to soothe Jack and reassure the enraged Marcella, who kept repeating that she had a plane to catch that night. Finally, at four-thirty, the scene was wrapped to Lloyd's satisfaction.

That night Anne took her phone off the hook and collapsed into sleep at six P.M. She slept all the way through until morning. The next day they didn't see a sign of Clint, but in the middle of the afternoon another mishap occurred. When Lloyd had said blithely they would be shooting "a lot of interiors," he'd passed over the necessity for certain exterior shots, such as one outside the Sedgby church, where hero Jack had come to get a glimpse of heroine Livie. An Associated truck drove by at the worst possible instant. It wasn't quite the disaster that the bulldozer had been, but now there was Livie to calm down.

At the end of that day's shooting Anne repeated the performance of the evening before, wondering why she felt so extraordinarily exhausted. Her weariness was suspiciously like depression, but she tried to stifle that idea; why should she be depressed over a cold-blooded, arrogant man like Clint Ward?

However, at the end of the third day's shooting she still couldn't get him out of her mind. That night with him had been so lovely, she mourned . . . as had that gray, exciting day in the writing room of the Halberd Inn.

It was four-thirty now. Feeling drained again, Anne saw Lloyd wave his arm and heard him call, "That's a wrap," then watched the crew pack up its equipment in the confined space of the Sedgby library.

At least, thank heavens, there hadn't been any overwhelming problems today. Hayward Gunn, who played the heroine's stern, cruel father—and who, in reality, was a perfect pussycat—was such a pro that nothing could bother him, it seemed. And Jack and Livie were in top form. If it can only stay this way, Anne prayed fervently.

She was going to have to keep "treating" Livie, just like a psychiatrist, to keep her on an even keel.

She watched Lloyd conferring with Harri Payne about the extras for tomorrow's takes. He was beaming as he strode toward her, saying, "I think we got some beauties, Anne. You were perfectly inspired about the filters." When he was beside her, he added, *sotto voce,* "You were wonderful with Livie. She's an awful pain . . . but then, when she's on camera, she's heavenly. I couldn't cope with these morons without you, my dear."

Anne smiled. She'd heard it so many times before. Actors, to Lloyd, were hardly more than animated chess pieces to be moved from this square to that one. Livie had told Anne privately that it was "nice to be treated like a human being." Always, of course, Anne tactfully kept each one's comments from the other.

"Look, darling," Lloyd rushed on with an amazing air of energy, as if he were starting the day instead of ending it, "I'm going to hang around while the boys take those exteriors. You look done in; I don't really need you for these. Why don't you head back to what is laughingly called town? I'll hitch a ride with someone else. As a matter of fact, I'm going to arrange for a driver tomorrow. I can't keep imposing on you to drive me. We can't be joined at the hip all the time."

She murmured a polite disclaimer, but she was privately glad. She welcomed a little solitary time to get her thoughts in order. The meeting with Clint had put her off her stride all week.

Then she almost wondered if the hypersensitive Lloyd had picked up her thoughts, because he said, "By the way, I like the way you handled that straw boss the other morning."

She unhappily recognized the familiar prickle of irritation when Lloyd denigrated Clint, and she thought what a dangerous sign that was.

"But there's nothing like a pretty woman to manipulate the adversary," Lloyd added, with a probing glance at her.

She managed to retort lightly, "You don't have to

butter me up. I'm on your side." She saw the actors emerging from the dressing trailers, looking strangely unreal out of costume.

"See you later, then." Anne hoisted her heavy tote bag over her shoulder and raised her hand to Lloyd. "I'll be in your suite at seven for the conference."

She climbed the ridge to her car, parked in a wooded spot, and thought longingly of a protracted bubble bath and an enormous early dinner in her room.

It startled her to see that someone was sitting in the passenger seat. As she came nearer she recognized the dark head and massive shoulders of Clint Ward.

She opened the driver's door and leaned in, demanding, "What are you doing here? This is childish."

"Damned right it is," he drawled. "No woman's ever made me pull a stunt like this." But he made no move at all to go, and when he grinned at her it was so infectious she found herself shaking her head in helpless wonder, then grinning back.

"Please, Anne. Get in. You must be exhausted by now." He sounded very gentle, but his last comment stung her vanity; she wondered if she looked as tired as she felt.

She got in and closed her door, unable to help thinking how damp and grubby she felt, absurdly glad that she had sprayed her neck and wrists with cologne a little while before simply to refresh herself.

"You smell lovely," he remarked. His look was so welcoming, so open, that she melted a little. "I'm glad to see you."

She realized that she was glad to see him, too, more than she wanted to be, but she didn't answer right away. Finally she murmured, "Isn't this a little much . . . materializing in my car like this? I do have a phone in my room, you know." She could feel her mouth relax into another smile.

He leaned toward her. "Yes, you do have a phone—which you didn't answer for two nights. And which you might not have answered this evening, either." His nearness was working its usual magic; she sensed the very hair of her head responding. An actual chill ran over her scalp. It was awful. And marvelous.

"How do you know?" she heard herself asking, almost as if she were listening to someone else. That positively scared her. Just yesterday she'd almost hated him.

His reaction was instantaneous; he absolutely glowed. He reached out and put his hand on her arm, and she had to restrain herself from crying out. Those fingers, on the skin of her wrist, felt made of fire.

"I couldn't take the chance. You're right, you know. We shouldn't be playing these kids' games. Please give me a little time with you . . . just a little time to breathe, time to talk, Anne. You remind me of me about ten years ago—and a lot of times now," he admitted wryly. "So wrapped up in work you won't give yourself any time to live. I know I haven't given myself time for that, and look at me now."

His voice was sober, and his self-evaluation touched her. There might be something in it, she conceded. She herself had had very little real living time for the last three years. But it had been different for her; she'd been running away.

Anne surprised herself again by saying the last two words aloud.

"From what?" he demanded softly, taking her hand. She quivered a little, but didn't take her hand away from his.

"Grief." Uneasily she saw the dressing trailers pass by, and then Jack's Porsche. But luckily the trailer drivers hadn't given her car a glance, too occupied with negotiating the mountain road. And Jack was too engaged in checking himself in the rearview mirror to notice her.

"Would you like to talk about it?" Clint's voice was so gentle, his attention so total, that they might have been the only people in the world. Just like that night, she reflected.

All of a sudden she did want to talk about it. Haltingly, she told him more than she'd told anyone in a long, long time. About the sudden, devastating shock of Dan's last illness, then his death. The empty years that followed; her conviction that she would never love anyone again.

When she paused, she gave him a sidelong look; his face was somber, vulnerable. "And you still think that?" he asked unsteadily.

A quick heat suffused her face and neck and breasts. "I . . . I'm not sure now." She was shaken, dismayed at how much of herself she'd revealed. It was so unlike her usual reticence that she had the uncomfortable sensation of public nakedness. But when she looked at Clint again the hope and triumph were so plain on his face that she found it unbearably moving.

She began to feel almost as she had on that first evening—that the two of them were utterly alone together here on the mountain. The waning light, the recent quietness, enhanced the odd, sweet illusion; the sun was sinking now on the other side of the mountains, the gently sloping blue-gray peaks assuming their mysterious cloudiness again.

Anne half closed her eyes and leaned her head back

against the seat. She had the strangest feeling of letting go, of wishing someone or something would take over.

What Clint said next completely surprised her until she realized that he was actually falling in with her silent, wistful desire to be looked after. He raised his hand to her chin and caressed it.

"When did you eat last?" he demanded.

"Eat?" Her glance slid sideways to him. His expression was almost paternal. "Eleven or so, I think," she murmured.

"Let's feed you, then. Would you like me to drive? I know a nice place on the other side of Sedgby. I think it opened after you left." He smiled at her.

"I have a conference in Warrenburg at seven," she temporized. This was insane, after what had happened on the set.

"And it's not even five yet," he persisted. "Come on. What do you say . . . shall I drive us?"

"I'd love it," she answered finally. "Yes to both." She was poignantly reminded of the old days with her father, newer days with Dan. She'd missed that so much, that feeling of being taken care of; she hadn't had that feeling in a long, long time.

He got out quickly, and she slid over to the passenger seat, tossing her tote bag in the back after retrieving her small clutch purse from its cluttered interior. Then Clint was beside her, starting the car, turning it around, heading back up the mountain and past the sleepy village of Sedgby.

As they passed some far-flung, random houses, she caught sight of women in their kitchens cooking the evening meal; that would be such a lonely sight now if she were driving alone. But she wasn't alone. She was with Clint. She wondered if he might be thinking something like that, too, because he'd given a swift glance at the houses and smiled a little as they drove on.

The restaurant *was* after her time, she realized when he braked outside a small, converted log cabin almost hidden in a stand of pine. Theirs was the only car.

"It's not exactly crowded," he chuckled, sounding very pleased.

She was, too, but it came to her that both of them were still in their work gear. "I hope it's not a fancy place." She grinned, with a gesture at her rumpled suit.

"Far from it. Besides, you look so beautiful you could wear a croker sack and nobody would care." He caressed her face again.

"Where *did* you pick up that expression?" she demanded, laughing, as they got out. It was a localism for a burlap bag, something she hadn't heard for years.

"I get around, lady. I get around." He put his hand lightly on the small of her back, inviting her to go in. The simple touch, the natural sound of the Tennessee expression on his lips, gave her a sudden, warm, deep sense of *déjà vu,* as if they'd been there together before, long ago, and belonged there. As if their conflict had never existed.

When they entered the one-room restaurant, she took a quick breath with pleased surprise. It was a spotless, homey place lit dimly with lanterns, smelling of pine, with only a few widely spaced tables covered in homespun clothes. There were sprays of dogwood in pottery vases at each table. From speakers attached just under the low ceiling folk music was unreeling like a ribbon of silver; she recognized the words from "Greensleeves" in the crystalline tenor of a famous singer she had almost forgotten until now.

"It's heavenly," she whispered, looking around.

There was no one else in the room at all. Their entrance had been announced by a tinkling bell attached to the door.

"I didn't make reservations," he quipped, and waved expansively. "Take your choice."

"That one." She nodded toward a table in the corner. "We'll be out of the traffic there," she added, laughing softly. He grinned and followed her, then pulled out her chair.

"Where *is* everyone?" she asked, also softly; it seemed so quiet, even with the gentle music, that anything above a whisper would be inappropriate.

He answered just as gently, "It's early. Later there'll be lots of people, maybe even the high-and-mighty Cannons of Sedgby."

"Oh, *no*. Wash out your mouth," she said with mock horror, feeling better, more at ease.

"Sorry I brought it up. Cancel," he ordered. Then his wide smile faded and he looked deeply, seriously happy. "You're like a dream, Anne Reynolds. This is like a dream . . . again. I never thought I'd be sitting here with you." His steady look held hers; then his hand reached out and delicately lifted hers from the table. The loose khaki sleeve fell back from her long white arm. He kissed her wrist, the palm of her hand, and her heart seemed to leap from her breast to her throat.

There was a pause in the music; then she heard, sweetly and as if by magic, the first haunting words of the song she'd remembered that morning. This time it was sung aloud in a frail soprano voice as clear as mountain water. "Black is the color of my true love's hair."

Her fascinated gaze wandered to the wild, deep blackness of Clint's hair, shining in the lantern light, then to the straight, heavy brows of equal blackness over the unique and piercing eyes the shade of a cat's-eye gem. Where had her coldness gone?

She recalled with a little quiver of excitement how his mouth had tasted, like apple wine; how his mouth had hungered and explored her own submissive, trembling lips. Her hand moved in his; her fingers tightened on his.

She felt a strong tremor in him that seemed to extend all the way up his heavily muscled arm. "Anne," he whispered. His own look swept her now, from her head to her face and mouth, down over her narrow torso, then back to her hair, and he said quietly, "Your hair lights up this room, too, just the way it did that parlor the other morning."

Anne smiled and glanced around the room. Yes, this room, too, was done in quiet, subdued colors, with its polished wood and creamy homespun and pale dogwood blossoms.

At last a slender, smiling, middle-aged woman came in from a doorway beyond. She, too, was all in quiet colors, from her gray-brown hair and unmade-up face to her loose beige blouse and long brown cotton skirt. She had very kind brown eyes and an easy, friendly manner. "Sorry to keep you waiting," she said in the high, sweet twang of the mountains. "But I reckon you-all didn't mind too much," she added with a discreet glance at their entwined hands.

"We didn't mind at all," Clint agreed, answering her smile. "What are you feeding us tonight?"

"I can fix you-all some steak or chicken," the woman said. "And we have some real good scuppernong wine, if you want a glass."

Clint looked at Anne. She opted for steak, and he

said, "Double that, please, ma'am. And do bring us some wine." He turned to Anne again. She nodded.

When the woman had gone, Anne murmured, "I don't believe this wonderful place. And the music is exquisite. I would have expected country. . . . As much as I love that, I like this better." The song had changed now to "On Top of Old Smoky."

"So do I. Even when we do-si-doed that night, I was thinking that this music is the kind that suits you. The first time I saw you, you looked like the ladies in the old folk songs, Anne. So sweet, so . . . delicate. There's one song in particular you reminded me of. Something about a lily, and the snow. I wish I could remember."

She said softly, squeezing his fingers, "'Have you seen but a white lily grow, before rude hands have touched it? And marked the fall of the snow, before the earth has smutched it?'" As she remembered the words of the old folk song, Anne could feel tears gathering in her eyes; she had loved it all her life. And he knew it, loved it, too. Even compared her to it. Somehow this whole enchanted interval was growing more and more like the far-off, bewitching dreamworld of her childhood, resembling the fondest wishes of her yearning heart.

"Oh, yes," he murmured. "Yes." He raised her hand to his lips again and pressed it with a long, long kiss. "That's it. That's the song. You're the song; you're that music."

He broke off. The proprietress was bringing their wine. She set their glasses before them and left at once.

Clint and Anne, still looking at each other, touched glasses and sipped the rich, fruity wine. "This tastes like *auld lang syne*," she remarked, smiling.

But she could still hear the lovely things he'd said just

a moment before, and she marveled that a man like him could talk like that. An engineer, who believed in the "evidence of the senses," nothing else. He was remarkable in ways that she had not imagined.

And what he'd said about the music opened her heart. Softly, with utter frankness, she told him what she had felt when they were first together, as if she were thinking not in words, but music.

His eyes lit up. "The first time we heard that country music, I thought the damnedest things . . . how I'd like to hear all kinds of music with you: Wagner in Bayreuth, and jazz in New York, and calypso in the Islands."

Then their dinner arrived, and they began eating, talking about music and cities and everything under the sun. Anne was almost high with delight at the ease of the transition from solemn tenderness to mirth. Even with Dan, she hadn't felt anything quite like this. Especially with Dan, she admitted, feeling faintly disloyal but facing it squarely. Dan had been an artist like herself, and highly sensitive; more than once she'd jarred him with her abrupt departure from a mood of high seriousness.

He had been so different from this man across from her, she reflected. Clint had seemed to be her diametric opposite—a scientist who could never understand the artist that she was, and yet . . . Yet he had a core of solidity, a way about him that made her feel he had a strength she could lean on. When she looked back now, it seemed to her that she and Dan had been sensitive babes in the wood, clinging to each other. Clint Ward would never lean on anyone like that. She marveled at the breadth of his interests and knowledge.

How much of it, though, was the best face a man

showed in ardent courtship, and how much was real? Where that sad little thought came from she didn't know, maybe from a furtive glance at her watch that told her time was flying, reminding her of Lloyd and Warrenburg . . . that Clint was an adversary.

Apparently Clint intercepted the glance and noticed her silence, recognizing how much of the talk he had been carrying on alone. "Anne, why are you looking like that all of a sudden? What are you thinking?"

At that point four other diners walked into the cabin. Somehow their entrance was the final pinprick in the magic bubble.

She could almost hear it pop when she answered in a newly sane, matter-of-fact voice, "A lot of things. About what a poetic scientist you are."

"I'm not, as a rule. But you make me break rules, Anne. And I've been thinking what a different woman you are from the drill sergeant who yelled at me the other morning. Not working agrees with you." He grinned a bit uncertainly, trying to gauge her expression. "What else were you thinking? Tell me."

"Of time . . . and obligations." She wondered where the magic had gone, if it would come again. "How you dismiss things."

"*Must* you be in Warrenburg at seven?" he asked eagerly.

She thought about it. She really didn't have to be; she and Lloyd had gone over the next day's shooting schedule at lunch. The truth was, it was only a habit, these nightly meetings, a habit she'd clung to for three years simply because her nights had been so empty. She could always phone.

"No," she admitted. And suddenly the voices of the intruding diners had faded to an indeterminate buzz;

the music was clear and silvery in her ears again, and she was almost drowning in the amber depths of Clint Ward's eyes. "I couldn't bear it."

That hot light leaped up in his eyes. "*Don't* bear it then, Anne. Please . . . be with me," he pleaded in an undertone, keeping her hands captive in his, oblivious to everything around them.

Anne could feel the urgency of his need flow into her. She was suddenly awake to the strength of his desire; a new heat suffused her skin, persuading her cautious body to answer in kind. Again that sweet weakness washed through her the way it had the first time they'd looked into each other's eyes.

Looking back at him now, she knew that they would be together tonight, wholly together. All her little mental debates with herself, her reasons and reservations, were being torn from her as easily as leaves from a wind-battered tree.

Yes, they would be together. She let that message go from her eyes to his and saw his gaze change, brighten, felt his hands squeezing hers more tightly.

"But not . . . in Warrenburg," she murmured, and saw that he understood. There, surrounded by everyone she knew, their secret would no longer be a secret; their lovely apartness would be intruded upon. She saw that he understood at once, because he smiled and said, "Oh, no, not in Warrenburg. I'm not at the inn anymore," he added softly. "I've got myself a place up here, in the mountains. Probably," he said, smiling at her, "because I was hoping this night would come to pass. I rationalized, of course, about being near the job." He grew quickly solemn. "Oh, Anne, I never dared to believe that this would happen."

She didn't answer, letting herself feel the strange new joy, that warm letting-go. There was no more wondering now, no hesitation. Her own body had taken command, urging her to him with an unswerving passion, a deep inevitability. Whatever had made her hesitate before was utterly irrelevant now, almost as if another woman had been bothered by those far-away considerations.

Clint grinned and reached in his pocket for something; he held out his hand to her, palm upward. A shiny dime rested there. "Do you want to make your call now?" he asked with a touching eagerness. "The phone's back there, by the kitchen."

"Yes." Grinning back at him, she took the dime and sought out the phone. She reached Lloyd at once, amazed at the calmness of her voice when she told him she wouldn't be coming to the conference, that she needed to rest tonight.

"An excellent idea. You put in quite a day."

You don't know the half of it, she answered in silence.

"Everything will be roses in the morning."

She almost retorted, "More than you know." But she just said levelly, "I'm sure it will."

When she walked back to their table, Clint was already rising, smiling at her with glowing eyes. "Shall we go?" he asked with gentle eagerness.

She nodded, and then they were leaving the pine-scented room of dewy dogwood and lantern light that echoed again with the sounds of "Black is the color . . ." and were alone in the green-smelling dark.

In the car she could barely make out his face, but his powerful head was silhouetted against the faint gold streaming out from the cabin behind him. Her quivering nostrils caught the titillating odor of his skin's fresh muskiness when he lowered his head and his demanding mouth found hers.

This kiss was wilder, sweeter, different from all those that had gone before—surer, more familiar, a vow and a commitment. The apple-rich taste of his lips on hers aroused in her a new, whirling delirium; whatever desire she had known in the past turned into mist, nonexistent in the sweeping fire of this emotion. Now she could let his strong, insistent hands have their way at last . . . and hers.

The sounds he made, deep and ravenous, pierced her with such yearning and such tenderness that she was shaken. His fingers tangled in her hair, traced the shape of her face and throat, shakily descended to her breasts, caressing them with exquisite, gentle lightness. Then that touch became savagely hungry, taking possession of her curving waist, her quivering upper thighs, until she moaned softly against his ardent mouth. Her own wondering touch lingered on the hard, smooth planes of his face; she stroked his warm ears and strong neck, slid her hands slowly down over his massive shoulders, down, down to feel the muscular sides of his torso through the rough khaki.

When he raised his lips just long enough to say her name softly, wonderingly, and then to repeat it once again, even that momentary separation gave her an awesome sense that her heart was being torn from her body, that no power on earth could keep her from him now.

As if he had sensed the extreme depth of her surrender, he started the car and, keeping an arm around her, drove into the wooded night.

Dreamily, through half-closed eyes, she watched the headlights spear the blackness unreeling before them; once he swerved to avoid an animal whose frightened, phosphorescent eyes appeared from nowhere. Clint returned both hands to the wheel, and Anne leaned back, realizing dimly that it had been a deer. There had been a deer on the sunny ridge the morning they had found each other. It was a happy omen.

Now they were leaving the main road, turning onto a smaller road that led upward. In the headlights she saw a little cabin.

For the first time in hours she experienced something that was almost dread, mingled with her anticipation. She wondered if he really knew what a momentous thing this was for her after her long isolation . . . after she had pegged him as nothing but trouble for her.

She felt that she was holding her breath, her whole body suspended in time.

Then, when he'd stopped, when he'd gotten out and opened the door for her, and she looked up into his eyes that were bright in the light from the house, she recognized with elation that he did know what she felt.

His face was tender with understanding.

Chapter 5

CLINT HELD OUT HIS HAND, LOOKING DOWN INTO HER face.

He saw such vulnerability there that he burned with an oddly protective feeling, and his mind whispered, Go slow. Go slow.

This was a lot for her to overcome: their newness with each other; her anxieties about the work. Unlike him, she was all of a piece; he was used to compartmentalizing things, taking them as they came, one thing separate from the other.

He would have to be careful. The night was like an overfull cup that could be spilled in a careless second.

He stood there not speaking, still holding out his hand. At last he saw her smile, and the sweetness of it made him catch his breath. She put her small hand in his. Exerting the lightest pressure, he urged her to get out of the car.

She looked so fragile, so breakable, he thought, and yet he could infer in her a core of strength as strong as steel. He was so afraid to hurt her physically that it made him shake inside.

With utter grace she unfolded her long legs and stepped from the car; he could not let go of her hand for a minute. He felt as awkward as a kid, which stunned him. A guy who'd been on this planet for thirty-eight years, known countless women. But never, never one like this. To cover the strangeness of their posture—his hand still holding hers in such a way that he couldn't even put his arms around her—Clint lifted her hand to his mouth and kissed it. Then he let her hand go and put his arms around her, pulling her to him, feeling that astonishing softness like . . . mist, like thistledown, amazing in a woman so compact and so slender.

Her breasts were crushed against him, her shapely body closer to his body than his skin, and he felt his control slipping. He wanted her so much it hurt.

But his mind reiterated coolly, Take it slow.

He let her go then and ushered her into his house with a soft touch on her waist. He shortened his steps a bit to match hers, and together they went up the few small stairs to the cabin door.

He'd left it unlocked—nobody ever intruded in these mountains—so he pushed the door open and stood aside for her to enter, glad he'd left the lights on, because it looked more welcoming.

Swiftly it occurred to him to wonder if the place was
all right, if it would please her. He seldom thought of
things like that, and he suddenly realized how long
it had been since he'd entertained a lady in his quar-
ters. Too damned long, he thought wryly. Like this
lovely thing beside him, he'd been so preoccupied
with his work that he'd almost forgotten the rest of
living.

She went in and, to his gratification, murmured, "I
like your house."

"I'm glad," he managed to say, and he thought that
he sounded funny, not like himself at all. He was afraid
it was too cold, though—the night was chilly—and he
hated overheated places. "Make yourself at home," he
invited, wishing to hell he could speak in something
besides clichés.

She was relaxing a bit, he could see, and he was glad
of that. She looked around with a little smile and
wandered across the room.

"Why don't I build us a fire?" he suggested, still
puzzled by the odd sound of his own voice in his ears.
Before she could answer he went to the hearth, stooped
and picked up a piece of wood. His back was to her for
the moment.

He was almost stunned when he felt her small hand
on his shoulder, thinking swiftly, She moves like a cat,
with hardly any sound. Then he heard her say quietly,
"We're not going to need one."

Clint turned around and looked up at her. She was
smiling down at him, her beautiful, clear eyes heavy-
lidded in the lamplight.

He couldn't believe it; she had referred to more than
the fire in the hearth. And the marvelous face, which
had looked so fresh and new when he first saw her, was

very different now. She looked like a man's dream of every seductress in the whole world.

He got up slowly, holding out his arms.

Anne could hardly believe what she had said; the bold, suggestive words had come to her from nowhere, almost as if another woman had said them.

She was positively dizzy now with astonishment and desire.

When he turned around and looked up at her, his eyes were full of amazement . . . open, vulnerable. He, too, looked like another person now.

This wasn't the smooth, worldly man who'd taken her to dinner that first night, not even the demanding and passionate lover who had tried to urge her into his bed after they'd known each other for less than a day.

Nor, she thought swiftly, was this the relentless pursuer of some mysterious goal that he could not even reveal, the man who trampled everyone who crossed his path. This man looked almost like a boy, achingly young, gentle.

Slowly he rose. She moved to him, putting her arms around his neck as he encircled her body with his arms. She knew what his control must have cost him, was costing him now. There was an awful tremor in his big, hard body, pressed so close, so thrillingly to hers. It came to her in a kind of daze that all that iron self-control was for her . . . because he cared for her.

She whispered against his neck, "There's fire enough in me for both of us." Then, surprised at her own boldness, she let the tip of her tongue caress the tanned skin below his ear.

He didn't say a word, but his hands answered with a wonderfully barbaric abandon, descending to her hips,

urging her even closer to him until she was fully aware
of the urgency of his need, his almost exploding passion; then he took a step backward, unbuttoning the
buttons at the top of her jumpsuit until it fell away, and
he marveled at the sight of her lace-covered breasts, his
eyes on fire.

With a slow solemnity he undid the rest of the
buttons, slowly peeling down the khaki fabric until it
fell around her feet. He drew in his breath when he saw
the rest of her exposed, her body covered only by the
sea green wisp of her bra and her harmonizing bikini.

She stepped out of the jumpsuit and watched him
fling it aside. Her flesh was hot and quivering, and she
gazed at the top of his dark head as he took off her
shoes, then stooped to plant nibbling kisses on her
naked feet. He held her ankles and his fingers slid like
burning bracelets up her trembling calves. She watched
as he clasped her thighs, so weakened with excitement
that she wondered that she could still stand.

Sharp arousal knifed through her, followed by a
hotter longing. His hands were peeling the scrap of
green lace from her vibrant body, freeing it from her
ankles as tenderly as if she were a child.

"Oh, Anne." He was kneeling, looking up at her,
and his eyes were blazing. "You look so . . . little in
your clothes," he whispered in magnificent surprise.
"And you're really so soft . . . so voluptuous." He
raised his hands again and stroked her on each side, all
the way from her narrow waist over her rounding hips,
down her long legs to her feet.

"Come," he invited, urging her down beside him on
the thick, round rug. She knelt with the lyrical motion
of a dancer as Clint, in utter silence, let his bemused,
dark amber stare play over her naked flesh.

Now they were face-to-face. Still with a look of

unbelieving wonder, he lifted both hands in an almost prayerful gesture to her head. Each hand stroked her hair, testing its silky texture, and he smiled with a kind of ecstatic drunkenness. It was the most profoundly arousing look she had ever, in all her life, seen on a man's face. She was too overwhelmed to take a breath, bewitched to stillness by the moment. With one hand still in her hair, he raised the other to her face for an instant; then both of his hands slipped over her shoulders and her lace-covered breasts. Then his warm, magical hands were reaching behind her, fumbling with the back of her bra.

The surprising lack of practice in that attempt moved her to an even deeper tenderness and, perversely, to stronger desire. Laughing a little, she put her own hands behind her back, stroking his, and undid the constricting lace. His gestures were no longer slow and smooth, but almost desperate; again this made her want him more than ever, and she flung the green lace wisp away.

He gasped at the sight of her total nakedness and, groaning, bent his head to her breasts to caress them with his mouth. The kisses sent a leaping flame over every trembling inch of her bare skin, and she took his head in her hands and held it to her breast, rubbing her face against his hair. She was almost mad with her need and yearning.

Her hands were shaking so that she couldn't manipulate the buttons of his heavy shirt; the rough khaki rasped her seeking fingers, and she cried out.

"Let me; let me." His voice was so tight that she could barely make out the words, but she dropped her hands and closed her eyes, feeling rather than seeing him as he wrenched his shirt from his torso, hearing the small buttons hit the uncarpeted part of the floor.

She sank back on the thick rug, hearing the sound that was torn from his throat, the faint sounds of his undressing.

Half opening her eyes, she glimpsed his naked body for a moment and was dazzled by him—the tanned, hard-muscled torso fully exposed, the corded middle, and the narrow loins giving evidence of his urgent arousal. She called his name, and wasn't even sure she had called it aloud; it sounded so far away, like a cry being carried away on the wind.

He lowered his body to hers until they were melded together, and now her flesh could experience what only her eyes had before; she folded him in her arms and stroked him, letting her fingers perceive that smooth, hot texture of his skin. Her heart thudded with such force it threatened to break free of her body, and she felt like an erupting volcano, with molten blood leaping and coursing through her veins. She waited eagerly to receive him.

But to her sweet puzzlement he raised himself and, staring down at her, pulled away. She saw that he was seeking out her lower body; feeling his eager caress beginning on her inner thighs, she let her eyelids close and gave herself up to the stunning pleasure of his touch. There was a narrow, piercing dart of swift delight, quick and subtle as a wing-brush on her secret flesh, and then a nearly unbearable sense of pleasure rocked her, overwhelming her. She was climbing and rising, struggling like an eagle in flight to reach the topmost height of the highest mountain.

On the utmost summit she let forth a cry, then subsided. In a dreamlike haze she was aware of his smooth and mighty hotness melded to her body once again, their meeting flesh a mingling of fire with fire. Renewed and astonished, having thought that there could be no greater joy than what she had just experienced, she rose to him again and took a deeper joy. She was unable to tell one body from the other in their wild converse of pleasure. Nothing had a name or meaning anymore; dimly, madly, she realized that she was past all thought. There was nothing, nothing anywhere but this.

At some unnameable and timeless instant she felt as much as heard his outcry, sensed the last explosion of his fulfilled and so fulfilling body. Holding him as tightly as her strength allowed, she opened her shaken lips against his neck and ran her hands repeatedly up and down his body.

He raised himself and lay beside her again, pulling her to him, inviting her to lay her head against his chest. Her cheek encountered the pleasing rasp of dampened hair, and under it, the thundering rhythm of his heart. He still took gasping breaths, like a runner at the end of a grueling race; she kissed him on the chest and smiled.

A sound like a contented growling rumbled from him. "I feel you smiling," he whispered. He lifted one lazy hand to cap her head before his strong fingers slid down again to savor the texture of her hair, trace the outline of her cheekbone, then her nose and chin and lips.

When his big thumb was resting on her mouth, she kissed it; he winced with pleasure, drawing her tightly to him. "Oh, Anne," he murmured, "how I wish I could think of something splendid enough to say. Splendid enough for you . . . and this."

She waited carefully to answer, aware of what care, what wistful yearning was hidden in his hesitant statement. Gladdened, she found the gift of a soft response to give him, one she hoped would let him know what this had meant to her, how much his effort touched her. "No one has *ever* found anything to say that's splendid enough. How can we?"

Apparently the gentle and rueful answer, her coupling them in the same dazed, happy, inarticulate state, pleased him; when she looked up he was smiling, his eyes closed, and he hugged her even closer.

He kissed her eyebrow, and she was warmed again. "You are not only the most beautiful woman I've ever known . . . you're also the most generous."

Now she wished that she could tell him what those nameless wonders had been like for her. Astonished, she reflected that she, Anne Reynolds, who had written and devised so many beauties for the screen, was almost dumb now in the aftermath of this profoundly greater beauty, this stupefying pleasure. Haltingly, with new shyness, she tried to tell him and spoke of the eagle's flight above the mountains.

He was silent for a moment after listening to her intently. Then he asked abruptly, "Have you ever been to Clingman's Dome? You must have, living here so much of your life."

Clingman's Dome. The highest point in the Tennessee Smokies—a place of strange desolation, awesome power and loneliness. What an odd thing for him to bring up now. Anne recalled it vividly. It had seemed so stark and cold, and the vegetation there was practically Arctic in contrast to the near-tropical leafage far below. Once she'd seen a buzzard crouching like a black statue on the stump of a dead tree. "Of course," she murmured. "It's an almost haunted place."

"Yes. But when I was there I had the feeling of being in at the Creation. I had a tremendous sense of awe. I felt incredibly lonely," he confessed, and she began to see the connection in his mind between the dome and her imagined eagle's flight. "I decided then that I could never love a woman who would be diminished by these mountains," he added in a sober voice. "You aren't diminished by them . . . or by anything. I told you that first day that you seemed to belong here. It was a bit too soon to say why." He kissed her head.

All the feelings of closeness warmed her again, and she wondered why such foolish fears should have intruded at all at a perfect time like this.

"Oh, Anne, you would always be perfect anywhere." He went on with eagerness. "I want to take you everywhere with me—to the cities of Europe and the Orient, to South America . . . and everywhere in this country, needless to say."

At once she understood the origin of her earlier unease and she almost started to say, "How could you?" There was always her work . . . and his. And that thought was the engine hauling an unhappy train of thought. It reminded her of the competitive lives they led by day, of the mystery of his work. Surely he wouldn't keep it a secret from her now. She gave an involuntary little shiver.

"I must be crazy," he exclaimed. "You're cold. I'm going to find you something to put on." He scrambled to his feet; she was treated again to the sight of his magnificent, trim body before he hurried into his trousers.

"Pajamas would be fine, or part of them," she suggested companionably, deciding to dismiss intrusive notions.

Walking away into his bedroom, he called back over his shoulder, "Never touch them. Rather, they never touch me."

She chuckled. But the small idiosyncrasy teased her into wondering what his life had been like before. He must have lived in some very primitive places; he seemed to be a very tough and able man. Plain, despite his status. She liked that.

He came back smiling, with a creamy flannel shirt over his arm. "Here," he said protectively, opening it out to receive her. Before he slipped it on her, he kissed both her shoulders, murmuring, "Mmmm . . . delicious."

With apparent delight he observed her in the shirt and buttoned it up for her. "A shame to obstruct such scenery," he commented with a wicked grin, "but you will feel warmer."

"Thank you." She put a hand on either side of his face, pulling him toward her for a kiss. The shirt felt wonderful, soft and cozy from many washings, like fleece against her cooled skin.

"You were absolutely right, lady. We both had fire enough without one in the hearth, but now's the time." She curled up and watched him go to the fireplace. He did things with wood and paper, and soon a small blaze had caught and begun to build. A lovely smell drifted to her.

"Ooooh . . . what *is* that?" she demanded.

"Sweet gum. It makes a very nice fire. But nothing," he amended, striding toward her and kneeling to caress her face, "is quite as sweet as what I'm touching right this minute."

He lowered his mouth to hers and gave her a lingering, eager kiss.

"I'd like to improve on that," she murmured, still a bit breathless. "Would you direct me to your shower?"

"Yes. With reluctance." He grinned at her.

"Reluctance?"

"You may not believe this, but the sight of you in that shirt is giving me ideas. It never looked that good on me." He studied her with an affectionate, delighted amusement blended with obvious excitement. The shirt was huge on her, the cuffs falling over her hands, the shoulder seams drooping halfway down her arms.

She held her arms out, laughing, making flapping motions.

"Stop that and take your shower," he ordered. "Or you won't get it. That shirt is almost the color of your skin. Speaking of which . . ." He stooped and planted a fervent kiss on one of her bare knees, then the other. She was almost tempted to postpone the shower.

But she couldn't. She leaped up and took her tote bag from the chair where she'd dropped it. "I'm going; I'm going."

She could feel his admiring gaze from behind as she headed for what was obviously the bathroom. She went in hurriedly and shut the door.

Examining her wide, glowing eyes and her bright, disheveled hair in the mirror, she was amazed. She almost looked like another woman. Satiety had weighted her eyelids, and her eyes sparkled back at her, not quite serene.

No, not quite, she thought, giggling. Clint was not the only one who was getting new ideas.

She slipped the shirt off, showered hurriedly, and dried herself off. After spraying herself liberally with her cologne, she ran her brush through her unruly hair until it gleamed. Then she hung her bag on a hook and padded back to the living room. The sweet gum's aromatic scent filled the empty room. She saw an open door beyond, revealing only darkness; the gray smoke from a cigarette whorled out along the blackened space.

Suddenly she felt wild and utterly abandoned. She unbuttoned the capacious shirt and let it fall on a chair, then slowly walked into the darkened room.

She could perceive the darkness of his big, sun-weathered form against the whiteness of the bed. Apparently he hadn't heard her soundless entry. But as soon as she was silhouetted in the door, she saw him come to attention, heard his deep exclamation of surprise. He stubbed out his cigarette, then rose and came to meet her. He picked her up in his arms and carried her back to the wide whiteness of the bed, to another meeting of their newly vibrant skin. The fragrance of the sweet gum was all around them, incense burning for their rite.

Anne felt the pressure of soft brightness on her lids and, stirring, opened her eyes. She knew they'd been asleep for hours, because the room was transfigured in the coral glow of sunrise. Still half-asleep, she reached out. The other side of the rumpled bed was empty. Now she could hear a cheerful bustle and banging, apparently from the kitchen. She stretched and smiled, thinking what a racket men always made in kitchens.

Elated, she thought, It's been so long since I've heard sounds like that. It was endearing, companionable. She lay back for a moment and observed the room from beneath lowered lids. She liked its neat, austere look, strong and plain as the man who occupied it. Remembering the wonders of the night, she was conscious of a hot, sweet flood of tenderness, remembered desire and delight.

Through the narrow windows of the bedroom she could see the mighty trunks of the ever-present pines, the spreading mountain laurel coming into bloom, pale ash and poplar, giant oaks, and the new flames of redbud starting.

The essence of renewal, the heart of spring, the same lovely vistas she had known from childhood. It must be very early, she decided, from the color of the sun.

There was another rattle from the kitchen, and a cheerful whistle. She smelled the delicious odor of strong coffee and felt as new as the redbud blossoms.

Then she chuckled, realizing that there was nothing in the room—nothing visible, at least—to wear. She got up and crept into the living room, where she took up the discarded shirt from the chair and slipped it on. She padded barefoot toward the smell of coffee.

In the compact kitchen Clint was pouring the coffee out into two mugs; his back was to the door. She went in soundlessly and started to put her arms around his waist from behind, but he put down the pot and said, in imitation of an old-time private eye, "It's no good, sugar."

She jumped in surprise when he turned and grabbed her, capturing her in his arms. "I smelled your cologne." His hands had slid through the loose opening of the too-big collar, caressing her naked body. "Ummm . . . I'm so glad it's early," he murmured. His arms encircled her under the shirt, and she nestled close to him, kissing his neck.

"What *do* you mean by that?" she demanded in mock puzzlement.

"I mean it's five o'clock in the morning, lady. Which means we don't have to face the world quite yet." He drew her nearer, and she was aware of his renewing need, amazedly conscious, too, of hers. Her own body already felt filled with melting warmth.

"If you're nice to me," he said, leering down at her, "I'll fix you flapjacks later."

"Flapjacks! I haven't had them since I was so high," she said, grinning. "How *much* later?"

"Not much, I'd figure, from the way I'm feeling." His hands were caressing her naked sides. She laughed softly, feeling very close to him. It felt as if they'd known each other forever, she marveled.

But she persisted in her teasing. "Can't I even have coffee?"

"Do you want coffee?" he asked her with great seriousness.

"Later. Later," she decided firmly. Laughing again, he pulled her upward and slung her over his shoulder in a fireman's carry; as she shrieked and giggled and protested, he strode with her through the living room back into the coppery red light of the bedroom and tossed her gently on the bed.

The shirt's buttons had come undone, and he knelt over her, no longer laughing. He folded the shirt back on either side and gazed at her with a worshipful solemnity.

Now, even more than last night, there was an edge to their desire, a desperate urgency, as if something might snatch them away from each other. They came together with a lovely swiftness, a hot immediacy that shook her. At the peak of her splendid forgetting, her shattering delight, she felt a more pervasive pleasure than she had ever thought to find, even with him.

They lay together for a timeless moment, spent, wondering, and short of breath.

"Right at this minute," he whispered, "I wish we never had to go anywhere again."

"So do I," she answered, raising herself on one elbow so she could look down into his face. She bent slowly over him and found his mouth with hers, kissing him deeply, then lightly, over and over again.

"Oh, Anne. Anne." He slipped one arm about her upper body and crushed her close to him, his lazy fingers trailing down her back, stroking her singing skin.

"But we must," she said reluctantly against his chest, her lips encountering the crisp mat of black hair that sprang from his moist, sea-scented flesh.

"Yes." He sighed. "What time," he asked with a blandness that didn't deceive her at all, "do you have to be at work?"

"Well, we're doing a night scene today, so . . ."

"That's great!" He looked elated. "You mean *to-night?*"

She felt laughter bubble in her. "No . . . sorry. I was trying to get my thoughts together. Which isn't easy right now," she added. "We're doing a so-called night interior, at the Halberd Inn. It's a matter of lighting. But to answer your question, I have to be on location at the civilized hour of nine for a change."

"Oh." He looked so dashed that she gave him another brief, consoling kiss. "Well, I'm not so lucky. I'm meeting my crew at six-thirty."

That dogged curiosity assailed her for an instant. But she told herself, Not now. Not yet. Don't let anything spoil this for you. So she said, "All right. Let me make the flapjacks, then."

"Really?" He looked at her uncertainly.

She laughed out loud at his expression. "Really. I'll love it." It had been so long since she'd cooked breakfast for a man.

"You're wonderful." He sat up with great reluctance, lighting a cigarette. "Okay. I'll take a shower while you're starting. Or maybe you want to take one first."

She nodded. He lay back smiling on the pillows, pulling at his cigarette while he watched her put on his shirt again. "You're so beautiful," he said.

She hurried through her shower feeling as light as a balloon, giddy with happiness. She felt strange getting back into yesterday's clothes, but dismissed the minor concern. She decided that she'd leave with him, drop him off and drive back to Warrenburg for fresh clothes.

By the time he went to shower, she had breakfast well organized; they ate with sharpened appetites while she told him about the movie.

"What's the name of it?" he asked after a swallow of coffee.

"When That April."

" '. . . with its showers sweet,' et cetera," he finished the quote, smiling.

She was surprised and pleased that he remembered the famous first line of Chaucer's *Canterbury Tales.* "Well, well," she teased him. "That's pretty good for a filing-cabinet mind."

"Oh, yes, I had my exposure to all those pretty little things, too." There was a certain condescension in the way he said that, an indulgence in his smile, but she let it go.

"Did you see *Winter Kind?* This is a sequel to it," she explained.

"Good Lord, yes. That was quite a film." She could hear a kind of grudging admiration in his comment. "That was yours, then?"

"Strictly speaking, Lloyd's and mine," she amended. There was the slightest darkening in his expression, as if the very mention of Lloyd Eliot's name recalled their rather awkward situation—competitors in a kind of territorial dispute. More than that, it reminded her of how diametrically opposite they were. He was a scientist, governed by objective absolutes, while she had always been an artist, sure of nothing beyond her own intuition, following no rule but inspiration's instinct. Which had so far, she thought drily, been infallible. It always amused her, for example, when the country's space engineers slowly began to catch up with science fiction.

"You're very quiet," he remarked, studying her with that tender anxiety that always melted her, made her forget other issues. His golden brown eyes were startling against the weathered tan of his face, the whiteness of his teeth positively stunning. A lock of thick black hair was brushing one of his shaggy brows, and his sensuous smile was one-sided, questioning.

When he looked at her like that, it was hard to consider anything but him. "I'm just so . . . happy," she said softly, to reassure him. "And so awfully unwilling to leave."

He grabbed her hand across the table and squeezed it. "That makes two of us." Glancing at his watch, he said, 'I'd better get going." He pushed back his chair hesitantly, then got up with enormous unwillingness. "Look, I can walk to my site today, and to the Rover later. Why don't you stay awhile and relax here? It'd be nice to think of you here, Anne."

That warmed her heart, but she shook her head and told him her plans.

"Even better." He grinned. "I can be with you a few minutes longer."

This time she drove, glorying in the loveliness of the warm spring morning, in his presence at her side. In the near distance, mist was moving away from the Smokies' rugged peaks; now and then one of the summits was wrapped in the embrace of clouds that took fairylike shapes, some like smoke wreaths, others like castles and towers.

I belong here, she thought, elated. And this is the man I belong with. When he told her where to slow to let him out, he leaned over and pressed her khaki-covered knee with his big, strong fingers. She tingled at his touch.

He said soberly, "I think my place is . . . the place for us to be, don't you?"

She nodded, feeling a wild exhilaration. He took it for granted that they would continue being together. She hadn't really been sure until he said that, because of the constant hail-and-farewell, the light-ness with which so many people now conducted their lives.

"Oh, yes," she agreed softly. "Absolutely."

"Then maybe you'd think about . . . well, bringing a few of your things there, to save you all this nonsense. Would you think about it, Anne?" He sounded eager.

Smiling, she answered, "I will. Think about it, anyway."

He raised his black brows at that, but apparently decided to let it go. "Now, look, about tonight . . . how shall we arrange it?"

"I'll come to you," she said, "because right now I don't know exactly what time I'll be able to get away."

"It'll seem a long time from *now,* I know that much," he retorted. He took her face in his hands and gave her a lingering caress. Then, with great suddenness, he got out and stood in the road with his hand raised to her, as if he'd had to tear himself loose.

She gave him a long look and waved in response, then drove slowly off. When he had disappeared she accelerated, barely glancing at the village of Sedgby as she passed, making good but careful time down the winding road to Warrenburg.

It was only a little after seven, to Anne's pleased surprise, when she let herself into her room. She could use a little extra time; there was a lot to take care of.

Her luggage had arrived from the Coast, the suitcases neatly lined up just by the door. Bless the never-failing Emma. With a pleasure that was deeply feminine she began to unpack the bags, examining various things for wrinkles and creases. She separated the uncrushables from the items that needed to be pressed. Holding up a soft and sexy pajama suit against herself in front of the mirror, she reflected, Clint will love me in this. It was a low-cut frivolity in an unusual grayed lilac, and it did great things for her coloring and hair.

Suddenly the full significance of the previous night struck her. Still holding the pajamas to her breast, she sank down on the bed opposite the mirror, staring at her own reflection. Once more she had the sense of being someone new, a whole other person. Giving herself to him had had such deep meaning for her, and it had happened so quickly. She had only known him for a matter of days.

It had happened so fast, in the midst of so many other pressures, that she'd hardly had a chance to think. And there wasn't that much time to think about it now, either, she decided wryly.

With an ironic little twist of her mouth, she thought, there's the small matter of my whole career. Lloyd's promising remarks, his admiring praise, recurred to her. She had to pull herself together, go over her notes for today's shooting. Last night, this morning, she'd almost forgotten that there *was* a film.

She jumped up and started to hang several things in the closet. Hesitating, she put one or two of them aside; she would take those to Clint's place. That decision slowed her thoughts for a minute, but then she hurried on with her tasks, laying the clothes that needed pressing over a chair and calling the desk for valet service.

She hurried into the bath and turned on the shower, then washed her hair and blew it dry. The soft water of the mountains, she noticed, gave her hair an almost phosphorescent shine; it surrounded her face like a sculpted bonfire, behaving well on this dry, sunny day.

It was nearly eight when she sat down at her desk, dressed in a dark gray shirt and jeans, to consult her notes. A cold idea intruded: How much was she going to *care* today? All she wanted at this moment was to get through the day as quickly as possible, to hurry to Clint this evening. If he kept affecting her like this . . . She shook her head and made herself attend to what she was doing.

The phone's ring was sudden and loud, surprising her. She hurried to answer.

"Anne." Lloyd was crisp. "It looks like I'm going to have to fly to New York this morning to see my man in person. You direct today."

Her heart thudded. She exulted, It's here—the day I've been waiting for. "Of course," she said breathlessly.

"You can handle it if anyone can," Lloyd went on. "I may be back tomorrow afternoon. I'm not sure yet. If I'm not, you know the drill." Tersely he told her his ideas for the scenes. "These are the numbers where I can be reached. All right?"

"Very much all right," she responded in the same even tone as his. "Bon voyage. And good luck."

He hung up without a goodbye.

She sat on the bed for an instant, holding the receiver in her hand, then softly replaced it.

It was frightening . . . exhilarating. She was in charge! She was in command now, after all the years of waiting. And she knew exactly how those scenes should go. They would incorporate Lloyd's ideas and hers, but they would go beyond that: They would be touched with the magic she herself had glimpsed.

She put her notes in her canvas briefcase with the other things she'd need on location, then slung the case over her shoulder, scooped up her packed carryall and donned her sunglasses.

Within fifteen minutes she was halfway to Sedgby, the scenes they were to shoot that day unreeling clearly before her inner eye. Triumphantly she realized that she'd been a fool to think anything could distract her; it was exactly the opposite. Being with Clint last night and this morning had positively inspired her. She was already discovering fresh nuances, inventing new beauties, for the ballroom scene.

None of them would involve script changes or departures from the basic outline; they would be a matter of new camera angles, subtle coloring, careful direction.

Soon the Sedgby church spire came into view and she was driving past the familiar nineteenth-century houses. When she pulled up behind the Halberd Inn she was not only eager, but more than ready.

She hurried through the rear entrance to the Halberd's ballroom, where the night scene would be shot in deference to Sedgby schedules—a retirement dinner would be held there that night, but it would be unused this morning. Excited local extras, dressed in old-fashioned evening clothes, crowded the corridor; a small group of them was being instructed by Harri

Payne, who seemed to have her hands full. Her short
gray-streaked hair was tousled, her solid, khaki-clad
body tense. Anne heard her say to an earnest-looking
fellow, "There aren't any speaking parts for the extras,
you see," and listened to him respond that he was a
history student, and . . .

Harri excused herself and greeted Anne. "Where's
His Highness?" she demanded.

Anne explained. Grinning, Harri commented,
"Great. About time," and turned back to the importu-
nate student.

Anne listened to him too. Sympathetically she murmured, "What a shame. That sounds like a marvelous
idea." Then she went on to outline to him the functions
of the extras, concluding with a brilliant smile. Dazzled, the student subsided, mysteriously satisfied.

Moving down the hall with Anne, Harri said softly,
"Thanks. You've got the magic touch."

The cast, in full costume, was already seated expectantly at one of the little tables edging the ballroom
floor. Anne went over to them. Jack Salem jumped up
when she approached, and she endured his bone-
crushing grip on her upper arms with a patient smile.
Livie was radiant in her new white ballgown; sullen and
sultry Marcella would not appear in this scene, or the
simpler one that would follow that afternoon. All to the
good, Anne judged; there would be nothing to upset
the finely balanced Livie, and Anne needed every
ounce of the actress's energy for this scene as well as
the one in the writing room.

The writing room . . . An uninvited picture of Clint
flashed through her mind. They had played a scene of
their own in that room.

Not now, she ordered herself sternly, and began to

block out the ballroom scene again for the actors. She took Livie aside.

"At the risk of beating the idea to death," she said, smiling at Livie, "remember . . . this is the very first instant that your love for Philip comes to light. I want to see it in your eyes, your mouth, your hands, your posture. I know it'll be exquisite . . . because no one, no one in the business, can handle it the way you can."

Gratified, she saw the glow in Livie's huge dark eyes. The actress said, "I'm *so* glad you're directing this, Anne. I can do things for you I can *never* do for Lloyd Eliot."

Livie never called him by his first name alone, as if to distance herself from him. Feeling a faintly disloyal satisfaction, Anne smiled, murmuring, "I'm glad."

Then she was busy, moving with swift, smooth confidence, conferring with the extras and the orchestra, with the photography director, the camera operator. Climbing into the seat in front of the photography chief's, she rechecked all the angles.

And at last, with a feeling of surprising calm, she raised her hand and called, "Take one."

The ballroom scene went like a dream, with only one retake of a minor part. Watching the rushes that evening, Anne wondered for a second if Lloyd would have done more retakes, if she had been overconfident. But then, hearing the glowing comments of the others, she decided not. It was perfection. The later scene had been just as good, she judged. Even the sun had cooperated—or she had cooperated with it, perhaps. She smiled to herself. She was almost beginning to think like Lloyd.

At a strategic moment a vagrant sunbeam had entered the narrow window of the writing room in such a way that the leaded pane cast a Mephistophelian shadow on the austere face of Hayward Gunn—the splendid actor who played the heroine's stern father—while he was confronting Jack, who had come to ask for his daughter's hand. Anne had had to restrain herself from exclaiming aloud at the perfection of it. She'd been operating the smaller camera herself, and had played it for all it was worth.

"Damned beautiful, Anne." The director of photography grinned at her ruefully. "If this keeps up I'll be collecting unemployment."

From him this was a rave, and she flushed at his approval.

"Maybe Napoleon will be, too," he added. "I must say, it's a pleasure doing business with you." Anne grinned back at him, reflecting that a little tact, like chicken soup, couldn't hurt. She'd listened very carefully to his advice before taking over the camera.

When the meeting was breaking up she glanced at her watch, uneasily seeing how late it already was. And she still hadn't heard from Lloyd.

She hurried out of the trailer that served as their miniature projection room and back to the inn. As she was about to pass the dining room, she realized belatedly that she'd had no dinner. She hadn't even been thinking of the rushes this morning when she'd planned to go right to Clint's place from the location. Now everything seemed to be piling up on her again.

Having decided to have something sent up to her room, she was heading toward the elevator when she heard her name called from the desk. Thank heavens. Maybe it was a message from Lloyd.

It was. He'd left a number. She flagged a passing bellboy and asked him to have a sandwich and coffee sent up to her, then headed for a pay phone in the lobby.

When she reached him, Lloyd demanded, without a greeting, "How did it go?" She told him, tactfully omitting her personal raves.

"Great. You'll have to carry on tomorrow . . . maybe the day after. There's more of a tangle here than I figured." There always was, Anne thought, but Lloyd seemed to thrive on problems, to enjoy dancing on the edge of disaster.

"I've got to romance another board member," he went on. "Way the hell in Newport. It's a bloody nuisance. You know how I hate these things."

Anne was silent. The exact opposite was true: Lloyd loved manipulations and ego wars. Only hè would have the gall to play footsie like this with the members of a rival corporation. She was torn between exasperation and delight; she'd still be carrying the picture.

"Are you there, Anne?" Lloyd snapped. She murmured her assent, and he asked, "You *can* handle it, can't you? I'm sure you can."

"Yes," she said firmly. "I certainly can."

"That's my Annie. Are the troops in line? Did Jack get his bike fixed? Any new trouble with Ward?" Her heart thudded.

"Yes to the first question, no to the second and third." She was tempted to add, "The only Ward trouble is heart trouble."

"Fine, fine." Lloyd sounded very pleased.

He asked her a few technical questions about the day's takes, then said goodbye.

Anne rushed up to her room, where room service was already outside her door waiting. She took care of the waiter, and the minute he'd left she started stripping off her work clothes, then headed for the shower.

Later, as she dressed, she wished fervently that Clint had a phone. He'd mentioned it that morning, declaring that when he wasn't working he was not to be bothered.

Anne took a last glance around the room. Her notes were in her briefcase in the car with her packed bag. She repressed an anxious thought about when she'd be able to review the next day's shooting and went out. Too impatient to wait for the elevator, she took the stairs down and sped to her car. The cabin now seemed half a world away, the time to come almost the dream of another person, not Anne Reynolds, who was carrying so much responsibility.

But as the miles unrolled behind her and she sighted the ridge where his cabin was, the world began to slip away again. And when she saw him on the cabin steps, waiting for her—he must have heard the car—she was convinced that nothing else really mattered.

Chapter 6

CLINT REACHED ANNE'S CAR JUST AS SHE BRAKED, THEN opened her door and leaned in to kiss her. His lips gave her a feeling of home. It was the first caress all over again.

Breathless, she looked up at him; he was still leaning over her, laughing at himself a little. "This is crazy as hell," he said, and his words were unsteady, "but today seemed like a week."

"To me too," she admitted, realizing that it was true.

He straightened and held out his hand. She took it and got out.

"Did you bring anything?" he asked eagerly, and his

eagerness moved her. He put his arm around her waist and, bending, peered into the car.

"Yes. In the back."

He released her, reached in and hoisted her big canvas bag as lightly as if it were a bunch of flowers. She watched the play of muscles under his tight T-shirt with warm pleasure. He grinned down at her with the delight of someone who has just been given a marvelous present.

Gazing up at him, taking in the jet black, tousled hair above the tanned face that was so relaxed and happy, she felt her insides melt.

"You look prettier every time I see you. I like that." His eyes were sparkling. "How are you? How did it go?"

He put one arm around her waist again, and they walked toward the cabin. "I'm marvelous. A little weary. It was a day and a half," she said.

They went rapidly up the few steps, and when they were inside, he said, "I want to hear about it, but first I'll stow this away."

He strode to the bedroom, dropped the bag and was back again in no time at all.

"And," he said, "I want to know if you've had dinner. I can manage a steak." He surveyed her again, very slowly and with a kind of amazement. "Never, in all my life, have I ever seen such hair."

He touched it, feeling its texture. "Get comfortable." His hands dropped from her hair and began to remove her jacket. She let him take it off, savoring the touch of his big fingers on her, feeling cared for and cherished.

Gently he laid the jacket over a chair and took her in his arms, hugging her to him. "How about it?" he asked. "Have you had dinner?"

"In a manner of speaking." She nestled close to him, kissing his neck. "I had no idea you were a chef."

Holding her, he chuckled. "Chef I'm not. With me it was a matter of survival; I've been on jobs where there was no restaurant for a hundred miles." With another powerful hug, he released her. Stepping back, he offered, "What do you say to a drink, then?"

That was the last thing in the world she wanted just then, and she told him so, with a new boldness that surprised her.

His face lit up. "Everything else can wait till kingdom come," he agreed softly. "There's only one thing, lady, that can't . . . something I've been thinking about all day."

"You are insatiable," she teased him. "Delightfully insatiable," she amended, realizing with amazement that her own body was throbbing, warming with renewed desire, that it had begun the minute she'd seen him standing there on the steps.

She also realized something else—something almost frightening. Her eagerness to talk about the day was gone. Everything else in the world seemed unimportant, far away.

She raised her face to his; with a look of solemn excitement he bent his head and kissed her with demanding hunger. As always, she sensed herself dissolving, melting against him as his commanding touch explored her willing flesh, his own body trembling, hard against her, his quivering mouth ascending from her lips to her cheek and temple, descending again in a fiery path to her parting lips.

"Anne. Oh, Anne," he whispered. "This . . . this is—" He stopped abruptly, words failing him, and kissed her once more, even more deeply. She leaned on him, weak with happiness and longing.

"Come," he whispered hoarsely. "Come with me." With his arm tight around her, he urged her toward the bedroom.

This time it was in twilight; a kind of lavender haze enveloped it. Dimly she saw the now-familiar wide, white bed; beyond lay the darker shadow of the trees. She was suddenly aware that he had let go of her and was standing before her, undoing the button at the waist of her trousers.

She slipped out of her shoes and watched him watch the soft garment sliding down from her body, revealing the nakedness her clothes had hidden.

He took a quick, shuddering breath, helping her step out of the blue trousers. He folded them carefully, laying them over a chair before turning bright-eyed to her again to unfasten her blue silk shirt and remove it.

"My God," he whispered, "you're so lovely . . . so lovely." He stared at her low-cut, gray satin bra, and then with gentle hands began to free her trembling breasts from it. He stooped to kiss her breasts, first one, then the other, with a feathery caress of the tongue. She trembled and cried out, her flesh so quivering and fiery now that her sudden need was torture.

He seemed to know that with the sixth sense he possessed in their intimate encounters, and suddenly he was divesting himself of his own clothes, baring that hard, magnificent body to her dazzled sight. She sank down on the bed, her legs so weak they could hardly support her, and as he stood there for an instant in front of her, on impulse she leaned over and planted a fervent series of quick kisses on his loins and upper thighs.

His body leaped at the first light caress; then he was urging her backward with his touch, lying beside her, stroking her all over, loving her in heavenly new ways, ways she had not even imagined, until she was pleading, "Love me, love me . . . completely."

With an instantaneous ease, an already practiced, joyous motion, they joined; immediately, to her utter wonder, she was on that climbing, straining flight to the highest peak of pleasure, aware incredibly soon of the bright, sweet explosion at the very moment that she heard him crying out.

He was holding her so close that her mouth was pressed against his ear; she could not tell, in that first dreamlike transition from breathlessness to breath, whether she had actually murmured the words she longed to say aloud or only sung them to herself.

But then, feeling his hold grow stronger, sensing the deeper trembling in his flesh, she perceived that she must have whispered to him, because he gasped, "Anne, oh, Anne. You make this so beautiful . . . so glorious."

She could almost feel them drift back together to solidity, floating like spent swimmers on an inward tide to rest on welcome sand. It was more than enough to be close and tender, to be themselves.

As if in an unspoken pact, they both seemed to know that for the moment they were in the world again, but the world was somehow glorified.

In companionable whispers they started to talk of other things; she heard their voices growing clearer and more natural.

"What did you mean, before," he said with playful sternness, "when you said you ate 'in a manner of speaking'?"

She told him.

"That's terrible," he scolded her softly, and once again she had the marvelous feeling of being cared for.

"Why don't you let me fix something . . . while you 'ablute.'"

She giggled.

"I know you will," he went on. "You wash yourself all the time, just like a little cat. So, while you ablute . . ."

"And slip into something less comfortable . . . " she quipped.

"Yes, and that . . . I'll shower quickly and put some steaks on." He patted her in a private spot and kissed her shoulder, then started to get up.

"Wait." She stopped him with her hand. "First, I'll pay the bill." She drew his head down to hers and kissed him soundly.

"I like the way you think," he said admiringly. "Paying the bill in advance."

Anne laughed, lying back in the bed and listening to the brief rush of the shower before he came back out with a towel draped around himself like a lavalava.

He approached her, grinning. "You forgot the tip," he said as he lay back down beside her.

"How shocking," she murmured, submitting to his caress.

"Mmmmm. I'd better get up," he muttered, but made no move to do so.

"I'd better be careful, molesting the cook like this. It could spoil dinner." She nibbled at his ear.

"If you're *that* hungry . . . " he teased her. Then he got up with a groan. "On the contrary, lady, when you molest the cook like that, you get *cordon bleu.*"

Grinning, she watched him toss away the towel, get into his discarded jeans and pad off barefoot toward the kitchen.

She stretched out her arms, feeling newly born, and slowly rose from the bed. She went to her canvas bag, unzipped it and took things out, hanging some in the closet, keeping a whisper-soft robe of turquoise jersey.

She picked up his damp towel and took it into the bathroom with her, then hung it to dry. She showered rapidly, then donned the robe and a pair of slippers. Satisfied, she scented herself with cologne and went back to the bedroom. In seconds she had it tidy again. Noticing that the air was cooler, she went to join him in the kitchen, carrying his T-shirt with her. A bottle of Bordeaux, two glasses and an appetizing-looking salad were already on the table.

"You look lovely, although I must say I like the way you are now best of all." He grinned evilly.

"That makes two of us." She let her gaze wander over his splendid torso, his heavily muscled arms. "Your tan's a heap better than this." She indicated the T-shirt. "But I thought you might need it."

"I do." He came to her and held her. "You're so sweet, Anne." He freed himself and put the T-shirt on.

She stood near him and rubbed his back while he asked her how she liked her steak. "Very, very well done."

He protested that that was barbaric but, nevertheless, soon served up a perfectly done steak. They ate with great enjoyment; touching glasses, savoring the ruby-colored wine. Afterward she helped him clean up the kitchen, although he protested, "Leave it for the maid."

"A maid?" she scoffed. "In this wilderness?"

He told her that a woman came in from Sedgby every afternoon to do the housekeeping.

"You enjoy quite a few amenities, considering," she commented as they strolled back to the living room. Looking around, she was able to notice for the first time just how luxurious the whole place was.

"As a matter of fact," she said appreciatively, "this is quite a place for a mountain cabin."

"Only the best for you," he said very seriously, stopping to look down into her eyes. Her evaluation had pleased him, though. She could tell because there was a trace of a smile on his sensuous mouth. "I sublet it from an old pal of mine," he explained. "A professor at the university. This is his weekend and summer place, but he won't be using it; he's going on a European sabbatical. And, speaking of pals," he said with an eager inflection, "I found an old favorite of ours." He headed for the handsome music unit among the bookshelves, selected a tape and inserted it.

Expectantly she settled on the couch and, kicking off her slippers, curled her legs beneath her.

Clint watched her in anticipation, his eyes shining, his mouth touched with the ghost of a tender smile.

"Have you seen but a white lily grow . . . before rude hands have touched it . . ."

She recognized at once that exquisite song they had reminisced about, the song whose words he had forgotten until she had remembered them for him.

Clint came slowly across the room and sat down beside her, looking down at her as the song went on.

". . . or smelt the 'nard in the fire, the bud of the briar, or tasted the bag of the bee . . . ? Oh so white, oh so soft, oh so sweet is she."

His look was full of meaning, as if to say, "This is you." Anne felt happy tears gather in her eyes; this music and this moment were so perfect that she almost wondered if they were real, if all of this would fade like a dream that one longs to hold, but cannot.

She put out her hand and touched his face to reassure herself of his reality.

At a break in the music, before the next mellifluous

song began—it was, to her immense delight, "Barbry Ellen"—she whispered to Clint, "You *are* real, then."

Over the next song's beginning words, "In Scarlett Town, where I was born, there was a fair maid dwellin'," Clint said softly, "That's my line, Anne. I've had to tell myself a hundred times in the last few days that you're the one who's really real."

He kissed her on the temple; then they leaned their heads back in glad, close silence to listen.

Anne drifted, almost drugged with pleasure, listening to the familiar words "a red rose and a green briar." Abruptly an idea for the next day's bedroom scene occurred to her: roses, a feminine symbol; the tough and stubborn briar for enduring, relentless male passion.

Ridiculous that the cabin had no phone; she wanted to call Harri and give her some directions about this. Lucky they were filming interiors tomorrow, too. . . . With equal suddenness she remembered the painful scene with the bulldozer.

The music ended. Clint murmured, "What would you like to hear?"

She gazed at him for a moment, unhearing. For an awful instant he looked almost like a stranger. Tonight they were lovers who had shut their door against the world; tomorrow they could be enemies with no hope of compromise.

"Sorry," she murmured. "Anything."

He gave her a swift look but inserted a new tape. She heard the gilded, rushing fountain of Bach at gentle volume. Clint sauntered back to her and sprawled on the couch beside her, stretching his lean length out, one big arm hanging relaxed, the other one about her shoulders.

She closed her eyes, wondering what was the matter

with her. Now she found the matter-of-fact possessive-
ness of his embrace disturbing. And such a little while
before . . .

"I hear small wheels turning," he commented softly.

Anne opened her eyes and glanced sidewise at him,
smiling a bit tightly. "I'm afraid you're right. I'm a
haunted woman. The music gave me all kinds of new
ideas for a scene we're doing tomorrow."

"Nothing wrong with that." He grinned down at her.
"You're not the only haunted one. By the way, you
never did tell me how your day went." There was a hint
of laughter when he added, "I didn't give you much
chance, though, did I?"

"You never do." She patted him to draw the sting
from the remark. "And I wasn't exactly unwilling."

He looked very pleased. Then he asked, chuckling,
"How was your day . . . he asked two hours later!"

She told him.

His hand kneaded her shoulder. "That's a break for
you, then. You told me you've wanted this for a long
time. I'm glad." He sounded so sincere that she was
moved to warmth again and snuggled against him. He
kissed the top of her head. "Funny, though," he went
on, and she could feel his breath against her hair, "for
Eliot to take off at this point."

It was more of a question than a comment. Anne
debated. How could she come right out and say Lloyd
was trying to sabotage him? Clint might be forced to
reciprocate. Yet, how could she not . . . when they
were this close? And yet . . . Clint hadn't been exactly
up-front with her. She still didn't know what he was
doing in the Smokies.

It was a poser. She took a quick breath and compro-
mised. "There was something he had to take care of out

of town." Surely that sounded all right; it might be anything.

But Clint was too sharp for her. He asked lightly, "It wouldn't be something to do with our little territorial war . . . about where we'll be allowed to play with our marbles?"

His insight, his ironic smile and careless tone stung her. She pulled away from him slightly. "It's not exactly a game, you know. We have more than money sunk in this film. There are other things in the balance— Lloyd's career, mine, the actors'—and we think this picture will be another award winner, like *The Winter Kind*. Besides, it's more than that for me," she admitted softly. "It's a kind of . . . grail, if that doesn't sound too purple." She smiled at her own seriousness.

She'd meant it, though. The film was a shining standard to uphold.

She looked up. Clint was staring down at her, an indulgent smile playing over his sensuous mouth.

Indulgent, she repeated silently. He still didn't really understand, she decided, feeling cold. Somehow that took a bit of the glow from this enchanted interval, alleviated her guilt about deceiving him.

But she went on, wanting desperately to make them close again, to make him see. "This picture is more than a film," she said. "You see, it's like trying to preserve a rainbow, make a cobweb as permanent as a sculpture of silver. I want to make dreams solid."

Good heavens, she thought, what a lot of high-falutin' stuff. She paused, feeling a little silly.

He traced her earnest lips with his fingers. The tender, indulgent smile was still on his mouth; his look, she thought, was uncomprehending.

"If you'll pardon the sermon," she said lightly. Her

voice sounded flat and cool to her own ears, and she felt irrationally lonely. Dan would have understood without being told.

"It didn't sound like one," Clint assured her. "It sounded quite . . . lovely." But his assurance was that of a man who didn't understand at all, but just didn't want to rock the boat, she concluded sadly.

"Did Eliot go to New York?" he asked her suddenly.

It was such a swift attack that she blurted, "Yes," almost before she thought.

"I see." Clint removed his arm from her shoulder, leaned over to an end table and found a cigarette. While he lit it, she studied him, wondering uneasily why he was so interested in Lloyd's destination, annoyed with herself for letting the information out. "I'll bet I know exactly who he's going to see."

Oh, dear, Anne mourned, I've done it now. "Do you?" she asked weakly.

He nodded with a grim smile. "Oh, yes, my nemesis on the board. That's my educated surmise."

Anne couldn't let herself admit it. "I don't know for sure. But, Clint, you know, we've been circling around this whole matter from the first. We might as well talk about it. After all, we can't keep having a repetition of that morning on the ridge."

Clint put out his cigarette and took both her hands in his. "I know that, honey. But you've both bitten off a mighty big bite here. We're just going to have to do the best we can with this thing. Our paths will keep crisscrossing. That's the way it is. Believe me, I'd do anything to make it easier for you, and I will, as much as I'm able. But there are certain . . . things that we won't be able to avoid. We'll have to take them as they come. And you're right, we have been dancing around the subject. I've been doing that on purpose. What we have together has nothing at all to do with our work; I want to keep it separate . . . special."

She was moved by his words, but she protested, "How can we, Clint? We *are* our work. We're all one piece. You have the kind of mind that lets you shut me away in a neat little drawer. I don't think that way. I can't. To me the self is . . . all one thing, intermingled and . . ." She struggled for expression. Philosophy always made her impatient; it was something she preferred to live, not talk about.

"The old art-versus-science war," he commented. "It's a tempest in a teacup, sweetheart. And it doesn't have a thing to do with the price of . . . marbles. You won't be working forever." He grinned.

He must be kidding, she thought. "You have me at a disadvantage. I tell you all about my work, and you never tell me about yours. What *is* your project, Clint? Surely you can tell me . . . now, after all that's happened." Her cheeks felt hot.

He looked very uncomfortable. "I'm sorry. I can't, not even now. Would you believe that most of my crew don't even know what they're working on?"

"That's . . . incredible." She tried to subdue an almost childish feeling of hurt. Surely, she reflected, he could trust *me*. But then, she hadn't trusted him enough to tell him about Lloyd's trip.

"All I can tell you is that the project's incredible . . . quite 'far-out.' " He had a peculiar smile on his face when he used the rather dated expression, which tickled her curiosity even more.

Then he rapidly switched the subject. "What's your itinerary for tomorrow, darling? At least we can talk about *that*. Maybe if we have a daily private session"—

he leered at her teasingly and brushed the tip of her nose with his finger—"I can save you a lot of grief."

Part of her resented his almost paternal attitude; another was touched by his consideration. "Well . . . tomorrow we do two interiors, both at the Cannon house."

"Any outdoor shots?"

"It depends on the weather. Two, if we can manage them. Lloyd and the crew have already caught up on a lot of the other outside building shots," Anne told him, at ease again.

"Then it should be full speed ahead," he assured her. "Unless I decide to kidnap you from the set. I never knew before how long a workday could be."

He leaned toward her, and she watched his mesmerizing eyes come nearer and nearer, his sensuous mouth approaching hers. She let her lids veil her eyes and raised her face for his caress.

With his mouth exploring hers, it was almost impossible to think anything at all, but dimly she reflected that when they were close like this, she had no more questions.

His eager hands were tracing the contours of her willing body once again, and all her doubts began to turn into absurdities.

"What do you say to an early night?" As he spoke he dropped light, nuzzling kisses on her submissive lips, and she tingled.

"I think that's a lovely idea."

They got up from the couch, and he bound her to him with one arm, walking close beside her, matching his steps to hers. They moved to the stereo, and he shut it off, then turned off the lamps with one hand.

"I feel better when you're not too far away," he said, chuckling. She went along with him, still close beside him as they entered the bedroom, lit now only by the pale reflection of the moon.

He turned her in his arms and pulled her close; she felt the familiar wonder of his big, hard body.

Later, when she drifted at last toward sleep, she vowed to take this gift from one day to the next, to take things one lovely day at a time. She wasn't going to ask for trouble anymore, at least not more than they had already. It was unimaginable that anything was big enough to destroy this perfection, this deep happiness. They would work it all out; she knew they would.

Driving toward Sedgby early the next morning, Anne marveled at her jubilance, at how much doubt had seemed to disappear overnight. She savored the memory of his waking kisses, their pleasant breakfast, the almost married way they'd parted at the fork where Clint took off in his Rover for his own site.

It was the greatest paradox she'd ever run across: On one hand, he was a threat and a complication; on the other, every moment with him inspired her, dyed her very thoughts with magical beauty that would color *When That April.*

She looked forward to shooting the interiors in the ancient Cannon house because one was an intimate love scene, and she felt she could direct it as she never could have before. The last enchanted night, this morning, still glowed through her body and all over her; that glow would be captured, transmitted to the lovers, shining through the film.

She glanced at her watch. She had plenty of time for some errands she wanted to do before she went to the location. She decided to make her calls from the filling station. First she'd call the Warrenburg Inn to see if there were any messages from Lloyd; next she needed to speak with the florist in Warrenburg, to have him rush the exact kind of roses she needed to the Cannon house. Then would come a visit to the marvelous Sedgby library to do some lightning research on folk songs. The music had eluded her before, but now she was convinced that mountain folk songs, which had, after all, originated in Great Britain, would be perfect, some vocal, others instrumental.

Anne pulled into the filling station, where she was greeted warmly by the attendant, who was also an extra in the film. She quickly took care of her calls. There were no messages from Lloyd.

Still with a feeling of being on holiday, she drove into Sedgby, past the church and the sprawling Halberd Inn, toward the Cannon house. The sky over the Smokies was gray and overcast, the air almost chilly. Rain was imminent.

Perversely, Anne loved "bad" weather like this; it made her feel wildly creative. Besides, Clint had told her that if it rained hard, the weather would cut his workday short and he might drop by her location. And tonight . . . tonight, her heart sang, we'll have another sweet gum fire. Everything was coming up roses at the moment.

She could use a few metaphorical ones, she thought wryly. There'd be problems enough, even if all went well on location. For instance, on the lot back on the Coast, doing the bedroom scene would be a piece of cake with a huge, wide-open fake room as a set. An actual interior wasn't so easy, simply because of logistics. She decided to skip the library until later.

She sighted the Cannon house, its squat gray outline rising above several gloomy oaks on a slight elevation. It was a travesty of Norman houses with its mansard roof and its two awkward chimneys rising like horns on either side of the structure. Of course, they would have to fake a weed-grown yard because this one was so manicured, but in the cloudy light the covered porch was full of threatening shadows. Marvelous, Anne mused. The whole house expressed the tragedy of the Winters, who were to be the subjects of the film.

Anne saw the equipment trucks lined up out of camera range, and Jack's and Livie's cars vivid among the plainer ones. Uh-oh! The silent exclamation jumped up in Anne's mind. It would have been a friendly gesture for either Jack or Livie to offer the other a ride. Anne hoped this didn't mean they were having problems again. She hoped, too, that the rain would hold off for a little while, because they had two exteriors of the house to shoot. One involved a dashing climb by Jack up the oak onto the roof and into Livie's room. He flatly refused to use a double for it.

On the other hand, there was only one dressing trailer, which must mean that Hester Cannon was allowing the cast to dress in the house, a sign that she was accepting them cordially and not making a fuss. Anne had had an uneasy feeling from the first that the rental agreement Hester had signed wouldn't mean zilch to her if she suddenly became cantankerous, that any dispute would mean a time-wasting conference with lawyers and heaven knew who else.

Anne slung her tote bag over her shoulder and mounted the few wide steps to the shadowy veranda. There was a stir, a babble of voices inside. To her surprise, Hester Cannon herself opened the door. She looked more forbidding than ever in black, with an unwelcoming expression.

"Good morning, Miss Reynolds," she said coldly as

Anne came in. "I will not use that unpronounceable form of 'Mzzzzz,' which always sounds like a stepped-on bumblebee. I assume it *is* Miss. One can never tell these days whether a young woman is married or not."

Anne was stumped. How did you answer such a greeting? But she managed, "Good morning, Mrs. Cannon. And I'm not married."

"Where is Mr. Eliot? I have a matter of some import to take up with him."

Anne explained Lloyd's absence. Mrs. Cannon's hostile expression lightened somewhat, and she said grudgingly, "Well, it's about time The Woman came into her own. And I'm glad to see you so sensibly dressed; it's a raw day. Amelia Bloomer had the right idea, inventing those outdoor drawers."

Anne suppressed her mirth, assaulted by several conflicting emotions: utter bewilderment, resentment, dread and, oddly, sheer delight. She didn't even need to psych herself into the nineteenth century; here it was, alive and well, in the person of Hester Cannon.

"What," she contrived to ask calmly, "is the matter of import, Mrs. Cannon? I'm sure I can help you."

"I doubt that. However, come into the parlor," Hester directed, leading the way into a vast, somber room.

Said the spider to the fly, Anne thought, on the verge of hysterical giggles and yet very apprehensive. Damn it, she reflected, here it is. Hester's going to be the fly in the ointment. This was probably going to be the very cantankerous objection that Anne had been afraid of.

"Please sit down, Miss Reynolds," Hester commanded, as if Anne had come to be interviewed for the position of housemaid.

That tone was a little too much even for Anne's poise. "I hope we can be brief, Mrs. Cannon. The cast and crew are waiting for me now, as you must know. We must begin shooting right away."

"There will *be* no . . . 'shooting,'" Hester declared, "until we get something settled. Ridiculous expression. It sounds like a duel."

That was just what this might turn out to be, Anne decided, but she made no answer. Let the old biddy cackle on, she thought angrily. I'll be damned if I'll help her.

"I understood," Hester resumed in freezing tones, "that the scenes to be filmed here today—according to Mmmmmzz Payne, at least—would be done in our library and on the outside of the house. *Now* I am informed that there will be an immoral passage in a *bedroom* of the house. This is unspeakable, and I will not countenance the enactment of excesses in the home of my dear husband's ancestors."

Once again Anne had to control herself sternly. Hester's outlook and language were so bizarre that for a dizzy second Anne wondered if she was hallucinating. But she pulled herself together and answered quietly, almost wishing Lloyd were here to take this tiger by the tail.

"First of all, Mrs. Cannon, your . . . unwillingness to cooperate is in breach of our agreement. And it's unprecedented in all my experience. No owner has ever questioned the content of a film being shot on his premises, certainly not *after* an agreement has been signed. And neither the duchess of Talbot, whose castle we rented in England, nor the contessa di Pitti, whose villa we used, ever raised such objections."

Anne had a hard time keeping a straight face. The contessa, in fact, had thought they were stuffy.

Before Hester could speak, Anne rushed on. "As to 'excesses,' well, things like that couldn't *happen* in a movie of ours. Our actors are highly professional and are . . . discreetly clothed in intimate scenes. If they appear not to be, it's because they wear special costumes. And we use certain processes to dim the scene, to make it look like an Impressionist painting. You see, our movies are on much too high a level to allow any vulgarity. Mr. Eliot would be horrified by that. And so would I."

Good Lord, Anne thought, she's got me doing it. I'm talking like a Victorian spinster. All the same, every word she was saying was true: Livie and Jack would wear specially made body stockings in the supposedly intimate love scenes. Lloyd insisted on it; it was an Eliot trademark. Jack, who loved to display his magnificent physique, was forever grouching about it.

Anyway, if she had to keep talking, Anne decided, she would. It was certainly an improvement over a possible day's delay, consulting with lawyers and getting everyone into a tizzy. To her pleased surprise, Hester seemed to be thawing.

"I see. I really had no idea."

"Surely Ms. Payne explained this to you?" Anne asked, bewildered.

"Not with such eloquence, my dear." Hester was actually smiling. Wonder of wonders. "Well, I feel like a foolish old woman, Miss Reynolds. I should have known that an obvious . . . lady like you would never be involved in anything base." She practically twinkled at Anne. "Although my dear mother always said that a lady never used the word 'lady.' You will pardon me."

Anne murmured something, feeling utter stupefaction as well as enormous triumph and relief. She'd never run into anything like this in her life. She absolutely couldn't wait to repeat it to Lloyd . . . and to Clint.

She pulled herself together as best she could and said, "Well, thank you, Mrs. Cannon. I'm glad we've reached an understanding." She got up, retrieving her tote bag from the floor, and added, "Now, if you'll forgive me, I'm a bit behind schedule."

"Of course, of course," Hester said, smiling as she rose to her feet. "Perhaps you and the . . . er—cast, is it?—would enjoy a bit of luncheon. I'll go and arrange it."

Well, well, Anne exulted. The old girl's getting into the spirit of the thing. She smiled widely at Hester Cannon. "Thank you very much. I'm sure they'll be delighted."

When she and Hester were back in the hall, the old lady said, "One more thing, Miss Reynolds."

"Yes?" Anne paused, with an "oh-no, what-now?" sensation.

"Don't wait too long to get married. It's the best thing for any woman. I myself managed to marry and raise several children while conducting a number of worthwhile activities." Hester gave Anne a piercing stare.

Anne didn't know whether to laugh or cry, or possibly to throw her bag right at Hester. But she held on to her control long enough to respond, "I'll give that some thought, Mrs. Cannon," before she ran upstairs to join the crew.

She saw Harri Payne in the hall. "Anne . . . I'm glad you're early. We've got a bit of a—"

"Tell me about it," Anne broke in grouchily.

"I'm trying to," Harri shot back with her wry, crooked smile.

"Sorry." Anne squeezed the other woman's shoulder. "Me first, though, before I absolutely explode." She exploded instead into giggles, and was amused at Harri's surprised stare. "Not only do we have a war with Associated," she explained, "but you've got to hear what just happened downstairs."

With pungent brevity Anne told Harri about the conference with Hester Cannon.

"Un-be-liev-able," Harri gasped. Then she looked chagrined. "I hate to lay this on you, too, but here goes."

"Jack and Livie," Anne surmised.

"Bull's-eye! They had another dustup this morning about the body suits, and you'll be hearing about it. Jack, of course, said he can't work 'constricted' . . . the drill he always gives Lloyd. And our Livie did the usual 'vulgah, vulgah' routine, accusing Jack of being coarsened by his association with wildcat Marcella. From there it escalated into World War Three, which of course doesn't bode well for Undying Love in Take Next."

"Oh, no."

"I . . . er . . . tried to call you. I must have . . . missed you this morning," Harri said gingerly.

Here was another little complication. The widowed Harri, like Anne herself, was famous for her quiet private life but was utterly unjudgmental about others, taking everything in stride. It was obvious that she knew Anne was involved somewhere, but she'd be the last person to make any indiscreet comment. Anne longed to tell her the real situation, but decided not to for the moment. Better to let Harri believe Anne was involved in some kind of fling than to try to clarify the tangle of her personal life.

Anne hesitated so long that she became aware of Harri's probing look. "I was out very early," she evaded. "Okay. I'll go deal with the Great Lovers. Meanwhile, there's something you could do for me later today."

She told Harri about the expected delivery of the roses, how they should be placed, and then asked her to check out the library for certain information. "Gotcha," Harri assured her.

"Where are the duelists?" Anne asked lightly, trying to reassure herself by taking a calm and carefree attitude.

"At the very scene of the crime," Harri informed her, gesturing toward the master bedroom.

Anne thanked her and walked away in that direction, dodging a camera and stepping over a bunch of cables and wires.

Jack Salem was posed moodily against the mantelpiece, dressed in skintight faded jeans and a T-shirt that pointed up his magnificent torso. Livie, her face like a sulky doll's, was seated across the room before an exquisite antique dresser.

"Hi!" Anne smiled widely, forcing herself to pretend an awful cheeriness. "Somebody told me we have a *petite* problem here."

As they both began to talk to her at once, Anne's smile became genuine. She could see them beginning to unwind.

In just about half an hour, she predicted, these glorious and temperamental creatures would be absolutely ready to go.

"That's a very good point," she said ambiguously, as if to each of them. "But what can we do? Now, listen, both of you. I've got a dynamite idea for this scene . . . and you're the only two actors on earth who can bring it off. . . ."

In twenty minutes, by her watch, World War Three was over.

Chapter 7

THE RAIN WAS COMING DOWN HARD WHEN CLINT BRAKED his Rover in front of the gloomy Cannon house. A florist's truck was also pulling in. Clint glanced up at the second story; three of the windows were brilliant with light.

They're shooting here, he decided, wondering if he could get away with sneaking a look. Anne had told him it would be tough. The driver of the florist's truck got out, went to the rear and, opening the back door, began to take out masses of blood red roses. Clint grinned as an idea hit him.

He got out and sauntered over to the truck, thinking

that he had some lucky stars today, even if he couldn't see them now for rain.

"Can I give you a hand?" he asked the driver casually.

The man flicked a glance at Clint's khakis. "Thanks, that's mighty nice of you." He probably thinks I'm part of the film crew, Clint decided.

Feeling buoyant, Clint helped the man carry the roses into the house.

"Upstairs," the man said. "They'll be setting up the lights now," he added in a proud way, as if pleased to display his knowledge.

"You been in the picture too?" Clint asked.

"Yeah . . . I was an extra in the ballroom scene. Goin' to be in another one, too. It's great. That lady sure knows her onions, I tell you."

"You mean Ms. Reynolds?" Clint felt a deep, secret delight.

"Yeah. Knows what she wants and how to get it." As they reached the top of the stairs, the man chortled. "She has some time with those characters . . . temperamental and all that." They set down their burdens for a moment on the landing. The man looked at Clint a bit uncertainly, maybe thinking he'd said too much. "If you'll excuse me . . ."

"No skin off my nose, pal." Clint grinned. "I know what they're like."

At that moment a heavyset, rather harried-looking woman rushed toward them down the hall.

"Thank goodness!" she called out. "Follow me."

This must be Harriet Payne, Clint decided with amusement. She hadn't looked at either of their faces; her eyes had been glued to the roses.

He hefted the huge vase and followed the florist's man down the hall toward the camera at the end. "Just

put them there," the harried-looking woman said.
"We'll take it from here." She reached into the pocket
of her sweater and brought out two five-dollar bills.

The florist's man beamed and took his. Then it
occurred to him that it was odd for Clint to be tipped,
and he looked up, bewildered.

"Oh, no," Clint said, waving his hand.

"Come on, take it," the woman said with impatience, and thrust the bill into Clint's hand. Then she
dismissed them both utterly and called out to someone
to take the roses in.

"Well, thanks, pal, I'll be . . . seeing you," the other
man muttered, still giving Clint a funny look.

"I'll be seeing you, too, in the picture," Clint joked.
"Here." He thrust the five into the man's hand.

"Hey! Well, thanks a lot." Grinning, the man walked
away.

"*Excuse* me," someone said in a surly tone. A reedy
fellow in a jumpsuit elbowed his way past Clint, and
then the harried woman appeared again.

"I'm sorry," she said, "but you can't stand here."
She gave him a rather searching look, and Clint wondered if she recognized him.

"Are you Ms. Payne?"

"Yes. Who are you?" she inquired rudely.

"I'm . . . a friend of the Cannons," he said, smiling.
"Could I watch for a few minutes?"

Harriet Payne gave him an "oh-yeah?" kind of scan,
but it was obvious that her mind was on other things.
"Okay. I don't have time to argue about it now. But
stand exactly where they tell you. Don't get in the
way."

"I won't," Clint promised with every appearance of
humility, and she seemed satisfied. She rushed into the
brightly lit area again. Clint could hear a babble of

voices; then a woman's and a man's overrode the general noise. Finally he heard Anne's silvery, controlled alto overriding everyone else, and he felt as if he were smiling all over his body.

"Okay, now," he heard her saying clearly. "Remember, Livie honey, when you see him coming in the window, you take that ten-count pause. Okay? Hold it, then you take this rose—the *opening* one, right here. That's very important, because it's our symbol, and we're going to be right on your hands for a couple of seconds."

"It doesn't have any *thorns?*" Clint heard the high, fluting, crystalline tones of the other woman's voice.

After a moment (Clint grinned, thinking that *Anne* must be counting to ten by now) Anne said, "Livie, there are no thorns on *any* of them. We've settled that. Okay now . . . you walk to the window slowly—slowly, to make your dress float just the right way. Give me that blower again, will you, Billy?" There was another brief pause; then Anne resumed.

"Beautiful. Just like that, not a hair more or less. Have you got it?" There was a muffled reply.

"All right now." Anne's voice was raised, sounding expectant, a little tight, but still controlled and pleased. "Jack—out on the balcony."

There was more babble, then the sound of recorded music. It was an instrumental version of "Barbry Ellen." Clint remembered the night he and Anne had listened to the music together, and his heart hammered. He wished to hell he could *see,* but the last time he'd made a move he'd nearly collided with some guy.

"No, no! Lower, lower, just a hair!" Anne yelled. The music gentled. "Wait a second! I don't like that curl. Jerry—get that curl."

There was more flurry and babble, and Clint heard the cameraman say a rude word below his breath.

After a long pause he heard Anne calling, "Ready, now," and someone shouted, "Take one!" Her silvery alto followed. "Roll 'em!"

The camera began to move forward a bit, giving Clint an inch or two of view; he peered in on the set, fascinated. The first thing he saw was Anne, on another camera, looking intent and slender in her jeans and creamy sweater; her fiery hair was so brilliant in the glaring lights that Clint drew a quick, excited breath.

My God, she's so beautiful, he reflected, hardly hearing what she said, looking at nothing else. Then his gaze was inevitably drawn toward the actors. He was amazed at the transformation in Livie. He'd gotten a glimpse of the woman before, and she hadn't impressed him much, even if she was quite pretty. And she'd sounded like a spoiled, silly brat a few minutes before. But now she looked really beautiful and soft, like a woman touchingly, wildly in love. Clint thought, I'll bet Anne was responsible for that. . . .

Anne was still giving directions. Clint gathered that the music was just for mood, that later they'd put the sound track together.

Then she called out, "Quiet!" and there was an almost unbreathing silence except for the camera's faint grinding. Clint stood perfectly still, watching in fascination. Livie had been just a skilfully painted mannequin a couple of minutes before; now, through some mysterious alchemy, she had become a vulnerable and emotional woman. Clint found himself in an imagined past.

Livie appeared to hear something.

She sprang up from the dresser and very slowly turned her head, intently listening, gazing toward the windows. Her huge, dark eyes blazed with a series of emotions—disbelief, then dawning hope, and at last incredulous delight.

If Anne got all this out of that querulous woman, Clint thought, she's a genius.

The outline of a man's form appeared behind the rain-splattered windows, and a trembling smile broke out on Livie's tearful face. She went swiftly to a table where there was a low silver bowl of blood red roses, started to pluck a furled bud and then, smiling, chose an opening rose on a shortened stem. She started slowly toward the windows, and Clint could have sworn she was floating. Something about the thin white dress, the woman's fragility, gave him that impression.

The windows were flung open, and Jack Salem, tigerish with vitality, drenched with rain, sprang into the room. It was a device, Clint thought, that could be corny as hell, but the man—or the director—brought it off. Clint was reminded of many old films of derring-do that had impressed him long ago, films that he'd never quite forgotten.

Livie, at the windows, was holding out her arms to Salem, the rose in one of her delicate hands. The actor gave her a lingering look, and then his eyes touched the blooming rose. She handed him the flower, and at once Clint was aware of the symbolism—she was offering him her opening heart.

Just the way, Clint recalled, Anne had offered herself to *him*. He was amazed at how much the scene moved him. Once again, it wasn't a new idea, but the way it was done here was somehow new and fresh. Salem took the rose and put his lips to it, then thrust it into his breast pocket and gathered Livie in his arms. Salem's hands wandered over Livie's hair and face and shoulders. He pulled her closer and closer, until their bodies impressed the watcher as melding, dissolving one into the other, and they moved into an endless-looking kiss that was more like a vow than a caress.

Then they broke and began to talk to each other, still embracing, but Clint was so involved in his own thoughts that he barely heard the soft dialogue; he was still astonished at the depth of his own reactions, sure that the sweet, incredible encounters between himself and Anne had been their source. Moment by moment he was being drawn into this thing, and more and more he was becoming aware of what it meant to Anne. There had been no exaggeration in her passionate statements. He remembered her talking about a "kind of grail," solidifying dreams to present them for others' pleasure.

Now he could see Anne again, on the camera, whispering to the operator, making mysterious gestures with her long-fingered hands; Clint thought how much he loved the mind inside that beautiful body. The strong lights still made a glorious conflagration of her hair, in dazzling contrast to her creamy sweater.

Blinking, feeling a bit high, he heard her cry out, "Great! Cut! Perfect, people, perfect."

Salem and Livie, now entwined in a fervent kiss beside the big four-poster bed, abruptly broke their embrace. Clint almost laughed out loud. They looked so businesslike and unconcerned, about as shaken up as if they'd just finished a game of checkers.

Clint moved forward a little and saw Anne smile. She still hadn't spotted him. "That was gorgeous," she said, jumping down from her perch. "You two got exactly, *exactly*, what I wanted. More, in fact. I love you."

She turned to the camera operator and added, "Thank you, too, Paul. You were marvelous." Clint noticed that all of them were beaming, the actors like complimented children, and he reflected how well Anne handled her personnel. She was something.

Anne strolled toward Jack, who was lighting a cigarette, inhaling with relish, and felt his hair. "You're soaking wet. Why don't we break till after lunch? Two o'clock . . . in costume, okay?"

There was a general murmur again, a chaotic stir. Livie was complaining to the hairdresser about something, and Anne was now deep in conversation with the cameraman. All kinds of people were rushing past and around Clint. Finally Anne saw him, and her face broke into a brilliant smile of welcome.

She came toward him, and when she was closer, said, "Hello," in that silvery, almost husky alto that always had such a pleasant effect on his ears and caused such an agreeable tickle along his nerves, as if she were running her hands up and down his bare skin. She looked terrific, he thought, with her eyes still wide with excitement, color in her cheeks.

He bent down and kissed her on the lips momentarily, not giving a damn who saw them. She flushed, but she looked pleased nonetheless, and when he whispered, "Sorry about that . . . I just got carried away," she murmured back, "It couldn't matter less. This is one crowd that's so self-involved they probably don't even know we're here right now." His swift glance around confirmed that; apparently no one was giving them a thought. Clint was glad, for her sake, since she'd expressed a wish for privacy.

"Did you see it?" she asked eagerly. "Did you see the whole thing?"

"The whole scene. It was . . . superb, Anne."

She flushed more deeply with gratification. "Glad you liked it. I'll bet you'll never guess what inspired the rose gimmick."

"I can't wait to hear." He grinned down at her.

"Then let's get some coffee. I'm dying for some. Right down the hall." She put her hand through his arm, and he warmed at once to the light touch. They walked together into a little closetlike space at the end of the hall, where there were several big coffee makers. He was delighted that there was no one else there at the moment.

She drew coffee for them both, and when they were sipping it, he asked, "So what inspired the rose gimmick, lady?" She told him about "Barbry Ellen." He put his coffee down and kissed her soundly.

"I recognized the music," he murmured. And then he told her how he had felt watching the scene. Her eyes looked huge and soft and happy.

"You don't know how much that means to me."

Suddenly he became businesslike. "Where can we have lunch?" Anne explained to him about Hester's arrangements, concluding with a chuckle, "Are you up to that?"

"Not exactly," he admitted, smiling. He glanced out the narrow window and added, "Besides, the weather's making a decision for me. The rain seems to be slacking up, which means I should be getting back. I'll just grab something; then we can think of dinner. It'll be much better if we don't get . . . interrupted."

His significant inflection made her laugh. "*Much* better."

"Besides," he commented, "there happens to be a weekend coming up. And I'd like to talk about that. Will you be free Saturday and Sunday?"

"Oh, will I ever!" She grinned and finished her coffee.

"Okay . . . then I'll see you later. What time will you be through here?"

She told him, and they agreed to meet at the cabin.

He drew her close for a quick goodbye kiss, then was walking away when he stopped short, clapping his hand to his head. "I must be cracking up," he exclaimed. "I totally forgot something."

He turned around, smiling, and took a small box from his pocket. Handing it to her, he said, "I got this in Knoxville . . . during one of those bad days when I couldn't get you on the phone. It seemed so appropriate, considering the site where we met."

Puzzled, she gave him a long, tender look and opened the box, revealing a delicate gold ring hammered into the shape of a dogwood flower. "Oh, Clint," she said softly. She took the ring from the box and slipped it on the ring finger of her right hand. It was a perfect fit.

"It's exquisite. And yes, *very* appropriate," she added, her lovely eyes looking up again into his, glowing.

He was thinking, No woman with eyes like that could lie to me. And he was surprised to realize that he'd wanted to put a ring on her other hand; he'd been about to ask her to marry him, right then and there. But maybe that was crazy right now; maybe she wouldn't say yes yet. And maybe he wasn't even sure himself.

She moved into his arms again and kissed him lingeringly, and his confused ideas bothered him. He'd never been indecisive about anything in his life. Well, one thing was certain: He knew now that he loved her.

When they'd said a last goodbye, and he was going downstairs, Clint told himself again, No woman with such eyes could lie to me. She really didn't know exactly what Eliot was going to do in New York; it was all Eliot's idea. That had to be behind this new hassle with the higher-ups, this nonsense about the budget. He was going to enjoy having a little talk with Eliot when the man got back.

Emerging into the rain-remembering air, Clint sniffed with appreciation. Everything smelled new. No, he concluded, Anne had nothing to do with it at all, or she would have told him.

Yet something in him asked, Would she? He'd seen how much this picture meant to her this very morning. But he shoved the thought away, looking forward to the weekend . . . and the night.

All through the busy afternoon the gleaming golden blossom on her finger was a delightful distraction to Anne. At lunch, which to her surprise turned out to be a very pleasant interval, Harri Payne noticed the ring.

"Ummm . . . nice," she said softly under the buzz of talk around them. "New?"

"Yes." Anne was noncommittal, but she couldn't prevent the sudden warmth she felt coloring her face.

"I have a feeling I've been missing something," Harri remarked. Anne had a strong desire to confide in her because they'd always been relatively close, but somehow she couldn't. It was still too new, too complicated and awkward. How could she tell Harri that she was falling in love with the very man who had caused them so much trouble, and might cause more before the picture was ended?

So she said with equal lightness, "You never miss much, so I doubt it," and let it go at that.

Then, when they were back on the set, there wasn't any time to think about it. Livie pulled another fit of temper, enraging Jack, and Anne had to serve as psychiatric referee again. After they'd gotten going, however, the love scene went like a hot knife through butter, and Anne was restored to her earlier feelings of triumph and elation.

The sensations buoyed her right through the wrap. To top it off, a phone message from Lloyd was waiting. He wouldn't be back until Sunday night; he'd left a number in case she needed him. This puzzled her a little. It was so unlike him. Ordinarily he would have urged her to call him with a full report, and she was mystified by this evidence of *laissez-faire*, practically indifference coming from Lloyd Eliot. But at the same time she blessed her luck; the weekend would definitely be free now. The cast and crew practically cheered when she told them. Lloyd Eliot was such a twenty-six-hour-a-day type that he had no respect for weekends, vacations, or leisure. Now *their* weekends were in the bag, too.

She was bubbling with good spirits when she drove back to the cabin and found Clint waiting. He smiled from ear to ear when she told him the news; yet it seemed to her that at the mention of Lloyd's name a kind of shadow crossed his face. But she told herself she was imagining it. After all, Clint was every bit as elated as she was about the weekend, sweet and tender as ever.

That night they had dinner at their special place outside Sedgby and afterward went to have a sentimental dance at the roadhouse near Warrenburg, where they'd had their first date. Dancing close in his arms, Anne was able to forget everything else for the moment, convinced that she didn't have a care in the world.

The feeling lasted throughout the evening and the close, exciting night. The next morning they woke, as she put it, sinfully late and feeling marvelous. He volunteered to cook breakfast.

When they were lingering over their third cup of coffee, he suggested lazily, "What do you say to a little trip . . . and the theater tonight?"

"Don't tell me we're flying to New York," she teased him.

"Far from it. Driving, lady, driving." He grinned at her.

"Driving? You're very mysterious this morning. May I know where?" She chuckled.

"Not yet. I want it to be a surprise." He reached across the table, took her hand and kissed it.

"Okay," she said agreeably. "But at least give me a clue about what kind of gear I'll be needing. I don't want to sit in a dress circle in jeans."

He laughed. "Not to worry. I'd say casual all the way."

Now she was really interested.

"Bring some stuff for overnight . . . just in case. We'll still be in the mountains," he said.

"Wonderful. When will we be going?"

He looked at his watch and then at her, and his look was full of meaning. "That depends on you. I'm not in a terrible hurry." He was kissing the palm of her hand, and she experienced a fresh, delirious tremor deep inside.

"I don't think I am either," she answered softly.

"I'm glad," he told her, and the look in his eyes was excited.

They walked back to the bedroom very close together, and the interval that followed was the loveliest she could recall between them.

When they could talk again, he muttered, "This is so great I don't even want to move. But I guess we should start."

She kissed him soundly. "Don't move for a while. I'd

like to shower and wash my hair . . . and get my things together.''

"You've got a deal." He closed his eyes, smiling.

Happily Anne took a leisurely shower, washed and dried her hair, sprayed herself lavishly with faint cologne. It was fun, for a change, to take time to remember that she was a woman. The film had been so all-consuming, free time so scarce, that she'd hardly thought of things like clothes lately. She peeked into the bedroom and saw that Clint was napping.

So much the better; now she could really take her time with everything. And it was still only one o'clock. She tossed on a light robe and tiptoed to the closet, choosing a few items of mix-and-match clothes. She used to find such clothing boring and too-too practical —the Coast glamour women sneered at them—but in her hectic life, with her desire to travel light, they were utterly essential.

The weather was gloriously warm that day, but there was always an evening coolness in the mountains at night. She'd save a skirt and sweater for later, and wear pants now.

She quickly packed a few items, including an outrageously sexy nightgown that had been shipped with the other things from the Coast. She'd bought it once on impulse, although, she thought drily now, she'd had little use for it before. It was a vivid blue-green. When she was finished dressing she examined herself in the mirror, pleased with the way her hair looked, and the healthy, relaxed glow of her skin.

Clint was waking up, calling out, "How are you doing?"

"Never better." She presented herself for his inspection.

"Better's not the word. You're the best thing I've

ever seen in my life." She felt a rush of tenderness and went to the bed to kiss him.

"Enough, enough," he gasped when their mouths parted. "You look too nice to mess up. Unhand me, woman."

She laughed and obeyed. He jumped out of bed and headed for the shower. Anne went to the kitchen and tidied it up a bit, thrusting their dishes into soapy water.

When she was walking back to the living room she heard him call out, "I'll just be a minute."

"Take your time." She heard him heading for the bedroom, opening drawers. In the living room she casually surveyed the books on the shelves. His friend was apparently an English professor, she reflected. Most of the books were poems and novels and literary criticism.

For the first time, though, she noticed books that must be Clint's—some adventure novels, technical books, and one volume whose title intrigued her: *The Earliest God*.

She took it from the shelf and riffled through it. How odd, she thought. It was a kind of history of the sun, from ancient myth to modern astronomical data. The sun. Now why would he be so interested in that?

This reminded her of his secretiveness about his project, which took a little of the bloom off her feeling of well-being.

However, when he joined her, looking big and fresh and vital in his light shirt and snug brown denims, she found it utterly impossible to linger on that thorny problem, to feel anything but happy. He had a jacket and a small canvas bag slung over his shoulder, and her bag in his hand.

"Ready?" he asked her eagerly. His wonderful

amber eyes were bright, as excited as a young boy's; his face was almost mischievous, and she could tell he was looking forward to springing his surprise.

She thrust her doubts aside determinedly and grinned at him. "Ready and waiting. I even did a little K.P. Let's go."

They hurried out into the sun. The whole world looked green and magical to Anne at that moment. He locked up and headed toward her car, raising his brows as if to ask her permission. "I think it'll be more comfortable for you," he said.

"Fine. Of course." He tossed their bags in the back and drove off.

She'd never seen the mountains look so beautiful as they did this afternoon, and she reflected happily that beauty really was in the eyes of the beholder. When she was with him, everything took on a new dimension, she realized.

Soon she recognized the road to Warrenburg. "It's that near?" she asked, smiling.

"Warrenburg?" He chuckled. "No way."

She decided to be a sport and ask no more questions, and they drove on in companionable, contented silence, crossing the Tennessee border into North Carolina. "I remember this place," she said delightedly. "Now I know where we're going. Oh, Clint, this is marvelous; I haven't been to the Cherokee reservation for years and years."

"Then it *will* be a surprise. I think you'll be amazed at what it's like now." She was. There were startlingly modern, graceful buildings on the green plateau nestling at the foot of the mighty mountains, interesting shops and stores all operated by Cherokees. They took a fascinating tour, watching calm, adept women beading moccasins, making baskets of river cane, hammering out silver jewelry. Clint insisted on buying Anne samples of all three, the last a wonderful silver bracelet of unusual design.

Deciding they were hungry, they entered one of the restaurants. Anne was impressed. It was sunny and gracious and very attractive, the diners both tourists and a number of soft-spoken Cherokees.

They were about to order when an impressive-looking Indian in his fifties, dressed in a well-tailored lightweight suit, approached their table. He was quite handsome, with classic features and glittering black eyes, but he looked fearsome until a wide white grin slashed his reddish brown face.

"Clint Ward," he stated in a basso voice, holding out his strong hand.

"Sequoyah!" Clint was smiling too, and jumping up to shake the man's hand. "I was going to look you up after dinner. This is great." He introduced Anne. Sequoyah bowed to her courteously, with an old-world grace. His black eyes swept over her hair.

"The lady of *Cheera*," he murmured to Clint.

"He's saying your hair is like fire," Clint explained to Anne. "Like the Cherokees' national name—*Cheeratahge*, 'men possessed of divine fire.'" Anne thought how lovely that was. Clint said to his friend, "Sit down and join us."

Sequoyah laughed. "You can't eat here," he protested, laughing. "This is tourist stuff. Come home with me and eat at my house. Jack is home, and he'd love to see you. I can take off now. How about it?"

Clint beamed. "Well, I'll be damned. I haven't seen him since we worked on that job together out west." He turned to Anne. "Shall we?"

"Of course." They left quickly and drove in Sequoyah's car to a modest, beautiful house in the hills. On the way Clint explained to Anne that Jack was Sequoyah's son, and that he was now teaching engineering at the university. Anne liked him on sight; he looked very much like his father, but had gentle eyes that must have come from his mother.

Jack obviously looked up to Clint. During dinner and the conversation afterward, Clint entertained them with stories of his jobs around the world. It wasn't a center-stage performance, Anne thought, but a matter-of-fact recital that emphasized the job he'd done with Jack, making much of Jack's talents in the telling. Anne was seeing a side of Clint she hadn't really known before, and it made her feel more loving than ever.

In fact, the very house and its inhabitants, who were very much of the twentieth century yet still retained their ancient pride, cast a kind of spell over Anne, which deepened that evening when she and Clint attended the Mountainside Theater and saw the Cherokees' Eagle Dance, a highlight of their pageant *Unto These Hills.*

The splendid red-brown bodies, the pounding of drums and the rattle of calabashes aroused a primitive pounding in her blood.

At the pageant's end she was too moved to say a word. She and Clint looked at each other silently, and in perfect accord found a motel in utter quiet. That night they made the most exciting, almost savage love they had ever known, then joined together in another cataclysmic encounter late the next sunny morning.

"It was so wonderful," she murmured as they drove away from the reservation the next afternoon. "It's as if we were living in another world."

"I know," he agreed quietly. "These people are as unchanging as the sun." There was that odd inflection in his voice again. The sun. She remembered the book on his shelves and was teased anew, in the midst of her deep serenity, by her constant need to know what was behind it. There was always a little pang when she thought, He doesn't trust me enough to tell me everything.

Yet when she glanced aside at his relaxed, happy face, she was reluctant to break the spell. She couldn't break it, she repeated to herself, not yet. Then his next remark drove the matter from her mind.

"Do you know what Jack said to me right before we left?" Clint asked softly. "He said, 'Your lady is *ottare*, like you, like us.' *Ottare* in Cherokee means that you belong to the mountains. Isn't that amazing?"

"It certainly is. I wonder how he knew," she marveled. She had said nothing about her origins during the visit.

"I don't know. He said something else, too." Clint was smiling broadly. "He advised me not to let you get away from me."

"And what did you say to that?" she inquired. Her heart was racing.

"I said that was superfluous advice." They were nearing the turnoff to the cabin, and he slowed, reaching out to touch her. She moved inside the circle of his arm and hid her face against his chest. They didn't speak again until he had parked the car before the cabin.

Then he turned to her and with deep seriousness asked, "What do you think about Jack's advice . . . and my answer?"

She looked into his eyes, groping for the right reply.

"Anne?" His expression of grave anxiety was touching.

At last she murmured, "I think . . . it's beautiful."

He studied her and seemed about to say something

else, but apparently changed his mind and suggested, "Let's go in."

She nodded, almost fearing that her answer had been too evasive, too noncommittal.

When they were inside he took her in his arms and said softly, "That it's 'beautiful' is not quite an answer."

"And I think there was another *question*," she retorted.

He led her to the couch, and they sat down. As he drew her to him, he said, "There was. The question is, will you marry me?"

She drew in her breath, feeling an overwhelming joy which was succeeded by consternation and an odd reluctance, a reluctance that she couldn't withstand.

"Oh, Clint . . . Clint. I . . ."

"Will you, Anne? You've *got* to," he said roughly, grabbing her by the upper arms and squeezing them until she cried out. "I'm sorry. I'm sorry," he muttered, looking away, shaking his head from side to side. Then he looked back at her, and his gaze was utterly open and vulnerable and pleading. "I just love you, want you, so damned much. Say you will, Anne. Marry me. Give up that crazy job."

"Clint . . ." She reached up and touched his face gently, with a tentative, almost fearful motion.

"Don't you love me?" he demanded. "You must . . . or all this could never have happened."

"Of course I do." She pulled his face to hers, and he kissed her with desperate urgency.

"Well, then," he said shakily, "you will . . . you must."

"I can't, Clint, not now," she said miserably, leaning against him.

"Why not? What is there to stop us, Anne?" He

urged her upright, turned her face toward him and, holding her chin gently, stared into her eyes.

"So many things. You've never even trusted me enough to tell me what your work is. How can there be love without trust, Clint?"

"So we're back to that again," he said bitterly. "I've tried to explain that to you. . . ."

"And you can't," she responded sadly. "Besides, there's the picture, there's my obligation to—"

"To that run-down thespian, Eliot?" he interjected, and his ugly name for Lloyd hurt her.

"No, not just to Lloyd." She was having a hard time controlling her voice; she was afraid that at any moment she'd burst into tears. "To the cast and the crew, the production . . . to myself."

The last words gave him pause, and she remembered the understanding he'd shown after he'd seen her direct the scene in the Cannon house. Pursuing her advantage, she asked softly, "How would *you* feel if someone asked you to give up your project?"

He frowned. "It just isn't the same, Anne. Talented as you are, it's not the same. My project is . . . My work will affect the entire civilized world."

There it was again, she thought with a hot rush of resentment. His almighty project—hinted at, teasing her, withheld from the very woman he'd asked to be his wife. As much as she loved him, he was arrogant, impossible. He still hadn't learned to understand what her own goals, her profession, meant to her and to millions of people.

"And do you think that *When That April* won't affect a great many people and their way of looking at things?" she protested softly. "Don't you know that we're upholding standards that are dying out: love, honor, fidelity, and compassion and pride? That's what

our pictures have been about. That's what I struggle
for, Clint—to restore to people some of the beauty and
magic that have been lost to them . . . to give them
back belief in work and love, the two things on earth
that matter. The unchanging things, the things we
experienced at the reservation." Her voice trembled.

"Oh, Anne, I don't want to fight with you," he said,
and drew her close to him again.

Suddenly she realized that this was the worst possible
time for her to tell him what she had planned to do that
evening. But it had to be done. "Clint . . . I think I'd
better go back to Warrenburg tonight."

He thrust her backward a little and stared at her,
dismayed. "Why?"

"Because . . . Lloyd's coming back late tonight. And
I think I should be there in the morning." An angry
frown creased his brow when she said Lloyd's name.

"Are you sure that's the real reason, Anne? Or are
you just running away?" he asked bluntly.

His tone hurt her. "No, I'm not running away, Clint.
I'm just not ready to . . . reveal our private business to
Lloyd. He's so . . ." She stopped, unwilling to go on,
reluctant to tell Clint about Lloyd's blasé, unseeing
attitude, to reveal that to Lloyd, nothing on earth was
more important than their work.

"I can imagine," Clint remarked with contempt. "I
may as well warn you, Anne, that I'm going to have a
little conference with Eliot myself tomorrow. But
meanwhile"—his voice softened—"I don't see why you
have to go back tonight. Please, darling, stay. I'll drive
you down in the morning."

She shook her head. "It's just not practical. I . . . I'd
better leave. Soon, as a matter of fact." He was still
staring at her, and his expression almost made her

waver. But she knew now that she had to get away; she had to have some time alone to think things over.

He sighed. "All right." He took her in his arms again and hugged her. "But you'll . . . think about what I asked you," he added urgently, "and we'll see each other tomorrow."

"Yes. Oh, yes, Clint, I'll be thinking about it, all the time."

Chapter 8

ANNE WAS SO DEEPLY SHAKEN THAT SHE DROVE WITH extra caution down the mountain and consequently found to her consternation that it was already nearly twilight when she pulled up in front of the Warrenburg Inn.

Her head was pounding. She might just have made the biggest mistake of her life. And yet . . . The alternatives pitched back and forth like the deck of a small boat in a storm, and the pounding in her head worsened.

Feeling absolutely haunted, she parked and made her way into the inn. There were several messages at the desk. Without looking at them, Anne stepped into the elevator.

It was surprising how impersonal and strange her room looked to her now, and yet for the first time she saw it more clearly—just the latest in a series of impersonal hotel rooms in different cities over the last few years. In contrast, the homeyness and beauty of the cabin made her almost ache. She wondered why she hadn't stayed with Clint after all, why she'd rushed back here instead of waiting until morning.

Anne tossed her bag on the bed and sat down. Because, you idiot, you promised yourself time to think. And things were difficult enough now without exposing herself to Lloyd's reactions to the love affair.

She glanced at the messages in her hand. One was from Harri; that was odd. Even the dedicated Harri had seemed happy about the thought of an undisturbed weekend, and Anne couldn't imagine what she could want. The other two were from Lloyd and were even more surprising; the first said he'd be arriving on an early-evening plane, the second on a later one.

This wasn't like Lloyd at all. It seemed to indicate an unwillingness to come back. But Anne told herself that that was absurd; she wasn't thinking straight because of her rotten headache, her indecision about Clint. She went to the bathroom and took some aspirin, deciding that she'd find out what was behind Lloyd's delay when he came, that there was no point in worrying about it now. What she could do was get in touch with Harri.

"My goodness, you're early." Harri sounded puzzled. "I had a feeling your weekend would last longer than this." When Anne didn't answer that, she went on, "I hate to break this to you, sweetie, but I thought you should be prepared."

"What now?"

"Our Jack's going to be laid up for a day or two," Harri began reluctantly.

"No," Anne moaned. "What happened? He got his bike repaired?"

"You got it in one try." Harri's answer was gloomy. "He took a minor spill yesterday evening, and his leg was sprained. All taped up, looks worse than it is, fortunately. The doctor says he'll be operative again by the end of the week."

"Damn. Well, we'll have to shoot around him." Anne's head was throbbing again. This was all she needed right now.

"I understand Napoleon"—Harri gave it a humorous French pronunciation—"arrives late tonight. Do you suppose we'll be burning the midnight oil? I'm available."

Her loyalty, her calm, reassured Anne. "I love you," she said warmly. "I really don't know yet. Let's wait and see. I'll be in my room for the duration if you need me, and of course I'll call you when I hear from Lloyd. Right now I'm going to go over the shooting script and see what we can come up with for the next few days."

"Right."

They hung up, and Anne realized that, oddly, she almost welcomed this new crisis; at least it would take her mind off Clint for a while, and his confrontation with Lloyd tomorrow. That in itself would be a treat, she thought wryly.

She got out the shooting script and began to go over it, trying to find places where Jack didn't appear. It was no easy matter, of course, since he and Livie practically *were* the picture. There were a couple of places, she discovered, where he could be just plain written out. Thinking it served him damned well right, Anne slashed away at his part with a thick blue marker, scribbling in changes with a narrower pen.

If his agent got antsy, she grumbled to herself, then let him chew on the insurance aspect and Jack's carelessness being interpreted as breach of contract.

Anne dropped her pen. I'm acting just like Lloyd, she reflected. Somehow that was very significant. This business is in my blood and bone, she said to herself. And Clint seems to think I can just walk away from it. That's utterly insane.

She blinked and looked at her watch. Good heavens, she'd been working for nearly two hours, almost without realizing it. The room was in twilight; she'd practically been working in the dark, so absorbed that it hadn't made that much difference.

She got up and turned on some lamps. There were still the maps to go over, just to make sure. She'd marked hers to accord with Clint's; of course the scenes she'd worked on were all right as far as their respective territories went—she knew them all by heart now—but she wanted to make doubly sure.

Anne went over the maps; everything looked fine. She was elated over the workmanlike job she'd done, and leaned back in her chair, feeling in command for the first time that day.

Now for a nice long shower, she decided, then some food from room service. After that she'd just read or watch TV and not think at all, if possible, until she heard from Lloyd.

She took the shower and ordered from room service, but before she could snap the TV on, her phone rang.

"Anne, darling." It was Clint.

Her newfound peace dissolved, and her heart gave a painful leap. "Hello, Clint."

"You sound so strange," he said. "Tired. Has something happened?" She could hear soft music in the background; it sounded like "Greensleeves."

"Nothing special. Where are you?"

"Not eating dinner," he responded wryly, "at the Dogwood Place."

When he used her name for their special restaurant she was pierced with longing and a disproportionate sense of desolation. If only a few hours apart could affect her like this, what would it be like to say goodbye to him for good?

All of a sudden she forgot the movie, even forgot Lloyd and Jack and Harri, in her renewed emotion. "Oh, Clint, I wish I were there, too," she said impulsively.

"I'll come to *you,*" he said, the words rushing out. "Right this minute, if you say."

Oh, no, I've done it now, she thought. She should have been more discreet, but it had all just spilled out. "Clint, I'm sorry, I really am. I shouldn't have said that, I guess. It's impossible tonight. Lloyd's coming in late, and then something's come up with one of the cast, and . . ."

There was a pause, a long one, while she listened to the faint background music. Then he sighed and murmured, "It's okay, honey. I understand. Really. It's just that . . . time has a whole new value when I miss you like this. Or *lack* of value, I should say." He laughed a little, but it had a sad, hollow sound.

"Look, I'm sorry if I was a bear this afternoon. I know you've got commitments. We both have. I just miss you like hell."

"I know, I know," she answered softly. "It's the same for me."

There was another pause, and then he said in a very different tone, "Speaking of commitments, which I don't enjoy doing right now, I've got to talk to Eliot tomorrow. And of course that means talking to you, too. Do you think a breakfast meeting might be feasible, at the inn?"

"It sounds all right to me. Not too early, though; Lloyd's plane doesn't get in till nine, which puts him here about ten . . . and which will put our conference late."

"I'll check with him in the morning, about eight. You poor kid," he added, sounding very tender.

Her heart fluttered like a rising bird. "I'll survive. Oh, Clint, I love you. I really do."

"I love you, Anne." His words were profoundly solemn, caressing. "We'll work it out. You'll see. We *have* to."

"I guess we do," she admitted, smiling now. "Until tomorrow."

"Try to take it easy while you can," he urged her in that same caressing way.

"I will," she promised.

After they had said goodbye, she lay back on the bed, feeling a sudden drowsiness. Sleepily she reflected, As long as we feel this way, he's right . . . we'll have to find a way to work it out.

Anne's first waking thought, when the phone's loud ring assaulted her ears, was, Why, it's ten-thirty at night already. But when she opened her eyes, she was amazed to see vivid sunlight.

Morning! she thought fuzzily. What had happened to last night? She blinked and reached for the phone. The bedside clock read seven.

"Annie." Lloyd's booming voice sounded unusually subdued and gentle. "Sorry to wake you at this ungodly hour."

He must be sick. He'd never apologized for such a thing before. "Lloyd? Are you all right? I thought I'd hear from you last night."

"We've got a lot to discuss, sweet child." He still had that strange softness in his voice, and it totally mystified her. He sounded like a different person. Where was the raging vitality, the self-centeredness, the utter disregard for other people that were his trademark? "Shall we breakfast about eight downstairs . . . will that give you enough time?"

"Of course." There it was again—that uncharacteristic consideration. "See you then."

She hung up and shook her head a little, as if that would clear it. She sat on the edge of the bed and a horrible idea occurred to her: He'd felt unwell in New York, consulted a doctor, and the doctor had told him he had an incurable illness. Oh, my God. That would account for this sweetness, this gentleness.

Then Anne shook her head again and laughed aloud at herself. The idea was right out of a 1940s tearjerker. Feeling more rational, she got her papers together and put them in her canvas briefcase.

She opened one of the windows wider—it was a glorious spring day, the air just warm enough, the sun already brilliant. She looked for an outfit to wear, one that she could work in, but that would also be pretty enough to wear when she greeted Clint at breakfast. He might be calling Lloyd right now to arrange it.

She realized that she should have brought it up with Lloyd, but decided that she couldn't think of everything, and promptly forgot it in her perusal of clothes.

She ended up with a three-piece outfit, easy slacks and camisole and slouch jacket of cotton ticking striped in ivory and lavender.

She decided to go down to the dining room and fortify herself with extra coffee while she went over her notes again. She felt that she needed to be a little ahead of the game; Lloyd would go up in smoke when he found out about Jack. And then there was the matter of Clint. As much as she looked forward to seeing him, this would not be the ideal way of meeting.

One or both of them would be bound to reveal their feelings for the other. And this might be a pretty explosive confrontation, considering what Lloyd had been up to.

And Clint could well find out that she'd known about it all along and hadn't told him. Anne wondered why this hadn't occurred to her before. The idea dimmed her morning optimism.

It was a relief not to see either Clint or Lloyd when she entered the dining room. She tried to dismiss the fresh problem as she ordered coffee and got her notes into final shape.

She was feeling a little more together when she saw Lloyd coming to join her. Good heavens, he *looked* like a different person, too. He was more relaxed than she'd ever seen him, the lines in his face smoothed out, his blue eyes genial and his smile benign. He actually seemed to move more slowly.

Apprehension gripped her. Was he ill after all? But no, his color was fine and his eyes bright. She wondered what had happened to make him look this way, reflecting that she'd have plenty to adjust to this morning, what with Jack and Clint, the production, and now the new Lloyd to deal with.

"Anne, you look wonderful," Lloyd said when he got to the table. He bent to kiss her cheek.

"So do you. Intrigue does you good, obviously." She

grinned and poured him a cup of coffee. "You're really taking it easy on me," she added as he sipped. "I expected you to call me last night."

"I figured it could wait till the light of morning."

Now she *was* at a loss; this was definitely not the Lloyd Eliot she knew and sometimes hated, sometimes loved. The old Lloyd always equated three or five in the morning with the same hours in the afternoon.

"I don't believe this," she murmured. "Have you . . . er . . . talked to Harri yet?" Surely he couldn't know about Jack and still appear this calm.

"Oh, yes," he responded easily. "Have you ordered?"

She shook her head, and he signaled for a waiter. Out of long habit he ordered for both of them, while Anne stared.

"Really, I don't have egg on my face *yet*," he quipped. "Breakfast hasn't even been delivered. What are you gawking at?"

"An impostor, I'm convinced," she shot back. "You haven't asked me a single question about what's been going on here; you haven't told me a word about what happened in New York." Anne was grinning, but then she turned serious. "What's happened to *you,* Lloyd?"

He patted her hand. "A lot, Anne." There was a wistful expression in his eyes, a poignant note in that magnificent voice.

I knew it, she told herself. Something earthshaking had happened to him. Anne's longtime affection for Lloyd was fully aroused. "Are you going to tell me, or keep me dangling till the perfect dramatic moment?" she demanded, smiling.

"Dangle you, of course." Their breakfast arrived, and Lloyd attacked his with an appetite. "In the fullness of time, my dear," he said between bites of scrambled egg, "all will be revealed."

Here we go again, Anne thought, biting vindictively into her toast. First Clint, now Lloyd.

"Meanwhile," Lloyd said casually, "I suppose you've worked out the small matter of Jack."

"Small matter," she echoed. Just a week ago Lloyd would have had a positive shouting fit over Jack's accident. "Yes." She took her notes from her briefcase and handed them to Lloyd.

He scanned them. "Excellent." Handing them back to her, he added, "I've already seen the rushes of the scenes you directed, Annie. I dragged the boys out of their beddy-byes last night." He grinned. "They were perfectly superb. You make me feel almost superfluous." She thought he said that with a special inflection, and his grin widened. "Now," he went on briskly, "let me tell you how I gummed up our grease monkey in New York, before he joins us."

"He's joining us?" she asked weakly, trying to show some surprise. The lack of it would have aroused Lloyd's curiosity, and she still wasn't ready to reveal the true state of affairs between her and Clint.

"Yes, indeed. In about"—Lloyd glanced at his watch —"ten minutes. He phoned me at cockcrow to arrange it." Lloyd chuckled. "And there may be hell to pay, so you'd better finish your eggs before round one. You see, I was quite successful with those board members. Apparently they've been opposed to Ward since day one. Personally, because of his arrogance, and financially, because of his outrageous budgetary requests."

"I suppose," Anne interjected, "you didn't find out what the project *is*."

"Oh, no. Even my oldest claim to friendship couldn't

accomplish that. It was all hems, haws and hints. The upshot was that Ward claims the project is of gigantic social significance." Lloyd's tone mocked the phrase. "And my pals think it's visionary hogwash. Anyhow, without going into all the gruesome, boring details, I managed to stir up a nice little hornet's nest, in my inimitable way; one member stirred another, et cetera, domino fashion, so we ended up with a kind of slowdown for our mechanic."

"Which means . . . ?" Anne prompted. She was full of conflicting feelings: hope for a full-speed-ahead signal, a nagging guilt for conspiring against Clint.

"Which means that we might not have a single problem from now until the wrap." Lloyd grinned even more widely. But he added, "Of course, we can't be absolutely sure until we talk to Ward. And speak of the devil . . ." he said softly.

Anne looked toward the entrance. Clint was coming toward them, smiling into her eyes, and he looked so appealing that her breath grew short and her heart skipped a beat. If things had been complicated before, those complications were nothing compared to these.

"Good morning, Mr. Ward!" Lloyd spoke with suspicious geniality. "Have you had breakfast? May I order you something?" Anne hadn't spoken.

"Hello, Anne." Clint spoke to her gently, still smiling, before he sat down with them. To Lloyd he muttered, "Eliot."

"May I order you something?" Lloyd repeated with an awful bright persistence, and Anne began to feel very uncomfortable. This was going to be worse than she'd expected. Clint was looking at her, admiring her with his eyes, taking in her hair and face, her springlike, flattering clothes.

"No, thanks." Clint turned to Lloyd with a cool, neutral look. "Let's get to it, Eliot."

Lloyd raised his brows, as if to comment unfavorably on Clint's brusque manners. But he said in a level tone, "Proceed."

"Your maneuvers have slowed me down, Eliot," Clint said bluntly. "I assume all this started with Roger Samson."

Lloyd seemed nonplussed; he couldn't hide his shock. "How in the name of . . . how did you know *that?*" He turned his head slowly and stared at Anne. "Anne, you couldn't have let this out, I know."

"*Anne* couldn't?" Clint repeated, looking stunned. Now he was looking at Anne too, with a pained and angry expression.

"What is going on here?" Lloyd demanded, but Anne barely heard him. She was thinking that Lloyd had done it now. Now Clint realized that she had known all the time and hadn't told him. He'd never forgive her for what he considered her treachery.

But that was idiotic. Even he couldn't expect her to betray her own interests to that extent. And what about his behavior all along . . . not even trusting her enough to tell her what his precious project was? She was becoming indignant now, impatient with her own self-reproach.

"Of course I couldn't, Lloyd," she said quietly, avoiding Clint's eyes.

"Will you please tell me," Lloyd insisted, "what is going on . . . what's happened here in my absence?"

"Apparently," Clint answered in a cold, bitter tone, "there's been one hell of a mistake."

Lloyd studied them both and started to speak. Then he evidently decided against it. In eloquent silence he gave Anne another long look, then turned angrily to Clint.

But before he could say anything more, Clint said, "You've outsmarted yourself, Eliot. Since I've gotten static from the board I've had to revise my schedule. And if you recall, we had a *modus vivendi* of sorts before. Well, we don't have one now, my friend. It's going to be tougher for you than ever. Before you 'arranged' things so cleverly, my schedule called for blasting and leveling the week after next. Now, with a tightened budget, my schedule's been compressed. I'm going to have to do it this week."

"This week?" Lloyd exploded. He turned to Anne. "But that means our scene on the bluff will be totally ruined. And we've *got* to have that tree."

"What tree?" Clint growled, still not looking at Anne.

"It's a particular oak," she murmured. "It . . . stands alone, apart from all the other trees on that bluff, and it has a very special value, both visually and as a symbol."

Clint was looking at her now; their eyes met, and she saw a reviving tenderness in his, a kind of regret for the things he'd said just a moment before.

"I'm sorry about that," he said tightly. "But you both knew, under the terms of the agreement we reached, that the bluff would ultimately be disturbed by our blasting."

"Yes. But not this soon," Lloyd conceded.

"Well, I'm sorry, Eliot. But you brought this on yourself." Clint almost bit off the words, and Anne thought, Doesn't he realize that I'm in this too . . . that when Lloyd is hurt, so am I?

Surveying Clint's hard expression, his ungiving mouth and stubborn jaw, she decided, Of course he knows. But he doesn't really care now because I've hurt him by deceiving him. The brief hope that had awakened a minute ago at his softened look died outright. The feeling was succeeded by a dawning resentment, a heating anger. Damn him. It had been absurd to think they could ever go on as they were, anyway. She was feeling too angry now even to acknowledge her hurt.

"Well, there's no point in belaboring that," she said coldly. She was careful not to address him by name. "Mr. Ward" would be grotesque under the circumstances, but she'd be damned if she'd call him by his first name anymore, either. "I assume you've brought us a new schedule . . . if that's not asking too much?"

After one unreadable glance at her, Clint said tersely, "Of course." He took two folded sheets from his pocket and handed one to her, the other to Lloyd.

The next few moments passed in intent silence while they scrutinized the new schedules. Lloyd sighed. "All right, Ward. We'll have to live with this somehow."

"I suppose we will. I don't know how, either." Something in Clint's tone made Anne look at him again. In his eyes was a baffled anger, but mingled with it she thought she saw the old look of unchanging desire. Her heart thudded; she felt a whole new confusion. Now, as on that morning at the Halberd Inn, he seemed to be saying things with a double meaning. "That should wrap it up, then."

This time, as he got up, Clint avoided her eyes, and she had a sinking feeling. It was so unfair for him to blame her for her secrecy when he'd been secretive from the very beginning. Part of her still mourned the loss of their closeness; it was impossible not to remember the sweetness of their times together.

She watched him walk away. The tall, strong body,

the long, lean legs that gave him such a proud and swinging gait tugged at her heart and teased her senses even now.

Anne tore her gaze away and looked uncertainly at Lloyd, realizing too late that he must have read her expression. He was studying her with a mixture of exasperation and understanding. "It seems to me," he remarked, "that a lot happened to *you* while I was in New York, my dear."

Of course, she thought. What a fool she'd been to think that she and Clint could ever have hidden their feelings. A person far less sensitive than Lloyd would have known right away, picking up on Clint's look, his use of her first name, the gentleness with which he spoke to her in contrast to his brusqueness with Lloyd. Most of all, his obvious dismay when Lloyd had made that remark about her not giving him away to Clint.

She'd banked on Lloyd's usual self-centeredness, that myopia about other people that afflicted him when he was totally involved in his own concerns. But that, too, had evidently undergone a change while Lloyd had been away. Anne still wondered what was behind it, but her curiosity was lost in chagrin when Lloyd added, "Ordinarily it would be none of my affair, Annie. But when *your* affair is with our nemesis, it becomes my business. I must say, I find your choice of lovers a bit awkward."

She bit off a sharp reply. After all, he had a point. In fact, her choice was even more awkward than he knew. Clint was more than an obstacle to them; he'd managed, for a time, to threaten her whole independent future with the force of his power over her. Well, she wasn't going to let him.

"Anne?" Lloyd looked uneasy. "Forgive me if I was tactless. But you're not going to let this . . . interval affect your plans, are you? It's obvious that it hasn't adversely affected your work." He grinned. "I'll say it again. What you did while I was gone was utterly superb. But, if you'll allow me, how serious has this thing become? You have the ability to go a long, long way, Anne. I hope you're not going to throw away a brilliant career for this fellow."

He hesitated momentarily. "Surely we've known each other long enough for me to say this," Lloyd went on gingerly. "Even if you've always been a very . . . reticent lady."

"Of course it's all right." She tried to sound offhand, almost dismissive. After all, she'd known Lloyd for nearly a decade. They'd worked together so closely, and she'd always liked him so much, that he had prerogatives. She took a deep breath and said, "Have no fear, Lloyd. It was an interval . . . an indiscreet one. But I have a feeling that now it's over."

That was true enough, she thought. Clint had looked as if he could never forgive what he considered her betrayal.

"I'm overjoyed to hear it." Lloyd was beaming; he was himself again. "What do you say we get to work again?"

So Lloyd Eliot's in charge now, Anne reflected, and her few days of glory were a thing of the past, just as the glorious moments with Clint Ward were. Thinking of that, she felt cold all over.

Clint braked the Rover in front of the roadhouse, where an unnatural blue light rayed out and sliced the gathering darkness. He had the feeling he could really use a drink, a feeling he didn't have often. He just couldn't face the cabin without her there, not right now. All day long he'd had a kind of bruised sensation along his solar plexus, as if he'd taken a heavy punch without trading any at all.

Dourly he got out of the Rover and walked into the place, heading for the bar, not looking at anybody. The happy hour, they called it—five to seven in the evening, when other miserable characters like him crowded the wateringholes because they had no better place to go. Happy hour was a barrel of laughs, he decided gloomily.

Clint ordered tersely, got his drink and put some money on the bar. The drink tasted lousy, but at least there was that rush of fake, consoling warmth. The weather in the mountains, he grouched in silence, was as changeable as New York's. The morning that had started out so warm and golden had turned treacherous before noon and carried a kind of raw chill all day. Well, when he'd sewed up this preliminary part of the project, he'd take some time off, maybe fly down somewhere warm.

He finished his drink and ordered another. Somebody had put money in the jukebox and one of those damned she-done-me-wrong songs was playing. Almost without volition, Clint turned on his stool and stared at the empty dance floor where he'd danced with Anne.

There came another body punch. He vividly recalled how she'd looked this morning, with her fiery hair and her lovely face, in those clothes the color of some flower or other in his mother's garden. And the wide, blue, true-looking eyes. He'd thought that eyes like that couldn't lie to him. How wrong he'd been. The whole damned time she and Eliot had been plotting, using him to get that rotten movie made.

Clint turned around again and swallowed some more of his drink, going over all their times together in his mind. Well, just as the song said, you couldn't always believe those sweet faces, those pretty eyes. His third drink was a double.

He'd better watch it; he never drank this much. Tomorrow, and the days after that, would be rough enough even if he were in top shape. Roger and the other fossils had really pulled a fast one, and it had played holy hell with the schedule. For a little while technical headaches began to plague him, but he decided to forget them until morning.

He saw the bartender eye him. Probably hoping he wouldn't get too rambunctious; a guy his size could really lay the "Tennessee hurt" on the place if he got going.

Clint smiled to himself, recalling the expression he'd learned from Jack in Oregon; translated, it meant the damage inflicted by angry mountain men with boots and fists. He debated about having a fourth shot.

He couldn't stop thinking of how she'd shafted him. But then he realized, all of a sudden, that the booze was doing his thinking for him, and *he* wasn't doing it at all.

He was acting like a prize jerk. What else *could* she have done? Tip him off about Eliot's maneuvers and foul up her own job? Clint himself had asked her to keep their love separate from their jobs. And now he himself was mixing them all up together, condemning her for the very qualities that had attracted him from the first: her independence and talent and gutsiness, her determination.

Clint Ward, you're a sulky moron, he addressed himself. He was going to call her this very damned minute and try to make things okay again.

He paid for his drinks and got up a trifle unsteadily,

asking the bartender where the phone was. To his amusement the man looked relieved.

Clint glanced at his watch, hoping against hope that she might be in her room by now, that maybe he could catch her before she went to dinner or something.

As soon as he heard her voice, his heart slammed like a fist against his breastbone. "Anne?"

There was a painful hesitation. "Anne?" he said again.

Finally she responded. "Yes, Clint." Her voice was so cool, so neutral, that he could practically feel his heart drop to his guts, and his knees shook slightly.

"I want to see you." He cursed the series of bourbons; he was having trouble with his enunciation.

There was another little silence, and then she went on, "Is it you—or sourmash—that wants to see me?" He took courage from her thawing tone and imagined that she might even be smiling. He thought he heard a tremble in her feisty words.

"Please," he said simply. "We've got to talk. Everything went . . . haywire this morning."

"You sound a bit haywire yourself," she retorted, but he knew now that he had read her right, that she was warming up a little.

"Can I come over?" he persisted. This hesitation, he decided, was the worst one of all. If she didn't say yes he'd have a stroke right then and there. He was hyperventilating now, and going hot and cold.

"Get some coffee," she directed. "You shouldn't drive in that condition." Her way of saying yes revived him; he could feel the adrenaline pumping through his system.

"You've got it. Don't go anywhere, lady. Please. I'll be there before you know it."

He heard her softly hang up, and he strode back to the bar, feeling steadier now, but vastly impatient. He asked the bartender for two cups of coffee, and swallowed them both in a hurry, thinking that it was lucky the stuff was only lukewarm or he wouldn't have had any esophagus left. He tossed a bill on the bar and rushed out to the Rover; he'd always had a good head, and the coffee was working.

It seemed no time at all before he was rushing into the Warrenburg Inn, calling her on the house phone, taking the elevator to her floor.

When she opened her door he blinked a little. She was so pretty that she almost hurt his eyes, her hair all fluffed out, her eyes looking green because she was wearing the bright robe that always reminded him of peacock feathers. Her face was even lovelier than it had been that morning, but now she had a serious, tentative expression that worried him.

There were so many things he wanted to say, but he couldn't even think of them now. All he could do was look at her.

"Come in," she said with a half smile, reminding him gently that he was standing in the hotel corridor, goggling at her.

She stood aside, and he stepped in. As soon as she'd shut the door, he grabbed her in his arms, pulling her close, feeling the delicious softness of her small, slender body. His whole frame was pounding, it seemed to him, and his very insides shook. He felt hot and achy already, wanting her so much it was like a fever.

All he could say was her name, over and over, as he kissed the top of her shining head, running his hands up and down her sides. Finally he raised his hands to her head and tilted her sweet face up so he could kiss her.

Shakily, with a wild new feeling of grateful happiness, he sensed her melting against him.

He couldn't stop kissing her, couldn't let go of that small, perfect mouth that tasted faintly of new cherries, listening to the little sounds she made as she kissed him back so sweetly; on the edge of his blurred awareness there was a clear, triumphant thought: It's all right; it's all right again. She cares as much as I do.

He was gasping for breath when he drew back. He was still too moved, too excited, to speak. He traced the delicate features of her face, looking down into those wonderful eyes. They looked soft again, misty, full of love, but with the shadow of something else: a faint confusion, a distant hurt.

Keeping one arm around her tightly, he stroked her gleaming hair with his other hand and managed to say, "It's been a bad ten hours, lady."

"Very bad," she agreed huskily. She raised her lips to his again, and then she was kissing him, and he was holding her closer than ever. He knew now that there was only one way this could go, that neither of them could stop now if they wanted to, and he was wild and hot with his elation.

But he told himself to hold on; there were things they had to talk about, apologies he had to make for being such a fool. "I'm sorry; I'm so sorry," he muttered against her mouth. "I acted like a fool. We've got to talk about this thing, darling."

"Not now, Clint. Not now," she protested to his amazement and delight, drawing his face back to hers. Then her fragile fingers were very busy, starting to unbutton his shirt, and the idea of talking about anything became totally remote, absurd, unthinkable.

His last clear thought, when he began to help her with her pleasant task, was that she was the most wonderful woman who had ever existed, that there was no way in the world he would ever let her go. Not now. Not ever.

Chapter 9

SHE HAD PLANNED TO SAY SO MUCH, BUT NOW ANNE WAS beyond thinking. She watched him take off his shirt, baring his sun-darkened torso and his powerful arms while his bright amber look met hers.

She was all hot, whirling sensation; he was undoing the tie of her vivid robe, parting it to stare at her trembling nakedness. He was smiling a shaky smile, and his expression was full of yearning tenderness; the desire on his face looked almost like pain. "Oh, Anne," he whispered. "This is all there is. This is what it all means."

He slid his urgent fingers around her waist, and the

pressure was fiery on her skin as he pulled her to him. His excitement was very plain; his touch pleaded for her. As always, the power of his nearness was almost frightening. She could sense the inevitable weakening of her body.

He carried her to the bed, then finished undressing rapidly. After tossing his clothes helter-skelter across the furniture and floor, he was with her, close to her, caressing her with a new wildness as his eager hands disposed of her one soft garment.

Anne found herself so eager to receive him that she drew him to her at once and urged him to the ultimate nearness. With astonishing swiftness his glad outcries began to answer hers.

They lay breathless for a time, in utter silence. With his arm around her, Anne began to softly drowse.

There was darkness around them when she awoke, and his fingers were gently stroking her skin. Anne brushed away a vagrant lock of hair; she could see Clint's face dimly.

He was looking at her with adoration, begging her with his piercing eyes. She shut her eyes again and lifted her mouth for his kiss. He leaned toward her, urgently grasping her naked shoulders, lowering his parted mouth to hers for an endless, hungry kiss that left her feeling weak.

She couldn't let him go. Warm and boneless, she gave herself up to this new abandon. Nothing mattered anymore but this, his mouth and arms, his hard, demanding body. This moment had nothing to do with that other world that plagued them. This instant blotted out whatever she had known before; there was no compass to guide her in this fiery country but her own ignited senses.

He kissed her shoulders and throat and arms, bringing her to new arousal with his quick and unspeakably gentle touches, until she felt a sharp and sudden need, a twinge of needlelike sensation that ebbed and eddied, lost in a wave of fresh, barbaric pleasure. As he joined with her again, she felt the rocking tempo of the sea, and the waves were fire and softness that brought her a forgetting like the edge of sleep. She heard voices cry out . . . and they were his, and hers.

He was lying with her again, his breath gone, and she turned her head with languid slowness to look at him. His eyes were shut; his face was calm. Smiling, he whispered without opening his eyes, "My love, my love," and pulled her close in his arms. They felt like home.

"I love you so much," he said softly. "I must have loved you from the minute I saw your face across the clearing that very first afternoon."

She burrowed into his chest without replying, wishing that the magic of their encounter could carry them through the rest of their lives, obliterating everything.

But even now, to her regret, so soon after that ecstatic forgetting, her restless doubts were stirring.

Uneasily she realized that this time the spell had been broken very soon, and wondered what that meant. The answer came to her clearly, coldly: It meant that they couldn't go on living in a kind of dream when there was so much unexpressed between them.

"Anne . . ." It was a relief to hear him speak in that tone, the let's-talk inflection. "I'm sorry about this morning," he went on gently.

"Oh, Clint, it's—"

"Please, darling. Let me go on." She glanced aside at him; his face was sober, his words weighted with seriousness. "I realize that when I fight with Eliot," he continued, "I'm fighting with you, too. But I don't think you realize just what he's done."

She started to protest, but decided to keep still for the moment.

"You see, I have a lot of latitude in my work," he said. She remembered Emma's reference to his being Associated's wonder boy. "But even I," he admitted wryly, "have people to account to. And there are . . . elements in the company who've opposed my project from the very start, who've been waiting for the flimsiest excuse to foul me up. Eliot gave them that excuse—however he accomplished it." There was a significant pause, as if he were waiting for her to say something, as if he were aware that she'd known more about Lloyd's plans than she'd told him.

Maybe if she opened up to him, he'd open up to her. "Lloyd and Samson were very close friends at college," she volunteered.

"I see." His voice was neutral. "I can understand why you felt you couldn't confide in me. I know you thought you had a lot riding on this movie."

"Thought!" There it was again, his bland assumption that her concerns were somehow trivial. Now she was beginning to wonder if she and Clint could ever really make peace with each other. But she tried to suppress that thought. Just a few moments before they had brought each other such indescribable pleasure, such deep happiness.

"Sorry," he conceded, and stroked her hair. Yet even that gesture, she decided resentfully, was somehow indulgent, condescending.

"It's . . . all right, Clint." Then she realized that it wasn't all right. "You see, it's a little hard to take—the idea that I'm supposed to confide in you, when you've never really confided in me. And the idea that what I do is somehow less important . . . that the sun rises and sets on your project."

His hand stopped its gentle stroking, and he was very still. At last he said, "You might say it does, Anne."

That did it. "So instead of 'Me, Tarzan; you, Jane,'" she remarked with bitter humor, "your're saying, 'Me, man; you, woman.' *Ergo* subservient. 'Me, heap big scientist . . . deal in truth; you, only crazy artist, deal in nonsense.' Is that it, Clint?"

He chuckled and, turning, took her in his arms and hugged her. "No. I'm saying you're one fantastic lady."

But she was stiff in his arms, neither amused nor mollified.

"Anne . . . what are we fighting about?" he demanded softly. "We'll get through this thing, and then we'll still have each other. Anne, we can have a whole new life together." He sounded as if he were talking to a child.

"Where I follow you from secret site to secret site, never knowing what you're doing . . . giving up everything I hold dear?"

His arms relaxed their hold. "I haven't suggested anything like that," he countered reasonably.

No, he hadn't. He hadn't repeated his proposal of marriage, and she'd just assumed it. Her face and neck felt hot with embarrassment. "No, you haven't," she admitted, feeling miserable, chagrined.

He was quiet for so long that she felt impelled to break the silence. "Clint, I think . . . I think you'd better go."

He raised himself on one elbow and stared at her, bewildered. *"Go!* What is this all about, Anne? What have I said? We've just gotten started talking . . . I haven't even had a chance to—"

"I think we've talked enough, Clint," she broke in, pulling the sheet up over her body, feeling suddenly exposed, shy.

"You can't mean this, Anne." He grabbed her shoulder, and his grip was painful. She wriggled out of his grasp.

"I do mean it, Clint. We can't be together for an hour without quarreling. If that's the way it is now, what would it be like if we were—" She stopped abruptly.

"If we were what?" he asked.

Avoiding an answer, she repeated, "Please . . . just go."

He stared at her for another long moment; then his expression changed from one of puzzlement to anger. "This is so senseless I can't believe it. I can't figure out what's gotten into you." He paused again, then muttered, "All right, I will go. You're not making any sense at all tonight."

It was the first time in their acquaintance that he'd spoken to her so sharply, so coldly, and her heart sank.

She lay with closed eyes, already feeling the tears beginning to gather under her shut lids, listening to him get out of bed, hearing him mutter under his breath while he tried to find his clothes in the semidarkness.

She didn't have the heart to open her eyes until she heard the sharp closing of the outer door.

When she did, the room looked so desolate and empty that she let the tears come freely.

When she woke the next morning after a toss-and-turn night, Anne realized that it was the worst awakening she'd had ever since the morning after Dan died, three years ago. And she thought, If he means that much to me, I'm a fool to let him go like this.

Impulsively she reached for the phone. It might be late enough to call him at his site office.

But then she remembered their problems, their conflicts. Her hand stopped halfway. What good would it do? Nothing had changed.

Except that she was more miserable than she'd ever been in her life. She lay there racked with indecision. Finally she resolved not to call him. The same thing that had happened before would only happen again: the remorse, the reconciliation, the wild meeting of hungry bodies, succeeded by another conflict, another tempest of distance and alienation.

Maybe . . . maybe it had only been her body that had betrayed her; maybe her mind had never really been touched by him. After all, they were such opposites; perhaps he would never be capable of understanding her, of being close to her as Dan had been.

There was one thing she was sure of: Today was a workday, and she'd always been able to handle that. More than handle it—welcome it, escape in it, drown in it. And today was no exception.

Her resolve carried her through the whole tough day of shooting, helping Lloyd cope with Jack's irate agent, and with the mercurial Jack himself, who, the doctors assured them, would be able to work by Friday. Lloyd and Anne devoutly thanked heaven for that. Jack would have to appear in the big scene on the bluff on Friday, and Friday was the last possible day they could shoot that scene because Clint would start blasting on Saturday.

Even his name gave her a twinge, and that evening she ached as she remembered other evenings after work, at the cabin. But she determinedly thrust the memories away, shoving them into a deep, dark recess n her mind. Lloyd was probably right, she decided, work was really all you could count on, in the last analysis. Cold comfort, she commented in silence, but comfort was comfort, however you sliced it.

She left her phone on the hook that night, but Clint didn't call. He didn't call the next night, either, and she thought sorrowfully that she hadn't meant that much to him, after all. The conclusion left a piercing ache in her body, and she looked forward to the time when the ache would become a mere bruise, then fade altogether.

By Thursday morning she'd achieved a kind of grim resignation, telling herself that it had just been a passing affair, that they'd been thrown together because of that overpowering physical magnetism, but that was all. And yet something deeper in her kept protesting that it had been far more. Once again she made herself bury that distant protest even deeper.

She was feeling fairly calm that morning when she went into the dining room of the inn for an early breakfast. Lloyd wasn't there yet, which made her wonder again if he were keeping something from her, something about his health. He'd seemed extraordinarily tired, strangely routine yesterday when they were working. The new anxiety crowded out her somber reflections about Clint.

She was so deep in thought, gazing out the picture window at the mockingly sunny morning, that she didn't notice anybody entering the dining room, so when she heard that familiar, resonant voice quietly saying her name, she jumped. Startled, she turned her head and looked up.

Clint was standing by her table, staring down at her. She imagined that she'd caught him in a tender expression that immediately disappeared when she looked up, because she could see a ghost of that look in his golden brown eyes.

But now he was only neutral, polite, and her heart sank. She composed her own expression to match his.

The half smile on his sensuous mouth died away. "Sorry I frightened you," he murmured. "Is Eliot going to join you?"

"Yes. He should be here soon." She looked away for an instant, reluctant to let him see the welcome she thought must be there in her own eyes. When she felt calm enough she looked up again, meeting his eyes steadily.

"May I sit down? There's something urgent I have to discuss with both of you." His voice was that of an utter stranger, she thought sadly. What a horrible situation this was.

"Sit down, by all means," she invited coldly. "What's the 'something urgent'? Are you going to tell me we have to stop shooting altogether?"

He looked as if she'd slapped him; he tightened his mouth, and a tendon moved in his stubborn jaw. He sat and responded evenly, "That would be a very good idea, under the circumstances. But I know neither of you will sit still for that, so I'm just giving you this."

He took a folded sheaf of papers from his breast pocket and handed a sheet to her. Dismayed, she scanned it rapidly. It was a schedule of Associated operations for the next morning. They were going to do their blasting on Friday.

Friday, she repeated to herself, fuming.

"*Friday,*" she said aloud, meeting his eyes.

"That's the way it's got to be," he said gruffly. "I won't go into all the details—"

"You never do," she snapped.

"Because," he continued with maddening calm, "I am not obligated to do so. But the point is that it will be a risky business. The bottom line is, you should shoot that bluff scene today."

"We *can't* shoot it today!" she said sharply, her voice rising to an angry, almost hysterical pitch. She controlled herself rapidly, however, and said in a quieter tone, "Our male lead sprained his leg and is under doctor's orders not to work until Friday. We've got to shoot that day, because after that," she added savagely, "there may not be any bluff to shoot on, thanks to you."

His expression was a blend of exasperation and regret. But he said, as if she hadn't spoken, "If you'll allow me to tell you . . ."

When she didn't reply, he went on soberly. "Blasting can be extremely dangerous. With blasting of this kind, we can't possibly determine the exact safe distance from the center of the blasting area. There's a danger; flying rocks can be life threatening." Suddenly his voice was less steady, and the expression in his eyes changed.

"Damn it, Anne, I don't want anything to happen to you." He snapped his mouth shut, as if he'd made a damaging admission, and stood up suddenly. "Don't get near this—I beg you. And tell that . . . tell Eliot. Here, this copy's for him; these extras are for whoever else is concerned."

He tossed the sheets on the table and stalked away.

Anne stared after him, her emotions in turmoil. She was the one he cared about. For a moment her heart sang within her. She picked up the sheet and read it again. The warning was quite clear. And Clint had come to her because it was about her that he was primarily concerned.

Perhaps that was stretching it, though; he was responsible for the safety of everybody in the vicinity, didn't want anything to happen to *anybody*. Besides, he could be exaggerating the danger a little, like an overcautious doctor who tells a patient to take it easy for an extra week or so just to be sure. She looked at his map again; the section of the bluff they needed seemed well outside the danger zone."

But he'd said, "I don't want anything to happen to *you*."

"Anne, good morning." Lloyd was coming toward her table, smiling. "Wasn't that the Great Grease Monkey I just passed, storming through the lobby?"

Lloyd took a chair and raised a princely hand to a waiter.

"It was indeed." Anne passed one of the papers to him. He glanced at it rapidly before the waiter came and took his order.

Then he read it more carefully. "No. No! I don't believe this," he declared in his best tragic voice. He tossed the sheet down and ran his hands through his white mane of hair, like a tortured character in a Russian play. "Why, oh, why didn't we go the hell to England . . . or Scotland or France? Why did we have to come to this benighted place?"

His voice belled across the dining room, and the diners and waiters were staring interestedly.

"Because," Anne reminded him quietly, "you said last year—remember?—that this is a 'piece of Americana' and you wanted it shot on native ground. Also, there was the little matter of that truckers' strike in France. Then there was the geological survey in our Scottish spot, and on and on."

"You're right; you're right, of course," Lloyd muttered, watching the waiter set his breakfast before him. He surveyed his eggs as if they were some unknown, exotic dish to be mistrusted. "We both know that this is the perfect spot . . . hence all the cloak-and-dagger maneuvers, the hassles, the problems. And so far they've been worth it. But oh, Lord . . . *this* . . ." He speared his eggs savagely with his fork.

"Is there the faintest chance we can shoot the bluff scene today?" For the moment Anne had almost forgotten the matter of Clint; here, at least, was a problem she might be able to handle. "We've already blocked out Jack's action, you know, to accommodate his wretched leg."

"True. But we can't make the poor devil overdo. I'd like to horsewhip him," Lloyd added, grinning, "but we can't drive him to that extent."

"Of course not. I'm grasping at straws," Anne admitted.

"I know one thing," Lloyd said decidedly. "We've damn well got to have that tree. We just can't chance its being uprooted, or listing to starboard or something after that blasting."

They plunged into a discussion of shooting hours and the resulting problems with lighting, and finally came up with what seemed a workable solution, one that seemed to offer no possible danger to the cast or crew.

Lloyd, Anne thought, always trusted a great deal to luck, and usually he was vindicated. There was no reason why this job should be an exception.

She threw herself into that day's shooting with renewed vitality, and got so involved in planning the next day's work that when she drifted off to sleep Thursday night she was still planning, able to put aside even the thought of Clint for the time being.

That new sensation of enthusiasm and self-command carried her through the next morning, right onto the location. She, Lloyd and the sound and camera crew were there almost at dawn, well ahead of the actors. The blasting wouldn't begin for several hours, and, Lloyd told her with that manic confidence she knew so well, they might be able to wrap the scene before then.

The sound and camera crew, with whom they had conferred the night before, had calculated almost to the millimeter the possibility of noise and vibrations interfering with their equipment. The main thing was to shoot as expeditiously as possible and not move outside the prescribed safety area.

By the time Jack and Livie arrived, everything was ready as far as Anne could tell. Jack was in fine form, still doing some loosening-up exercises to limber his newly unbandaged leg; then he managed a trial run up the bluff without mishap. They started to roll.

The whole scene was perfection, with the lovers silhouetted against the morning sky a little apart from the stately, towering tree. To Anne's and Lloyd's exhilaration, there wasn't a single hitch. She'd never known a shooting to go so effortlessly before.

"Cut!" Lloyd's triumphant call rang out. "That's it! Magnificent, children," he cried out to the smiling actors, then added words of praise for the crew.

Anne blinked, feeling dazed; she'd never dreamed they could do it, that it could possibly go this well. Not in a million years. They'd finished ahead of Clint's crew, and everything was coming up roses. There still wasn't a sound of the distant blasting.

"We did it; we did it, Lloyd." He gave her a bear hug, but called out to the camera crew, "Hold it just a minute."

The photography director scowled, looking at his watch. "I thought we were finished here, Lloyd. We'd better not fool around."

"Just hold it!" Lloyd snapped. He started down the bluff.

"What's up?" Anne asked him, puzzled but following.

"I just had the most splendid notion," he told her, beaming. "Come down here a little way. I want to show you something. I think if we—"

A mighty explosion drowned out his words; Anne could feel the tremors in the very foot of the bluff.

"We'd better get out of here," she warned.

Lloyd shook his head. Then there was another blast, nearer, over the ridge, and a few clods of falling earth spattered them.

"Lloyd . . ." Anne was beginning to feel panicky. Still another explosion followed, and this time several good-sized rocks came flying their way.

Anne looked up. A man in khakis was climbing up over the other side of the opposite ridge. As his head and shoulders became clearer against the sky, she recognized Clint's familiar outline.

He was striding toward them, his face like a thundercloud. "What the hell are you doing down here?"

"Don't take that tone with me, Ward." Lloyd was glaring back at Clint, standing his ground. And the ground, Anne thought in rising hysteria, was very shaky at the moment.

To her astonishment, Clint grabbed her by the shoulders and practically dragged her up the side of the bluff. "Damn it," he growled. "You are the silliest, most muleheaded little . . ." He raised his voice and shouted to Lloyd, "Get up here, you idiot!"

Another deafening explosion split the air, much nearer this time, and larger rocks came flying toward them. Clint threw himself on top of Anne, and Lloyd dived to the ground near them. They lay there for an endless moment.

Finally Clint moved away from Anne and lay against the slant of the bluff, gasping. "All right. All right, it's okay now." He jerked Anne to her feet without ceremony and bellowed, "Both of you. I want you to look up there."

Lloyd got to his feet. They all stared up at the bluff. The tree was intact, towering there unharmed, splendid as ever.

"You could have waited," Clint told them coldly. "As it is, I risked my neck and you risked yours because you're both damned fools."

Anne gasped with indignation, and Lloyd began, "Look here, Ward, I've had just about enough of—"

"You look here, Eliot. I've saved your neck, and I don't expect any thanks for it." Clint was fuming. "But all that's incidental. You've risked us all for this idiotic bit of hogwash."

Hogwash. Anne felt her temper slipping.

"Incidental!" Lloyd's rage had reached a frenzied pitch. "Do you call our lives incidental, you fanatical grease monkey?"

Clint and Lloyd were facing each other like angry mastiffs. "I didn't say that, Eliot." Clint was still angry, but he was in greater control. "My job has suffered enough at your hands. All I needed was for you people to be injured, or maybe killed, through my negligence. Whatever the legalities are—and you had plenty of warning—there are those who would be happy to blame me for this and stop me altogether."

He was breathing hard. He hadn't looked at Anne

again. "Now," he concluded coldly, "if you'll excuse me, I've got to get back to work."

He stalked away, leaving them standing there, staring after him speechlessly.

Anne couldn't believe the things he'd said—that all he'd needed was for "you people to be injured." He hadn't been thinking of her, not as a person, only as a threat to his almighty status with his particular powers-that-be. At that moment she felt that she absolutely hated him.

He'd blurted out two things that were utterly unforgivable: He'd saved them only to save his project. And he'd called their work, their masterpiece, hogwash.

Anne was shaking all over; she hardly knew whether it was with anger or relief over their escape from danger. Probably both.

She thought of all the sweat and agony that had gone into this picture, all the effort they had poured into it, going past the point of exhaustion into literal danger. And Clint Ward had dismissed all that in a few careless, angry phrases. When she remembered his hard face it was impossible to recall the gentle, loving man with whom she'd spent those fleeting, magical nights and days. It was a sickening realization, and she felt her heart turn cold as ice.

That sensation, so close on the heels of her flaming resentment, made her almost faint. She swayed a little.

Lloyd grabbed her arm. "Are you all right, Annie?" he asked her anxiously.

She murmured an assent, thinking, I'll never really be all right again.

"It's been quite a day," Lloyd muttered. "We'd better get you back to the inn."

"That's the understatement of the century," she retorted, hearing her voice tremble and break.

"Anyway, we've done it, Annie," Lloyd assured her. "And no bones broken, if you'll forgive the expression."

She didn't answer while they struggled back up the bluff again. Something else *was* broken, she decided. In just a few brief moments the last great dream of her whole life had been shattered to pieces, for good and all.

All the way back to Warrenburg, from her absent *au revoir* to Lloyd until the moment when she regained the peace of her room and stretched out, fully clothed and still shaken, on the soft bed, she was haunted by the memories of the brief time she'd had with Clint Ward.

She felt exhausted, no doubt the aftereffects of shock, and slightly giddy from the brandy Lloyd had pressed on her a little while before.

She let the last few weeks run through her mind. First the original sight of him on the ridge, him coming toward her, smiling, holding out his hand. Remembering all of him so vividly, from his thick, black, shining hair to his weathered face with its sensuous mouth, white grin and hawklike nose, his remarkable eyes glowing against his sun-touched skin.

The feel of his body when they danced . . . and the way his fingers brushed her burning, naked flesh, the way his mouth explored her willing mouth and body.

A thousand little gentle, tender things came back to her. She never thought to experience them again; only he had given them to her, and now they were lost.

He'd destroyed all that loveliness in an explosion of angry, bitter, uncaring words that revealed his true concerns—himself, his status, his almighty, wretched project. Blasted it away, as his men had blasted the mountain.

Anne's eyelids fluttered; her vision was dimmed by tears. She closed her eyes again, feeling hollow.

Clint paced the living room of the cabin feeling haunted, riddled with remorse. He'd give anything in the world to unsay what he'd said to them this morning. Or to *her,* he amended silently.

Clint swore and kept up his pacing. He had that bruised sensation across his chest again, as if he had been repeatedly punched there by somebody who knew how. He threw himself on the couch and leaned his head back, too despondent to smoke, or listen to music, or get ready for the trip he had to make tonight, missing her so much that it was like a deep, perpetual ache.

This was the worst possible time to have to leave town, he thought. He had to leave her with his anger ringing in her ears, and no chance to undo it, to apologize. She couldn't know that his terror for her safety had translated itself into blinding rage and made him blurt out those idiotic things.

Clint heard a car turning into the drive outside the cabin, the light beep of a horn. Ben was here already to drive him into Knoxville, and he hadn't even put his gear together.

He got up and swore again under his breath, stalking to the door. Opening it, he sighted Ben Marley, his number one man, parked in his compact. He called out, "Come on in. I'll be ready in a couple of minutes."

Leaving the door ajar, he strode into the bedroom and, trying not to look at the bed, got into a suit while he raised his voice to Ben. "Help yourself. You know where the bar is."

"Right. But snap it up. We don't have much time."

They didn't. Clint glanced at his watch and proceeded to pack with the swiftness and ease of long practice. He didn't know what he had expected to gain by dragging his heels—maybe there'd been a wild, crazy hope that she would come to him there at the cabin. But that *was* crazy, after the way he'd acted this morning.

Clint zipped up his bag and swallowed the small, hard lump in his throat. He went back to the living room. Ben was standing in the middle of the room like an amiable giant, holding a cup of coffee in his hand.

He raised the cup to Clint, took another swallow and set it on the bar. "Here's to luck in New York," he said, grinning.

"I'm going to need it, pal." Clint followed Ben out of the cabin and locked up.

When they were driving away, he glanced back at the small house on the wooded rise, thinking that he'd been happier there than he'd ever been in his life. And I'll be damned if that's the end of it, he thought. There was no way in the world he was going to let her go for good. What they had was worth too much for him to throw it away like this. It made no sense at all. He'd call her one more time from the airport.

Clint glanced aside at Ben Marley as they sped through Sedgby. He was the best man Clint had ever worked with: loyal, able, silent as a clam. He must have known that something had been going on with Clint, something highly unusual, even if he hadn't said so.

They were halfway down the mountain before Ben opened his mouth. "Don't let 'em get you down, buddy. You know, we've handled tougher stuff than this." The easy voice, with its trace of a Southern accent that world travel had not obliterated, was sympathetic, encouraging.

"But nothing as big."

"No . . . nothing as big. Those desk jockeys don't really know what they're fooling with, Clint." For Ben, one of the few who knew what the project was, this was absolute eloquence, Clint thought wryly.

There was another long silence. Then, when they passed through Warrenburg, Ben spoke again. "I don't want to stick my nose in . . . but I get the feeling that something else big is eating you."

It wasn't a demand to talk; it was an invitation. Clint took a deep breath and accepted. It was the first time in years that he'd talked so much about personal things—except to Anne. They were almost at the airport by the time he'd finished.

Ben braked and looked at Clint steadily. There was an affectionate light in his sharp gray eyes. He grinned. "Well, you know how I got Louise."

Clint grinned back. He did know. Ben had told him that he had just kept battering away at his wife's defenses until she'd given up.

"You can do it, pal," Ben added. "Just the way you can do it in New York." He held out his hand. Clint gripped it and answered gratefully, "Thanks, pal. I think I can."

He got out of the car and hurried into the terminal to call Anne.

But there wasn't any answer.

Chapter 10

CLINT BUCKLED HIS SEAT BELT, TRYING TO GET HIS MIND off Anne. The best way to do that right now, he decided, was to go over that report again. It was going to be hard enough to put his arguments across; he couldn't chance leaving a hole the size of a pinpoint in this thing.

"Would you like earphones for the movie, sir?"

Clint looked up absently at the attendant, his mind still going like a calculator. "I beg your pardon?"

She repeated her question.

"No, thanks." Clint shook his head, only half-aware of the movie screen. Then he saw the title of the film and the name Lloyd Eliot.

"Miss, wait a minute. I think I would," he called out.

As he watched the film, Clint began to feel his scientist's disbelief slip away. The stuff was utter fantasy, the kind of thing he usually skipped, but Eliot—or Anne, he decided—had made it very real.

He thought of the scene he'd watched her direct and knew this spell-casting was Anne's doing as much as Eliot's. Clint was so wrapped up in the story that when the movie ended he actually felt a small pang. His heart thudded when he saw her name in the credits.

Clint took off his earphones and leaned back in his seat, gazing into the outer darkness.

He had a flash of sudden, distant recall—another movie, one that he'd seen when he was just a kid. A film about a guy who was hewing a path for a railroad through an impossible mountain; Clint couldn't even remember where, now, or what the name of the picture was. But there was one thing he remembered vividly. Seeing that movie had decided him on his whole career.

A movie, he reflected, was responsible for his current project, the instrument for new hope, a whole new way of life for people all around the world.

And he, Clint Ward, had had the everlasting gall to think that her work was not as important as his. With her brightness, her sensitivity and her unique gifts there was almost nothing she couldn't accomplish. And he had blithely assumed that she could walk away from that to marry him.

He decided to send her a telegram as soon as he got to New York.

No . . . he'd take care of it sooner. Right now. In a letter. He put aside his report and took out a blank sheet and an envelope.

Maybe this wasn't the right time for him to ask her again to marry him. She'd think he was pressing her;

besides, it would be grotesque after what had happened that morning. But at least he'd be able to tell her that now he understood.

On Monday evening Anne headed for the desk in the Warrenburg Inn to pick up her key; it had been a rotten day following an unsuccessful weekend, and she was totally washed out.

Her rest on Friday afternoon had revived her a bit, but dinner that night with Lloyd and Harri had been awkward because she'd had so many feelings to hide, prominent among them that relentless sense of loss. Lloyd, elated over their success in finishing the scene on the bluff, was in the best of spirits. And if he suspected some of Anne's feelings, he gave no sign. When she got back to her room, she had thought she heard her phone ringing, but when she'd let herself in, the ringing had stopped. Fortunately she was so tired out from the incredible day that she'd had no problem falling asleep.

But she woke very early Saturday, dismayed to feel the return of that familiar ache. She couldn't believe that it was over between them, but she'd have to accept it. Brooding about it would do no good at all. He hadn't called her again the night before—if, indeed, the earlier call had been from him—and she'd had a gloomy feeling that he wouldn't call that day, either.

She promised herself that she was going to put the man out of her mind. As soon as it was late enough, she phoned an old friend who lived in Knoxville; the friend was overjoyed to hear from her, and invited her for the remainder of the weekend. Anne packed some clothes and drove to the city, noticing what an enormous difference her decade's absence had made.

But it was pleasant and consoling to spend the weekend at her friend's spacious suburban house. They went on a shopping spree Saturday afternoon, dined at the country club, and were escorted by her friend's genial husband to a local theater production that night. Sunday passed just as pleasantly, with visitors from the university dropping in during the afternoon. Anne had declined to stay for dinner, saying she wanted to get back to the mountains before dark.

As she drove the winding highway to Warrenburg, the distraction the weekend had provided began to fade. At the first sight of the Smokies' cloudy peaks, melancholy purple-gray in the gathering dusk, Anne's spirits drooped, and she felt the unwelcome return of that sharp sadness.

Once again she heard the phone in her room ringing, and once again it stopped before she could unlock the door. She rang the desk to find out where the call had originated; the man told her it hadn't been made through an operator, so he had no way of knowing. The caller, he said, was a man who hadn't left his name.

That settled it; it could have been anyone, Lloyd or any of the crew. She'd just have to stop expecting Clint to call. Nevertheless, the thought persisted, and Sunday night was a restless one.

Monday morning started off badly, too. She dreaded the thought of running into Clint somewhere near their location, though it wasn't likely. They were shooting in the Sedgby church and didn't have any exteriors lined up. When Anne arrived on location she was greeted by a triumphant Lloyd, who told her the "great news": Associated's project was halted for the time being. Lloyd had gotten the word on the grapevine through Hobie Cannon, he said. "And best of all," Lloyd concluded, grinning, "the *wunderkind*'s away. And they don't know exactly when he'll be back. My guess he's in New York, trying to straighten himself out with the money men."

Anne heard the news with mixed emotions—relief on the one hand not to have to confront him, and on the other a new, swift dart of pain, terrifying apprehension. He might not be back at all. She might never see him again.

Noticing her expression, Lloyd asked her gently, "You're not still hung up on our archenemy, my dear?"

"Oh, good heavens, of course not," Anne lied, trying her utmost to sound totally indifferent. "That *is* good news," she added with effort.

"I'm glad you're being sensible, Annie, because I have a feeling it's going to be a rough day."

And it had been, Anne thought, as she walked toward the desk at the inn. Jack's leg had acted up in the newly damp weather, and Livie was off her stride, among a dozen other complications. They'd had to do take after take, but finally they'd gotten it after seven grueling hours. Seven hours, Anne grouched to herself, for a big ten minutes of movie. This had been the worst day they'd had since the beginning. Lloyd's estimate of a wrap by Friday seemed insanely overoptimistic.

Automatically Anne held out her hand for the key. The clerk took it from her empty box and handed it to her with a smile. "No messages," he said. "But wait a minute. Sorry. I have a special delivery for you. I was just about to put it in your box when you walked in."

Anne took the letter from him with a murmured thanks. There was no return address; it was postmarked New York, with her name and address written in a bold, thick pen. Her heart skipped a beat.

As soon as she was in her room, she tossed her key

onto a table and ripped open the letter, her eyes skipping down first to the signature. It was from Clint.

She sat down on the bed, aware that her knees were shaking. A wild feeling of hope was racing through her. She felt as if she were on a roller coaster.

Dear Anne,

I'm on a plane for New York, where I have to go for a very high-level meeting. I just saw *The Wand*, and in it I saw you and all that you bring to your work. It was wonderful. It made me understand why your work is so important, not only to you but to everyone who sees its results. Forgive me for not understanding before, and also for the things I said to you both that morning. My only excuse is that I was terrified for your safety, and fear makes me so mad I go a little crazy. I did want you to know that I understand fully now what you really are—someone who can't "belong" to anyone but yourself. Darling, I do hope it goes well.

There was nothing more, except for his bold, black signature.

She couldn't believe that that was all, somehow, and read it again, foolishly, as if with the second reading he would say he loved her, and was coming back to her.

Anne was touched by his respect and understanding, but there was no mention of love at all, no repetition of his wanting to marry her.

She burst into tears, crumpling the letter angrily. I've really lost him now, she thought darkly. The letter was only a kind of apologetic goodbye.

Then she smoothed the letter out and put it away. After all, that and the ring with the gleaming petals that she still wore on her right hand were all that she had left of him. She was sure she would never see him anymore.

Clint shifted his long body on the deep, soft couch of the V.I.P. waiting room, wishing he had gotten there later. After all, he thought sardonically, it's only the project's life that's on the line. He was itching to jump into the meeting right now, and the worst thing about extra time was that it gave him more leisure to stew about Anne. The fact was, he'd need every ounce of his concentration for this battle, but his concentration kept slipping each time he thought of her.

A passing secretary, apparently noticing his glower, asked brightly, "Can I get you something, Mr. Ward? A drink, coffee?"

"No," he growled. "Thank you," he added, appalled at his rudeness. "Thanks very much." He tried to smile at her. She nodded, and with another bright smile walked away.

The whole damned trip, Clint reflected, had been an absolute nightmare. First of all, he'd been a jerk to mail that letter. It had been pitifully inadequate, not saying a tenth of what he meant to say. He was no writer; he had to talk to her, but she was never there when he called. It seemed like some kind of malign quirk of fate.

Or maybe she just wasn't answering. Maybe if he had left his name she'd have told the desk not to put his calls through again. There'd been no answer the entire weekend, or last night. And what a weekend it had been. Rick Jason, probably his only ally left on the board, had pressed him to stay at his house on Long Island, where they had spent most of the time going over their strategy, with Clint feeling like he had only half his marbles. Rick had not been encouraging. The board, he said, would have to concede that the project was feasible; whether it was *desirable* was what they'd be arguing.

It would be tough, Clint thought sourly. And worst of all was his nagging sensation that a part of him was missing, the part that had always sustained him, driven him, made him fight and win.

"Clint."

Startled, he focused on Rick Jason entering the lounge.

"They're ready," Rick told him. "Are you?"

"More than ready," Clint retorted in an aggressive tone that he assumed as much to reassure himself as Rick. "Let's go."

A half hour later, when they emerged, he felt as if he'd been hit by one of his own bulldozers. There was only one chance left now, and that was in Washington. That was all he could think of now; the prospect crowded out everything else.

"I can't believe it. I *still* can't believe it," Anne murmured to Lloyd on the way down the mountain. It was only a little after noon on Friday.

"I'm sorry for your surprise, my dear." He chuckled. "But it's sweet of you to chauffeur me."

"Why not?" she responded, smiling. "It *is* the last time . . . an occasion."

"The last time indeed." There was something in his inflection that made her hark back to their breakfast meeting right after he'd returned from New York. Ever since then she'd had the recurring suspicion that there was something he wasn't telling her.

This last week, though, she'd been so wrapped up in her own unhappiness that she'd hardly given Lloyd a thought, and she was stricken with guilt. Actually it was a relief right now to concentrate on him, on anything that could take her mind off her constant ache.

"Lloyd, you've been dropping hints like that ever since you came back. Why can't you tell me what's going on?" she asked him abruptly.

He was silent for an instant; then he said calmly, "All in good time, Annie. Tomorrow, before our celebration."

I was right, she said to herself. There *was* something. "Is it good?" she pressed him, newly anxious.

"Very good, I think."

That was reassuring . . . if he were telling the truth.

"And speaking of celebrations," he went on brightly, "I want everyone in their best costumes on location at two tomorrow." They were planning a huge and elaborate luncheon at the Halberd Inn. Anne imagined that Lloyd's emphasis on how people should dress was significant, and she realized that she hadn't paid much attention to her looks lately.

"Have no fear. Your second-in-command will be all smooth and polished for the occasion. As a matter of fact, I'm heading for the hairdresser's as soon as I drop you."

"Splendid." She felt his searching look on her. "Something's been bothering you, Anne, bothering you badly, I have a feeling." His tone was sympathetic, probing.

"Not a thing," she lied. "Except the usual pressure."

After she dropped him off at the inn and drove toward the center of town, Anne took a deep, ragged breath. It was good to be alone again for a while to suffer in peace, she decided with wry, dark humor. It would be even better when this whole thing was over and she could let herself relax and lick her wounds. Maybe she'd stay on here for a time. . . . No, that was an idiotic notion. She should go somewhere as different as possible, where she could start to forget. If she ever *could* forget.

She parked and entered the hairdresser's shop. Catching sight of herself in a full-length mirror, she almost shuddered, and suddenly wished she had changed before she came. Her face looked practically haggard, her hair dull; her khakis, worn for two days in succession, were positively grubby. She felt hideous among the well-dressed women waiting.

"Ms. Reynolds?" The receptionist could barely hide her surprise. That doesn't surprise *me,* Anne retorted silently; she didn't look like a movie mogul at the moment. "Marie will take you in about ten minutes. There are magazines and papers over there."

Anne thanked her and sat down in a vacant chair next to a small table laden with reading matter. Idly she picked up a Knoxville morning paper.

The headline jolted her. She blinked and looked at it again, then devoured the front-page story under it.

Associated Industries had just released the news of a unique nationwide research project headed by Clinton Ward, their chief engineer, a survey of sites for "solar windows," a whole new source of potential safe, cheap power for America, possibly the world. The survey had established the feasibility of the solar windows, but Associated, "under advisement," had halted the project, stating that "at the present time, many factors militate against our going ahead."

Anne knew without reading on just what—or who—those "factors" were. She understood at once the international complications, the entanglements of trade agreements and treaties, that would affect the project's chances. She had a feeling she'd see something about that on the editorial page; she turned to it, and there it was.

Solar power, safe and cheap as it was, was still regarded as a visionary idea, the editorial said, and could turn the international markets upside down.

Anne held the paper, staring unseeing into the mirror opposite. So that was what he'd been hiding. The reasons for Clint's extreme secretiveness, his arrogant air of dedication and rightness were wholly understandable now. He had been engaged in work that had significance for the entire world, the whole future of the human race. The concept was dazzling, overwhelming.

That was why he'd appeared to dismiss any other work but his; she could almost forgive that now in the light of this revelation.

"Ms. Reynolds." She was so engrossed that she barely recognized her own name at first, but she made herself fold the paper and rise, then follow the receptionist to the shampooer's cubicle.

Anne was only vaguely aware when the woman finished and showed her to Marie's chair. When the woman asked her questions about how she wanted her hair done, she was hard put to answer clearly.

It all hung together now—the book about the sun; the Indians' reference to it; Clint's odd expression every time she'd mentioned the word; his admission that his project was a "far-out" one.

Finally her hair was set and she was under the dryer, still feeling as if she were in a dream. She'd accused Clint of thinking the "sun rose and set" on his work; that was the greatest irony of all.

And she'd rejected one of the most brilliant and

courageous men in the history of the nation . . . more than that, the only man that she could ever love.

"Annie, you look *beautiful.*" Lloyd, at the door of the Halberd Inn, held out both his hands and took hers. "I particularly wanted you to look like that today . . . and I'm about to tell you why."

She heard him almost indifferently. Ever since yesterday afternoon, she'd been functioning automatically, with a robotlike detachment. Dressing today had been almost like dressing someone else, she cared so little. Nevertheless, she supposed it couldn't harm matters if her hair looked its tamed and glossy best and her dress was perfect. The dress was very appropriate to celebrate the wrap of *When That April,* with its last-century, romantic grace; it was mauve linen trimmed at the neck, hem and cuffs with crocheted lace.

Anne had chosen it simply to raise her morale, but she couldn't help thinking how much Clint would have loved it on her.

"Come on, kiddo," Lloyd said in his conspiratorial way. "I want to confer with you before I make the public announcement." He gently urged her down the hall toward the little writing room. Her heart lurched when she recalled the morning Clint had kissed her in that room.

Remembering Lloyd's words; she told herself that this really was "the unkindest cut of all," the irony of ironies. But she did her best to keep calm; she couldn't ruin this festive day by blubbering all over her lovely Irish linen, and Lloyd was glowing with his about-to-be-announced secret as if he were about to give her a magnificent present.

"There." He shut the door softly. "You'd better sit, my dear, because I'm going to knock you off your feet."

He remained standing and assumed his most dramatic manner. "Something remarkable happened to me in New York, Anne," he began with an offhand, quiet way that she knew would build to rising excitement. "It's positively dangerous, you know, for me to be there in spring—or rather, on the one rainy day when New York *has* spring. I was back in my green youth, Annie. And one afternoon I happened to drop in at a friend's rehearsal." His magnificent voice took on the tone of a skillful storyteller. "All of it came back." His big laugh went belling out from him and infected her with his happiness.

Then Lloyd sobered. "All my years of movie directing suddenly seemed unreal. I knew where I belonged." The splendid voice dropped an octave. "Walking the boards again . . . directing. I'm adding up the years, Anne, and I mustn't waste any more."

"Waste!" she blurted. "On pictures like *The Wand* . . . *The Winter Kind,* and . . ."

He looked at her so sternly that she almost giggled. It was the way he'd look at a stagehand who'd spoken during a rehearsal, interrupting the dialogue. He held up his hand.

"Allow me to rave on, please. The headline is this: I'm going to start rehearsing a Shakespeare series in New York this summer. *When That April* was my swan song. Anne Reynolds will direct *The Enterprise.*" He stood before her with another dramatic pause.

She was flabbergasted; she couldn't speak. Lloyd smiled at her expression. This had been a typical Lloyd Eliot performance. If there was anything he relished it was dropping verbal bombs and watching the after-math.

The Enterprise, she repeated silently, the new film they were planning for the fall, shot in Paris and London and Stockholm. International terrorism and intrigue, with two lovers whose commitment was so total, whose love was so all-encompassing, that it survived every disaster.

And she, Anne Reynolds, would carry it all. The only thing she could manage was to say, "Lloyd. Oh, Lloyd."

He sat down opposite her at the small round table and said matter-of-factly, "I've watched you all these years, Anne . . . absorbing my teaching, bringing your own gifts to the films. Last night I watched the rushes again, those scenes you did for *April.* You have a special eye, my dear. You're the only one I can entrust *The Enterprise* to. When you film, you give everything an aura of the timeless, the unchanging. Even a cynic like me can believe, for a while, that love can surmount anything, even the modern dark age we live in. You're someone who will always be young."

Lloyd smiled sadly. "I'm not, anymore. I need to turn back to an era that understands me, a long-ago time where I feel at home."

Anne felt a new exhilaration, an anticipation so bright that it even drove away the shadows of her emptiness and depression. Her delight when she had discovered she would direct those few scenes in *April* was nothing compared to this. Her old dreams had finally come true; she would have a picture all her own. She could tell from Lloyd's expression that he knew something of what she was feeling.

"It means a great deal to you, I know," he mur-mured.

"A great deal? It means *everything,*" she said breathlessly.

"Especially now, I'd say." His bright look held hers, and she realized something else: Lloyd's sensitive antennae had picked up her true feelings about Clint Ward.

I should have known, she thought. At the thought of Clint she felt like crying all over again. But she held on tight to her runaway emotions; she wouldn't spoil Lloyd's immense gift with sadness, though her voice shook when she admitted, "Yes. Especially now."

Lloyd patted her hand. "I suffered the love disease once, believe it or not," he said gently. "And work saved me from utter darkness. You'll see, it'll do the same for you. As a matter of fact, the picture may be better for it. Mine was."

He chuckled, and it was so infectious that she found herself laughing too. Everything was grist for Eliot's artistic mill. "Now let's join the party," he said lightly, and they walked together into the big dining room of the Halberd Inn.

It was, Anne conceded, a marvelous celebration. Livie was glowing and, now that the film was over, seemed not to have the slightest interest in Jack and Marcella's relationship with each other. Everybody had a look of bright polish, right down to the grips and gaffers and plain, indifferent Harri. Anne felt a slight twinge when she spoke to Harri—she wished now that she'd confided in her. It would be so nice to have someone to talk to today about how she really felt, in spite of the wonderful thing that had happened.

Lloyd made his promised announcement with enormous drama; the whole crowd was utterly still for an instant.

Then everyone broke into wild applause and stood

up, still applauding. Lloyd's eyes looked moist when he concluded softly, "I'll miss you." The applause became louder, and Anne's eyes felt wet with emotion.

At the end of the luncheon grim Hester Cannon, who looked unusually festive herself in ivory instead of her customary black, approached Anne and held out her wrinkled hand. "I offer you my congratulations, Ms. Reynolds. You are a shining example of the ascendancy of women." Then she gave Anne a piercing look and added, "However . . . remember what I told you. Don't wait too long to marry."

Anne murmured something, thinking, It's a bit late for that, old girl. But she smiled and thanked the incorrigible old woman.

The crowd was becoming hilarious, and all of a sudden Anne felt the need to get away. Her mouth was stiff with smiling, and she was uneasy in the face of Lloyd's and Harri's frequent looks. Both of them knew her so well.

She managed to slip away and hurried out the rear door of the inn toward her car. She'd just drive for a while, go someplace where she could breathe a bit and think things over.

Then she knew she was fooling herself about the place; she knew very well where she wanted to go. She parked her car on the shoulder above the dogwood clearing. It wasn't an easy descent in her fragile heels, so she stopped and took off her shoes, going the rest of the way on bare, tentative feet, thankful that the grass was so thick and soft.

The sun was lowering . . . the sun which had been a god to the Cherokees. She smiled a little, remembering that time at the reservation, recalling the book about the sun.

In its rose red, diminishing rays she thought of Clint's

abandoned project, begun with such courage and hope just as the ideal community of Sedgby had begun . . . and failed. But no, she amended, Clint's project hadn't failed. Sedgby had decayed because a group of naïve aristocrats from England had been too incompetent to deal with a primitive life. Clint's plan was nothing like that at all.

His project had been put aside because of forces stronger, for the moment, than all of them. She wondered how he was feeling now—perhaps discouraged, dejected. All of a sudden she had a vivid picture of him that tore at her heart. She missed him, missed him so achingly, and she always would, all the rest of her days. She asked herself again why she had ever let him go, and the tears gathered under her lids.

At least she could grieve in peace now, let go of the pent-up tears that had been dammed in her throat all through the loud afternoon.

She opened her eyes and looked at the shining stream inside the dogwood clearing. The blossoms were all gone now; their season was over. Like hers.

Blinking back the tears, she turned her head for a last glimpse of the opposite ridge; for a moment she thought she was imagining things—that her memory of Clint was so sharp and clear that her mind had summoned up his physical image.

But it wasn't her imagination: There was a man there, coming over the ridge. A tall man with thick black hair, a tanned, weathered face and a lean, strong body. He wasn't wearing khakis now; he was dressed in dark trousers and a white shirt that made his tanned neck look like mahogany. A dark jacket was slung over his shoulder.

Coming toward her, he called out her name. And just as it had on that first afternoon, the deep, resonant voice thrilled along her nerves. Today he wasn't smiling; his face had a pleading, uncertain expression. And his magnificent golden brown eyes didn't have their old twinkle. There was a sad, questioning look in them now.

He came nearer, staring at her, taking in her face and hair and dress eagerly, hungrily.

"I was right to hope," he said softly, standing before her. "They told me at the inn that no one knew where you had gone. I took the chance it would be here."

She still couldn't speak; her heart was pounding so much that words seemed impossible.

"I'm a very poor correspondent," he added with a half smile. "I had to talk to you face-to-face."

The admission touched her deeply; she could feel a rising, unconquerable tenderness, and her own smile began to answer his.

He tossed his jacket on the grass and stood there with his hands awkwardly at his sides, his smile widening. "I can't believe how beautiful you are. I never could. Right now you look like you should be appearing in a movie, not directing one." His eyes bored into hers, and she felt the faint warmth of new hope, a wave of almost forgotten joy. But she was still too overcome to say a word.

"They told me about your new project," he went on. "I'm so glad for you, Anne. Very glad."

He still hadn't touched her, she thought, still hadn't said a word of love, even if his eyes seemed to do that for him.

"And I'm sorry," she said huskily at last, finding her voice, "about yours, Clint. Really sorry."

A muscle moved in his jaw. "Thank you. But I didn't come here to talk about that. I came here to tell you I'm sorry . . . to talk about you. We never talked enough about you, Anne. Here." He spread out his jacket on the grass. "Sit down."

His sudden white grin split his tanned, solemn face. "It would never do for such a pretty dress to get grass stains on it."

She sank down to the ground, sitting on his jacket, looking up at him. He folded his long, lean legs and dropped down beside her on the grass, never taking his amber eyes from her face.

He still hadn't touched her, and now she was longing for him to, longing for it with a hot aching. Their shoulders brushed, and the minute contact sent a thrill of fire along her nervous body. She sensed that he was moved, too, because he made a restless motion, and a rush of blood darkened his face.

But he went on speaking quietly as he pulled up a handful of grass. "It took me so long to realize how terribly . . . valuable you are. Not to me," he said hastily, "because I knew that the first time I saw you. I mean to everyone else, to the whole damned world."

She listened intently, hardly wanting to breathe; her heart was pounding so hard now that she could feel it against her ribs.

"At first," he admitted, "I couldn't conceive of anything being as important to anyone else as my job was to me. I was really doing a messianic number." He grinned. "Clint Ward was out to save the world in spite of itself. I was tilting, like Don Quixote, against the windmills of all the nations' interests. So naturally I figured it was pretty silly for some moviemaker—even one so beautiful—to dare to tangle with me."

His tone of self-mockery was so generous, so open, that she felt a fresh wave of emotion. She'd never heard him sound like this before, never in all her wildest dreams expected to.

"Then I saw you work that day, and a lot of my arrogance began to crumble. But that still didn't convince the Great Ward," he added sardonically. "I still thought that if you loved me, you would put yourself in second place. Until I got on the plane to New York . . . and I saw *The Wand*. And remembered something else I had totally forgotten."

Haltingly he told her about the movie he'd seen as a boy, the film that had decided him on his lifework. "And today, when I heard that Eliot's giving you *The Enterprise*, I knew for sure what kind of lady I'm dealing with, what a wrong I'd done you by being so high-handed."

"But I was wrong, too, Clint," she protested. "Wrong in so many ways. At first I thought that you could never understand me, with your 'cold,' scientific mind." She smiled as she emphasized the words. "And then, when I found out what your project *was*, I realized a lot of things too . . . realized we *didn't* know what we'd been playing with."

His hand crept out toward hers. There was a gentler look in his eyes than she'd ever seen in them. "That's all irrelevant now. The main thing I wanted to apologize for was the unforgivable way I talked to you on the day of the blasting."

"I understand that now. You told me in your letter, you know." Her hand moved a little nearer to his. "It happened to me once before, with my father." She smiled at the memory. "He was driving my mother and me somewhere, and we nearly had a wreck. He was so frightened that he yelled at both of us and used the most awful words, words I'd never heard him use in front of me." She grinned at Clint.

His fingers grasped hers; a little point of fire expanded outward from her fingers, shooting up her arm, flooding her all over. "Oh, Clint, I'm sorry, too, for so many things. Most of all I'm sorry about your wonderful project. You must be so hurt."

He squeezed her hand, and then his hard fingers captured her wrist. She felt a shivering succession of cold and heat along her flesh.

"No, Anne. I'm not, oddly enough. I'm far from through. I've just started. Look over there." He nodded toward the ridge; the sun was sinking lower in a riot of fiery color. "The sun is stronger than all the economies and politics in the world; there's more power there than in anything we scientists can devise. It's disappearing now, but it will be up again tomorrow."

He turned to her again, and his eyes were blazing with unrelenting determination. His words, his look, ignited her own flagging hopes, and the shadows in her heart fled. She thought that he was like the sun himself, overpowering everything.

"Yes," he said, "we're going on, one way or another. . . . Look!"

She followed the direction of his eyes. A graceful deer was bounding along the darkening ridge. "The magic spell is still there," she murmured softly. "Just as it was the first time."

He must have recognized the love in her eyes, because he took her swiftly in his arms and lowered his mouth to hers for a long, starved, dizzying kiss, arousing her even more deeply than any kiss had before.

"Oh, Anne," he whispered when he was able to speak, "I love you so much, so much. Tell me, please tell me, that I still have a chance."

She raised her hand to his cheek and stroked it tenderly. "Clint, there's no chance for *me* without you."

He grabbed her in his arms again and held her close,

murmuring against her hair, "How would you feel about an escort in Europe? A constant escort. And a permanent escort to other spots around the world as we go along?"

"Glorious. Absolutely glorious. It would be the greatest thing under the sun," she said, half teasing.

"Of course," he said, releasing her a moment and staring into her eyes, "I don't expect to see my name on the credits."

"Why not? I like the sound of Anne Reynolds Ward. I think it's very stateley . . . don't you?"

"I think it's the greatest thing under the sun," he retorted, and hugged her close again.

"I intend to prove to you," he added, grinning, "that it's possible for me to change your name without wanting to change you. Nothing so perfect should ever be changed."

She stroked his arm, feeling a delirious happiness. "You *have* changed me, though, in many ways, and every change is for the better. You've given me the world again . . . the *real* world. You've made me see what giving is."

And that, she thought, as Lloyd would say, can only help the picture.

The giddy thought floated away, and she gave herself up to their spell of silent enchantment. Clint Ward had asked her to marry him on the very site of the proposal scene in *April*.

This was a dream-gift that made *The Enterprise* pale by comparison.

Clint smiled at her, a smile of total happiness, and got to his feet. Without a word he slipped her discarded shoes on her bare feet and held out his hand to invite her to rise.

They made their way quite slowly, in a dreamlike

state of joy, upward along the rise, then stood together at the top, staring at the place they had left behind them.

It would never really be behind them, Anne decided, watching the sun disappear in a circle of fire; they would always remember this greatest of all the love scenes that two lovers had ever played through time unending.

WIN

a fabulous $50,000 diamond jewelry collection

ENTER

by filling out the coupon below and mailing it by September 30, 1985

Send entries to:

U.S.
Silhouette Diamond Sweepstakes
P.O. Box 779
Madison Square Station
New York, NY 10159

Canada
Silhouette Diamond Sweepstakes
Suite 191
238 Davenport Road
Toronto, Ontario M5R 1J6

SILHOUETTE DIAMOND SWEEPSTAKES ENTRY FORM

☐ Mrs. ☐ Miss ☐ Ms ☐ Mr.

NAME _____ (please print)

ADDRESS _____ APT. #

CITY _____

STATE/(PROV.) _____

ZIP/(POSTAL CODE) _____

RTD-A-1

RULES FOR SILHOUETTE DIAMOND SWEEPSTAKES

OFFICIAL RULES—NO PURCHASE NECESSARY

1. Silhouette Diamond Sweepstakes is open to Canadian (except Quebec) and United States residents 18 years or older at the time of entry. Employees and immediate families of the publishers of Silhouette, their affiliates, retailers, distributors, printers, agencies and RONALD SMILEY INC. are excluded.

2. To enter, print your name and address on the official entry form or on a 3" x 5" slip of paper. You may enter as often as you choose, but each envelope must contain only one entry. Mail entries first class in Canada to Silhouette Diamond Sweepstakes, Suite 191, 238 Davenport Road, Toronto, Ontario M5R 1J6. In the United States, mail to Silhouette Diamond Sweepstakes, P.O. Box 779, Madison Square Station, New York, NY 10159. Entries must be postmarked between February 1 and September 30, 1985. Silhouette is not responsible for lost, late or misdirected mail.

3. First Prize of diamond jewelry, consisting of a necklace, ring, bracelet and earrings will be awarded. Approximate retail value is $50,000 U.S./$62,500 Canadian. Second Prize of 100 Silhouette Home Reader Service Subscriptions will be awarded. Approximate retail value of each is $162.00 U.S./$180.00 Canadian. No substitution, duplication, cash redemption or transfer of prizes will be permitted. Odds of winning depend upon the number of valid entries received. One prize to a family or household. Income taxes, other taxes and insurance on First Prize are the sole responsibility of the winners.

4. Winners will be selected under the supervision of RONALD SMILEY INC., an independent judging organization whose decisions are final, by random drawings from valid entries postmarked by September 30, 1985, and received no later than October 7, 1985. Entry in this sweepstakes indicates your awareness of the Official Rules. Winners who are residents of Canada must answer correctly a time-related arithmetical skill-testing question to qualify. First Prize winner will be notified by certified mail and must submit an Affidavit of Compliance within 10 days of notification. Returned Affidavits or prizes that are refused or undeliverable will result in alternative names being randomly drawn. Winners may be asked for use of their name and photo at no additional compensation.

5. For a First Prize winner list, send a stamped self-addressed envelope postmarked by September 30, 1985. In Canada, mail to Silhouette Diamond Contest Winner, Suite 309, 238 Davenport Road, Toronto, Ontario M5R 1J6. In the United States, mail to Silhouette Diamond Contest Winner, P.O. Box 182, Bowling Green Station, New York, NY 10274. This offer will appear in Silhouette publications and at participating retailers. Offer void in Quebec and subject to all Federal, Provincial, State and Municipal laws and regulations and wherever prohibited or restricted by law.

SDR-A-1

READERS' COMMENTS ON SILHOUETTE INTIMATE MOMENTS:

"About a month ago a friend loaned me my first Silhouette. I was thoroughly surprised as well as totally addicted. Last week I read a Silhouette Intimate Moments and I was even more pleased. They are the best romance series novels I have ever read. They give much more depth to the plot, characters, and the story is fundamentally realistic. They incorporate tasteful sex scenes, which is a must, especially in the 1980's. I only hope you can publish them fast enough."

S.B.*, Lees Summit, MO

"After noticing the attractive covers on the new line of Silhouette Intimate Moments, I decided to read the inside and discovered that this new line was more in the line of books that I like to read. I do want to say I enjoyed the books because they are so realistic and a lot more truthful than so many romance books today."

J.C., Onekama, MI

"I would like to compliment you on your books. I will continue to purchase all of the Silhouette Intimate Moments. They are your best line of books that I have had the pleasure of reading."

S.M., Billings, MT

*names available on request